# THE TRANSMIGRATION OF TIMOTHY ARCHER

## BOOKS BY PHILIP K. DICK

The Exegesis of Philip K. Dick

NOVELS

The Broken Bubble
Clans of the Alphane Moon
Confessions of a Crap Artist
The Cosmic Puppets
Counter-Clock World
The Crack in Space
Deus Irae (with Roger Zelazny)
The Divine Invasion
Do Androids Dream of Electric Sheep?
Dr. Bloodmoney
Dr. Futurity
Eye in the Sky
Flow My Tears, the Policeman Said
Galactic Pot-Healer
The Game-Players of Titan
Gather Yourselves Together
Lies, Inc.
The Man in the High Castle
The Man Who Japed
Martian Time-Slip
Mary and the Giant
A Maze of Death
Nick and the Glimmung
Now Wait for Last Year
Our Friends from Frolix 8
The Penultimate Truth
A Scanner Darkly
The Simulacra
Solar Lottery
The Three Stigmata of Palmer Eldritch
Time Out of Joint
The Transmigration of Timothy Archer
Ubik
Ubik: The Screenplay
VALIS
Vulcan's Hammer
We Can Build You
The World Jones Made
The Zap Gun

# PHILIP K. DICK

╪

# THE TRANSMIGRATION
# OF TIMOTHY ARCHER

╪

MARINER CLASSICS

Boston   New York

First Mariner Books edition 2011

Originally published by Timescape, a division of Simon & Schuster, in 1982.

marinerbooks.com

*Library of Congress Cataloging-in-Publication Data*
Dick, Philip K.
The transmigration of Timothy Archer / Philip K. Dick. —
1st Mariner Books ed.
p. cm.
ISBN 978-0-547-57260-4
I. Title.
PS3554.I3T7 2011
813'.54 — dc23
2011029336

*Book design by Melissa Lotfy*

Printed in the United States of America
23 24 25 26 27  LBC  13 12 11 10 9

*An Ode for him*

Ah Ben!
Say how, or when
Shall we thy Guests
Meet at those Lyrick Feasts,
Made at the Sun,
The Dog, the triple Tunne?
Where we such clusters had,
As made us nobly wild, not mad;
And yet each Verse of thine
Out-did the meate, out-did the frolick wine.

My Ben
Or come agen:
Or send to us,
Thy wits great over-plus;
But teach us yet
Wisely to husband it;
Lest we that Talent spend:
And having once brought to an end
That precious stock; the store
Of such a wit the world should have no more.

— *Robert Herrick, 1648*

# THE TRANSMIGRATION OF TIMOTHY ARCHER

# 1

BAREFOOT CONDUCTS HIS seminars on his houseboat in Sausalito. It costs a hundred dollars to find out why we are on this Earth. You also get a sandwich, but I wasn't hungry that day. John Lennon had just been killed and I think I know why we are on this Earth; it's to find out that what you love the most will be taken away from you, probably due to an error in high places rather than by design.

After I parked my Honda Civic in the metered slot I sat listening to the radio. Already all the Beatles songs ever written could be heard on every frequency. Shit, I thought. I feel like I'm back in the Sixties, still married to Jefferson Archer.

"Where's Gate Five?" I asked two hippies going by.

They didn't answer. I wondered if they'd heard the news about John Lennon. I wondered, then, what the hell I cared about Arabic mysticism, about the Sufis and all that other stuff that Edgar Barefoot talked about on his weekly radio program on KPFA in Berkeley. The Sufis are a happy lot. They teach that the essence of God isn't power or wisdom or love but beauty. That's a totally new idea in the world, unknown to Jews and Christians. I am neither. I still work at the Musik Shop on Telegraph Avenue in Berkeley and I'm trying to make the payments on the house that Jeff and I bought when we were married. I got the house and Jeff got nothing. That was the story of his life.

Why would anybody in their right mind care about Arabic mysticism? I asked myself as I locked up my Honda and started toward the line of boats. Especially on a nice day. But what the fuck; I had already made the drive over the Richardson Bridge, through Richmond, which is tawdry, and then past the refineries. The bay is beautiful. The police clock you on the Richardson Bridge; they time when you pay your toll and when you leave the bridge on the Marin side. If you arrive in Marin County too soon, it costs you big bucks.

I never cared for the Beatles. Jeff brought home *Rubber Soul* and I told him it was insipid. Our marriage was breaking up and I date it from hearing "Michelle" one billion times, day after day. That would be roughly around 1966, I guess. A lot of people in the Bay Area date events by the release of Beatles records. Paul McCartney's first solo album came out the year before Jeff and I separated. If I hear "Teddy Boy," I start crying. That was the year I lived in our house alone. Don't do it. Don't live alone. Right up to the end, Jeff had his antiwar activity to keep him company. I withdrew and listened to KPFA playing baroque music better left forgotten. That was how I first heard Edgar Barefoot, who impressed me initially as a jerk-off, with his little voice and that tone of savoring his own cerebral activity immensely, delighting like a two-year-old in each successive *satori*. There is evidence that I was the only person in the Bay Area who felt that way. I changed my mind later; KPFA started broadcasting Barefoot's taped lectures late at night, and I would listen while I tried to get to sleep. When you're half asleep, all that monotonous intoning makes sense. Several people explained to me once that subliminal messages had been inserted in all the programs aired in the Bay Area around 1973, almost certainly by Martians. The message I got from listening to Barefoot seemed to be: You are actually a good person and you shouldn't let anyone else determine your life. Anyhow I got to sleep more and more readily as time passed; I forgot Jeff and the light that had gone out when he died, except that now and then an incident would pop into existence in my mind, usually regarding some crisis in the Co-op on University Avenue. Jeff used to get into fights in the Co-op. I thought it was funny.

So now, I realized as I walked up the gangplank onto Edgar Barefoot's cushy houseboat, I will date my going to this seminar by John Lennon's murder; the two events are for me of a seamless whole. What a way to start understanding, I thought. Go back home and smoke a number. Forget the wimpy voice of enlightenment; this is a time of guns; you can do nothing, enlightened or otherwise; you are a record clerk with a degree in liberal arts from Cal. *"The best lack all conviction"* . . . something like that. *"What rough beast . . . slouches towards Bethlehem to be born."* A creature with bad posture, nightmare of the world. We had a test on Yeats. I got an A-minus. I was good. I used to be able to sit on the floor all day eating cheese and drinking goat's milk, figuring out the longest novel . . . I have read all the long novels. I graduated from Cal. I live in Berkeley. I read *The Remembrance of Things Past* and I remember nothing; I came out the door I went in, as the saying goes. It did me no good, all those years in the library waiting for my number to light up, signifying that my book had been carried to the desk. That's true for a lot of people, most likely.

But those remain in my mind as good years in which we had more cunning than is generally recognized; we knew exactly what we had to do: the Nixon regime had to go; we did what we did deliberately, and none of us regrets it. Jeff Archer is dead, now; John Lennon is dead as of today. Other dead people lie along the path, as if something fairly large passed by. Maybe the Sufis with their conviction about God's innate beauty can make me happy; maybe this is why I am marching up the gangplank to this plush houseboat: a plan is fulfilled in which all the sad deaths add up to something instead of nothing, somehow get converted to joy.

A terribly thin kid who resembled our friend Joe the Junkie stopped me, saying, "Ticket?"

"You mean this thing?" From my purse I got out the printed card that Barefoot had mailed me upon receipt of my hundred dollars. In California you buy enlightenment the way you buy peas at the supermarket, by size and by weight. I'd like four pounds of enlightenment, I said to myself. No, better make that ten pounds. I'm really running short.

"Go to the rear of the boat," the skinny youth said.

"And you have a nice day," I said.

When one catches sight of Edgar Barefoot for the first time one says: He fixes car transmissions. He stands about five-six and because he weighs so much you get the impression that he survives on junk food, by and large hamburgers. He is bald. For this area of the world at this time in human civilization, he dresses all wrong; he wears a long wool coat and the most ordinary brown pants and blue cotton shirt . . . but his shoes appear to be expensive. I don't know if you can call that thing around his neck a tie. They tried to hang him, perhaps, and he proved too heavy; he broke the rope and continued on about his business. Enlightenment and survival are intermingled, I said to myself as I took a seat — cheap folding chairs, and already a few people here and there, mostly young. My husband is dead and his father is dead; his father's mistress ate a mason jar of barbiturates and is in the grave, perpetually asleep, which was the whole point of doing it. It sounds like a chess game: the bishop is dead, and with him the blond Norwegian woman who he supported by means of the Bishop's Discretionary Fund, according to Jeff; a chess game and a racket. These are strange times now, but those were far stranger.

Edgar Barefoot, standing before us, motioned us to change seats, to sit up front. I wondered what would happen if I lit a cigarette. I once lit a cigarette in an *ashram,* after a lecture on the Vedas. Mass loathing descended on me, plus a sharp dig in the ribs. I had outraged the lofty. The strange thing about the lofty is that they die just like the common. Bishop Timothy Archer owned a whole lot of loftiness, by weight and by size, and it did him no good; he lies like the rest, underground. So much for spiritual things. So much for aspirations. He sought Jesus. Moreover, he sought what lies behind Jesus: the real truth. Had he been content with the phony he would still be alive. That is something to ponder. Lesser people, accepting falsehood, are alive to tell about it; they did not perish in the Dead Sea Desert. The most famous bishop of modern times bit the big one because he mistrusted Jesus. There is a lesson there. So perhaps I have enlightenment; I know not to doubt. I know, also, to take more than two bottles of Coca-Cola with me when I drive out into the wastelands, ten thousand miles from home. Using a gas station map as if I am still in downtown San Francisco. It's fine for locating Portsmouth Square but not so fine for locating the genuine source of Christianity, hidden from the world these twenty-two hundred years.

I will go home and smoke a number, I said to myself. This is a waste of time; from the moment John Lennon died everything has been a waste of time, including mourning over it. I have given up mourning for Lent . . . that is, I cease to grieve.

Raising his hands to us, Barefoot began to talk. I little noted what he said; neither did I long remember, as the expression goes. The horse's ass was me, for paying a hundred dollars to listen to this; the man before us was the smart one because he got to keep the money: we got to give it. That is how you calculate wisdom: by who pays. I teach this. I should instruct the Sufis, and the Christians as well, especially the Episcopalian bishops with their funds. Front me a hundred bucks, Tim. Imagine calling the bishop "Tim." Like calling the pope "George" or "Bill" like the lizard in *Alice*. I think Bill descended the chimney, as I recall. It is an obscure reference; like what Barefoot is saying it is little noted, and no one remembers it.

"Death in life," Barefoot said, "and life in death; two modalities, like *yin* and *yang*, of one underlying continuum. Two faces — a 'holon,' as Arthur Koestler terms it. You should read *Janus*. Each passes into the other as a joyous dance. It is Lord Krishna who dances in us and through us; we are all Sri Krishna, who, if you remember, comes in the form of time. That is his real, universal shape. Ultimate form, destroyer of all people . . . of everything that is." He smiled at us all, with beatific pleasure.

Only in the Bay Area, I thought, would this nonsense be tolerated. A two-year-old addresses us. Christ, how foolish it all is! I feel my old distaste, the angry aversion we cultivate in Berkeley, that Jeff enjoyed so. His pleasure was to get angry at every trifle. Mine is to endure nonsense. At financial cost.

I am terribly frightened of death, I thought. Death has destroyed me; it isn't Sri Krishna, destroyer of all people; it is death, destroyer of my friends. It singled them out and left everyone else undisturbed. Fucking death, I thought. You homed in on those I love. You utilized their folly and prevailed. You took advantage of foolish people, which is truly unkind. Emily Dickinson was full of shit when she prattled about "kindly Death"; that's an abominable thought, that death is kind. She never saw a six-car pile-up on the Eastshore Freeway. Art, like theology, a packaged fraud. Downstairs the people are fighting while I look for God in a reference book. God, ontological arguments for. Better yet: practical arguments against. There is no such listing. It would have helped a lot if it had come in time: arguments against being foolish, ontological and empirical, ancient and modern (see common sense). The trouble with being educated is that it takes a long time; it uses up the better part of your life and when you are finished what you know is that you would have benefited more by going into banking. I wonder if bankers ask such questions. They ask what the prime rate is up to today. If a banker goes out on the Dead Sea Desert he probably takes a flare pistol and canteens and C-rations and a knife. Not a crucifix displaying a previous idiocy that was intended to remind him. Destroyer of the people on the Eastshore Freeway, and my hopes besides; Sri Krishna, you got us all. Good luck in your other endeavors. Insofar as they are equally commendable in the eyes of other gods.

I am faking it, I thought. These passions are bilge. I have become inbred, from hanging around the Bay Area intellectual community; I think as I talk: pompously, and in riddles; I am not a person but a self-admonishing voice. Worse, I talk as I hear. Garbage in (as the computer science majors say); garbage out. I should stand up and ask Mr. Barefoot a meaningless question and then go home while he is phrasing the perfect answer. That way he wins and I get to leave. We both gain. He does not know me; I do not know him, except as a sententious voice. It ricochets in my head, I thought, already, and it's just begun; this is the first lecture of many. Sententious twaddle . . . the name of the Archer family's black retainer in, perhaps, a TV sitcom. "Sententious, you get your black ass in here, you hear me?" What this droll little man is saying is important; he is discussing Sri Krishna and how men die. This is a topic that I from personal experience deem significant. I should know, because it is familiar to me; it showed up in my life years ago and will not go away.

Once we owned a little old farm house. The wiring shorted

out when someone plugged in a toaster. During rainy weather, water dripped from the light bulb in the kitchen ceiling. Jeff every now and then poured a coffee can of black tarlike stuff onto the roof to stop it from leaking; we could not afford the ninety-weight paper. The tar did no good. Our house belonged with others like it in the flat part of Berkeley on San Pablo Avenue, near Dwight Way. The good part was that Jeff and I could walk to the Bad Luck Restaurant and look at Fred Hill, the KGB agent (some said) who fixed the salads and owned the place and decided whose pictures got hung up for free exhibition. When Fred came to town years ago, all the Party members in the Bay Area froze solid, out of fear; this was the tip-off that a Soviet hatchetman was in the vicinity. It also told you who belonged to the Party and who did not. Fear reigned among the dedicated but no one else cared. It was like the eschatological judge sorting the sheep, the faithful, from among the ordinary others, except in this case it was the sheep who quaked.

Dreams of poverty excited universal enjoyment in Berkeley, coupled with the hope that the political and economic situation would worsen, throwing the country into ruin: this was the theory of the activists. Misfortune so vast that it would wreck everyone, responsible and not responsible alike sinking into defeat. We were then and we are now totally crazy. It's literate to be crazy. For example, you would have to be crazy to name your daughter Goneril. Like they taught us at the English Department at Cal, madness was funny to the patrons of the Globe Theater. It is not funny now. At home you are a great artist, but here you are just the author of a difficult book about Here Comes Everybody. Big deal, I thought. With a drawing in the margin of someone thumbing his nose. And for that, like this speech now, we paid good money. You'd think having been poor so long would have taught me better, sharpened my wits, as it were. My instinct for self-preservation.

I am the last living person who knew Bishop Timothy Archer of the Diocese of California, his mistress, his son my husband the homeowner and wage earner *pro forma*. Somebody should — well, it would be nice if no one went the way they collectively went, volunteering to die, each of them, like Parsifal, a perfect fool.

# 2

Within a period of two days, two people — one an editor friend, the other a writer friend — recommended *The Green Cover* to me, both of them saying the same thing in effect, that if I wanted to know what was happening in contemporary literature I had goddamn well better know your work. When I got the book home (I had been told that the titular essay was the best and to start with it), I realized that you had herein done a piece on Tim Archer. So I read that. All of a sudden he was alive again, my friend. It brings fierce pain to me, not joy. I can't write about him, since I'm not a writer, although I did major in English at Cal; anyhow, one day as a sort of exercise I sat down and scratched out a spurious dialog between him and me, to see if I could by any chance recapture the cadence of his endless flow of talk. I found I could do it, but, like Tim himself, it was dead.

People ask me sometimes what he was like, but I'm not into Christianity so I don't encounter church people that often, although I used to. My husband was his son Jeff so I knew Tim on a rather personal basis. Frequently we talked theology. At the time of Jeff's suicide, I met Tim and Kirsten at the airport in San Francisco; they were briefly back from England and meeting with the official translators of the Zadokite Documents, at which point in his life Tim first began to believe that Christ was a fraud and that the Zadokite Sect possessed the true religion. He asked me how he should go about conveying this news to his flock. This was before Santa Barbara. He kept Kirsten in a plain apartment in the Tenderloin District of the City. Very few people went there. Jeff and I, of course, could. I remember when Jeff first introduced me to his father; Tim walked up to me and said, "My name's Tim Archer." He didn't mention he was a bishop. He did have on the ring, though.

I'm the one who got the phone call about Kirsten's suicide. We were still suffering over Jeff's suicide. I had to stand there and listen to Tim telling me that Kirsten had "just slipped away"; I could see my little brother, who had really been fond of Kirsten; he was assembling a balsawood model of a Spad Thirteen — he knew the call was from Tim but of course he didn't know that now Kirsten, along with Jeff, was dead.

Tim differed from everyone else I ever knew in these respects: he could believe in anything and he would immediately act on the basis of his new belief; that is, until he ran into another belief and then he acted on that. He was convinced, for example, that a medium had cured Kirsten's son's mental problems, which were severe. One day, watching Tim on TV being interviewed by David Frost, I realized that he was talking about me and Jeff . . . however, there was no real relationship between what he was saying and the reality situation. Jeff was watching, too; he did not know that his father was talking about him. Like the Medieval Realists, Tim believed that words were actual things. If you could put it into words, it was *de facto* true. This is what cost him his life. I wasn't in Israel when he died, but I can visualize him out on the desert studying the map the way he looked at a gas station map in downtown San Francisco. The map said that if you drove X miles you would arrive at place Y, whereupon he would start up the car and drive X miles knowing that Y would be there; it said so on the map. The man who doubted every article of Christian doctrine believed everything he saw written down.

But the incident that, for me, conveyed the most about him took place in Berkeley one day. Jeff and I were supposed to meet Tim at a particular corner at a particular time. Tim drove up late. Running after him came a gas station attendant, furiously angry. Tim had filled up at this man's station and then backed over a pump, mashing it flat — whereupon Tim had driven off because he was late for his appointment with us.

"You destroyed my pump!" the attendant yelled, totally out of breath and totally beside himself. "I can call the police. You just drove off. I had to run all the way after you."

What I wanted to see was whether Tim would tell this man, a very angry but really a very modest man in the social order, a man at the bottom of the scale on which Tim, really, stood at the top — I wanted to see if Tim would inform him that he was the Bishop of the Diocese of California and was known all over the world, a friend of Martin Luther King, Jr., a friend of Robert Kennedy, a great and famous man who wasn't, at the moment, wearing his clericals. Tim did not. He humbly apologized. It became evident to the gas station attendant after a bit that he was dealing with someone for whom large brightly colored metal pumps did not exist; he was dealing with a man who was, quite literally, living in another world. That other world was what Tim and Kirsten called "The Other Side," and step by step that Other Side drew them all to it: first Jeff, then Kirsten and, ineluctably, Tim himself.

Sometimes I tell myself that Tim still exists but totally, now, in that other world. How does Don McLean put it in his song "Vincent"? "This world was never meant for one as beautiful as you." That's my friend; this world was never really real to him, so I guess it wasn't the right world for him; a mistake got made somewhere, and underneath he knew it.

When I think about Tim I think:

> *"And still I dream he treads the lawn,*
> *Walking ghostly in the dew,*
> *Pierced by my glad singing through . . ."*

As Yeats put it.

Thank you for your piece on Tim, but it hurt to find him alive again, for a moment. I guess that is the measure of greatness in a piece of writing, that it can do that.

I believe it was in one of Aldous Huxley's novels that a character phones up another character and exclaims excitedly, "I've just found a mathematical proof for the existence of God!" Had it been Tim he would have found another proof the next day contravening the first — and would have believed that just as readily. It was as if he was in a garden of flowers and each flower was new and different and he discovered each in turn and was equally delighted by each, but then forgot the ones that came before. He was totally loyal to his friends. Those, he never forgot. Those were his permanent flowers.

The strange part, Ms. Marion, is that in a way I miss him more than I miss my husband. Maybe he made more of an impression on me. I don't know. Perhaps you can tell me; you're the writer.

Cordially,
Angel Archer

I wrote that to the famous New York Literary Establishment author Jane Marion, whose essays appear in the best of the little magazines; I did not expect an answer and I got none.

Maybe her publisher, to whom I sent it, read it and flipped it away; I don't know. Marion's essay on Tim had infuriated me; it was based entirely on secondhand information. Marion never knew Tim but she wrote about him anyhow. She said something about Tim "giving up friendships when it served his purpose" or something like that. Tim never gave up a friendship in his life.

That appointment that Jeff and I had made with the bishop was an important one. In two respects, official and, as it turned out, unofficial. Regarding the official aspect, I proposed and intended to carry off a meeting, a merger, between Bishop Archer and my friend Kirsten Lundborg who represented FEM in the Bay Area. The Female Emancipation Movement wanted Tim to make a speech on its behalf, a speech for free. As the wife of the bishop's son, it was thought I could pull it off. Needless to say, Tim did not seem to understand the situation, but that was not his fault; neither Jeff nor I had clued him in. Tim supposed we were getting together to have a meal at the Bad Luck, which he had heard about. Tim would be paying for the meal because we didn't have any money at all that year, or, for that matter, the year before. As a clerical typist in a law office on Shattuck Avenue I was the putative wage-earner. The law office consisted of two Berkeley guys active in all the protest movements. They defended in cases involving drugs. Their firm was called BARNES AND GLEASON LAW OFFICE AND CANDLE SHOP; they sold handmade candles, or at least displayed them. It was Jerry Barnes' way of insulting his own profession and making it clear that he had no intention of bringing in any money. Regarding this goal he was successful. I remember one time a grateful client paid him in opium, a black stick that looked like a bar of unsweetened chocolate. Jerry was at a loss as to what to do with it. He wound up giving it away.

It was interesting to watch Fred Hill, the KGB agent, greeting all his customers the way a good restaurateur does, shaking hands and smiling. Hill had cold eyes. According to the talk on the street he had the authority to murder those under Party discipline who seemed restive. Tim paid hardly any attention to Fred Hill as the son of a bitch led us to a table. I wondered what the Bishop of California would say if he knew that the man handing us our menus was a Russian national here in the U.S. under a fake name, an officer in the Soviet secret police. Or perhaps this was all a Berkeley myth. As in the many preceding years, Berkeley and paranoia were bedfellows. The end of the Vietnam War was a long way off; Nixon had yet to pull out U.S. forces. Watergate still lay several years ahead. Government agents rooted about the Bay Area. We independent activists suspected everyone of conniving; we trusted neither the right nor the CP-USA. If there was any single hated thing in Berkeley it was the smell of the police.

"Hello, folks," Fred Hill said. "The soup today is minestrone. Would you like a glass of wine while you decide?"

The three of us said we wanted wine — just so long as it wasn't Gallo — and Fred Hill went off to get it.

"He's a colonel in the KGB," Jeff said to the bishop.

"Very interesting," Tim said, scrutinizing the menu.

"They're really underpaid," I said.

"That would be why he has opened up a restaurant," Tim said, looking around him at the other tables and patrons. "I wonder if they have Black Sea caviar, here." Glancing up at me, he said, "Do you like caviar, Angel? The roe of the sturgeon, although they do sometimes pass off the roe of *Cyclopterus lumpus* as caviar; however, that is generally of a reddish hue and larger. It is much cheaper. I don't care for it — lumpfish caviar, I mean. In a sense, to say 'lumpfish caviar' is an oxymoron." He laughed, mostly to himself.

Shit, I thought.

"What's wrong?" Jeff said.

"I'm just wondering where Kirsten is," I said. I looked at my watch.

The bishop said, "The origins of the feminist movement can be found in *Lysistrata*. 'We must refrain from all touch of baubled love . . .'" Again he laughed. "'With bolts and bars our orders flout and —'" He paused, as if considering whether to go on. "'And shut us out.' It's a pun. 'Shut us out' refers both to the general situation of noncompliance and a shutting up of the vagina."

"Dad," Jeff said, "we're trying to figure out what to order. Okay?"

The bishop said, "If you mean we're trying to decide what to have to eat, my remark is certainly applicable. Aristophanes would have appreciated that."

"Come on," Jeff said.

Carrying a tray, Fred Hill returned. "Louis Martini burgundy." He set down three glasses. "If you'll excuse my asking — aren't you Bishop Archer?"

The bishop nodded.

"You marched with Dr. King at Selma," Hill said.

"Yes, I was at Selma," the bishop said.

I said, "Tell him your vagina joke." To Fred Hill I said, "The bishop knows a real old vagina joke."

Chuckling, Bishop Archer said, "The joke is old, she means. Don't misunderstand syntactically."

"Dr. King was a great man," Fred Hill said.

"He was a very great man," the bishop said. "I'll have the sweetbreads."

"That's a good choice," Fred Hill said, jotting. "Also let me recommend the pheasant."

"I'll have the veal Oscar," I said.

"So will I," Jeff said. He seemed moody. I knew that he objected to my using my friendship with the bishop in order to get a free speech — for FEM or any other group. He knew how easily free speeches got tugged out of his father. Both he and the bishop wore dark-wool business suits, and of course Fred Hill, famous KGB agent and mass killer, wore a suit and tie.

I wondered that day, sitting there with the two of them in their business suits, if Jeff would go into Holy Orders as his father had; both men looked solemn, bringing to the task of ordering dinner the same intensity, the same gravity, that they brought to so much else: the professional stance oddly punctuated on the bishop's part with wit . . . although, like today, the wit never struck me as quite right.

As we spooned up our minestrone soup, Bishop Archer talked about his forthcoming heresy trial. It was a subject he found endlessly fascinating. Certain Bible Belt bishops were out to get him because he had said in several published articles and in his sermons preached at Grace Cathedral that no one had seen hide nor hair of the Holy Ghost since apostolic times. This had caused Tim to conclude that the doctrine of the Trinity was incorrect. If the Holy Ghost was, in fact, a form of God equal to Yahweh and Christ, surely he would still be with us. Speaking in tongues did not impress him. He had seen a lot of it in his years in the Episcopal Church and it struck him as autosuggestion and dementia. Further, a scrupulous reading of Acts disclosed that at Pentecost when the Holy Ghost descended on the disciples, giving them "the gift of speech," they had spoken in foreign languages which people nearby had understood. This is not glossolalia as the term is now used; this is xenoglossy. The bishop, as we ate, chortled over Peter's deft response to the charge that the Eleven were drunk; Peter had said in a loud voice to the scoffing crowd that it was not likely that the Eleven were drunk inasmuch as it was only nine A.M. The bishop pondered out loud — between spoonfuls of minestrone soup — that the course of Western history might have been changed if the time had been nine P.M. instead of nine A.M. Jeff looked bored and I kept consulting my watch, wondering what was keeping Kirsten. Probably she had gone in to have her hair done. She fussed forever with her blond hair, especially in anticipation of momentous occasions.

The Episcopal Church is Trinitarian; you cannot be a priest or bishop of that church if you do not absolutely accept and teach that—well, it's called the Nicene Creed:

> ". . . And I believe in the Holy Ghost, the Lord, and Giver of Life, Who proceedeth from the Father and the Son; Who with the Father and the Son together is worshipped and glorified."

So Bishop McClary back in Missouri was correct; Tim had, in fact, committed heresy. However, Tim had been a practicing lawyer before he became a rector of the Episcopal Church. He relished the oncoming heresy trial. Bishop McClary knew his Bible and he knew canon law, but Tim would blow golden smoke-rings around him until McClary would not know up from down. Tim knew this. In facing a heresy trial, he was in his element. Moreover, he was writing a book about it; he would win and, in addition, he would make some money. Every newspaper in America had carried articles and even editorials on the subject. Successfully trying someone for heresy in the 1970s was really difficult.

Listening to Tim dilate endlessly, the thought came to me that he had calculatedly committed heresy in order to bring on the trial. At least, he had done it unconsciously. It was, as the term has it, a good career move.

"The so-called 'gift of speech,'" the bishop said cheerfully, "reverses the unity of language lost when the Tower of Babel was attempted; that is, its construction was attempted. When the day comes that someone in my congregation gets up and talks Walloon, well, that day I will believe that the Holy Ghost exists. I'm not sure he ever existed. The apostolic conception of the Holy Spirit is based on the Hebrew *ruah,* the spirit of God. For one thing, this spirit is female, not male. She speaks concerning the Messianic expectation. Christianity appropriated the notion from Judaism and when Christianity had converted a sufficient number of pagans — Gentiles, if you will — it abandoned the concept, since it was only meaningful to the Jews anyhow. To the Greek converts it made no sense whatsoever, although Socrates declared that he had an inner voice or *daemon* that guided him . . . a tutelary spirit, not to be confused with the English word 'demon,' which of course refers to an indubitably evil spirit. The two terms are often confused. Do I have time for a cocktail?"

"They just have beer and wine here," I said.

"I'd like to make a phone call," the bishop said; he dabbed at his chin with his napkin, rising to his feet and glancing about. "Is there a public phone?"

"There's a phone at the Chevron station," Jeff said. "But if you go back there you'll trash another pump."

"I simply do not understand how that happened," the bishop said. "I never felt anything or saw anything; the first I knew was when — Albers? I have his name written down. When he showed up in hysteria. Perhaps that was a manifestation of the Holy Ghost. I hope my insurance hasn't lapsed. It's always a good idea to carry automobile insurance."

I said, "That wasn't Walloon he was speaking."

"Yes, well," Tim said, "it also wasn't intelligible. It may well have been glossolalia, for all I know. Maybe there is evidence that the Holy Ghost is here." He reseated himself. "Are we waiting for something?" he asked me. "You keep looking at your watch, I only have an hour; then I have to get back to the City.

The difficulty that dogma presents is that it Strickens the creative spirit in man. Whitehead — Alfred North Whitehead — has given us the idea of God in process, and he is, or was, a major scientist. Process theology. It all goes back to Jakob Boehme and his 'no-yes' deity, his dialectic deity anticipating Hegel. Boehme based that on Augustine. *'Sic et non,'* you know. Latin lacks a precise word for 'yes'; I suppose *'sic'* is the closest, although by and large *'sic'* is more correctly rendered as 'so,' or 'hence,' or 'in that manner.' *'Quod si hoc nunc sic incipiam? Nihil est. Quod si sic? Tantumdem egero. Et sic —'"* He paused, frowning. "*'Nihil est.'* In a distributive language — English is the best example — that would literally mean 'nothing exists.' Of course what Terence means is, 'it is nothing,' with *'id,'* or 'it,' understood. Still, there is an enormous thrust in the two-word utterance 'nihil est.' The amazing power of Latin to compress meaning into the fewest possible words. That and precision are the two most admirable qualities of it, by far. English, however, has the greater vocabulary."

"Dad," Jeff said, "we're waiting for a friend of Angel's. I told you about her the other day."

*"Non video,"* the bishop said. "I'm saying that I don't see her, the 'her' being understood. Look, that man is going to take a picture of us."

Fred Hill, carrying an SLR camera with flash attachment, approached our table. "Your Grace, would it be all right with you if I took your picture?"

"Let me take a picture of you two together," I said, standing up. "You can put it on the wall," I said to Fred Hill.

"That would be fine with me," Tim said.

During the meal, Kirsten Lundborg joined us. She looked unhappy and fatigued, and she could find nothing on the menu that pleased her. She wound up drinking a glass of white wine, eating nothing, saying very little, but smoking one cigarette after another. Her face showed lines of strain. We did not know it then, but she had mild and chronic peritonitis, which can be — and was very soon for her — very serious. She hardly seemed aware of us. I assumed she had gone into one of her periodic depressions; I had no idea that day that she was physically ill.

"You could probably get toast and a soft-boiled egg," Jeff said.

"No." Kirsten shook her head. "My body is trying to die," she said presently. She did not elaborate. We all felt uncomfortable. I suppose that was the idea in her mind. Perhaps not. Bishop Archer gazed at her attentively and with a great deal of sympathy. I wondered if he intended to suggest a laying on of hands. They do that in the Episcopal Church. The recovery rate due to that is not recorded anywhere that I know of, which is just as well.

She spoke mostly about her son Bill, who had been turned down by the Army for psychological reasons. This seemed both to please her and to annoy her.

"I'm surprised to learn you have a son old enough to be inducted," the bishop said.

For a moment Kirsten was silent. Some of the worry that marred her features eased. It was evident to me that Tim's remark cheered her.

At this point in her life she was a rather good-looking woman, but a perpetual severity marred her, in terms of her looks and in terms of the emotional impression that she presented. As much as I admired her I knew that Kirsten could never turn down the chance to offer up a cruel remark, a defect that she had, in fact, honed into a talent. The idea seems to be that if you are clever enough you can insult people and they will sit still for it, but if you are clumsy and dumb you can get away with nothing. It all has to do with your verbal skills. You are judged, like contest entries, on aptness of phrase.

"Bill is only physically that old," Kirsten said. But she looked happier now. "What is it that comic said the other night on Johnny Carson? 'My wife doesn't go to a plastic surgeon; she wants the real thing.' I just had my hair done; that's why I was late. One time just before I had to fly over to France they did my hair so that—" She smiled. "I looked like Bozo the Clown. The whole time I was in Paris I wore a babushka. I told everyone I was on my way to Notre-Dame."

"What's a babushka?" Jeff asked.

Bishop Archer said, "A Russian peasant."

Regarding him intently, Kirsten said, "That's true. I must have the wrong word."

"You have the right word," the bishop said. "The term for the cloth worn about the head derives—"

"Aw Christ," Jeff said.

Kirsten smiled. She sipped her white wine.

"I understand you're a member of FEM," the bishop said.

"I *am* FEM," Kirsten said.

"She's one of the founders," I said.

"You know, I have very strong views about abortion," the bishop said.

"You know," Kirsten said, "I have, too. What are yours?"

"We feel that the unborn have rights invested in them not by man but by Almighty God," the bishop said. "The right to take a human life is denied back to the Decalogue."

"Let me ask you this," Kirsten said. "Do you think a human being has rights after he or she is dead?"

"I beg your pardon?" the bishop said.

"Well," Kirsten said, "you're granting them rights before

they're born; why not grant them equal rights after they're dead."

"As a matter of fact, they do have rights after they're dead," Jeff said. "You need a court order to use a cadaver or organs taken from a cadaver for —"

"I'm trying to eat this veal Oscar," I interrupted, seeing an endless line of argumentation ahead, and, emerging from it, Bishop Archer's refusal to make a free speech for FEM. "Can we talk about something else?"

Fazed not at all, Jeff continued, "I know a guy who works for the coroner's office. He told me one time they went into the intensive care ward at — well, I forget which hospital; anyhow, this woman had just died and they went in and ripped her eyes out for a transplant before the monitors had stopped registering vital signs. He said it happens all the time."

We sat for a time, Kirsten sipping her wine, the rest of us eating; however, Bishop Archer had not stopped gazing at Kirsten with sympathy and concern. It came to me later, but not at the time, that he sensed that she was latently physically ill, sensed what the rest of us had missed. Perhaps it emanated from his pastoral ministering, but I saw him do this again and again: discern a need in someone when no one else, sometimes even the person involved, recognized it or, if they recognized it, took time to pause and care.

"I have the highest regard for FEM," he said, in a gentle voice.

"Most people do," Kirsten said, but now she seemed genuinely pleased. "Does the Episcopal Church allow the ordination of women?"

"For the priesthood?" the bishop said. "It hasn't come yet but it is coming."

"Then I take it you personally approve."

"Certainly." He nodded. "I have taken an active interest in

modernizing the standards for male and female deacons . . . for one, I will not allow the term 'deaconess' to be used in my diocese; I insist that both male and female deacons be referred to as deacons. The standardization of educational and training bases for male and female deacons will make it possible later on to ordain female deacons to the priesthood. I see this as inevitable and I am working actively for it."

"Well, I am really pleased to hear you say this," Kirsten said. "Then you differ markedly from the Catholic Church." She set down her wine glass. "The pope —"

"The Bishop of Rome," Bishop Archer said. "That is what he actually is: the Bishop of Rome. The Roman Catholic Church; our church is a catholic church as well."

"They won't ever ordain women, you think?" Kirsten said.

"Only when the Parousia is here," Bishop Archer said.

"What is that?" Kirsten said. "You'll have to excuse my ignorance; I really have no religious background or inclinations."

"Neither do I," Bishop Archer said. "I only know that, as Malebranche said, 'It is not I who breathes but God who breathes in me.' The Parousia is the Presence of Christ. The catholic church, of which we are a part, breathes and breathes only through the living power of Christ; he is the head of which we are the body. 'Now the Church is his body, he is the head,' as Paul said. It is a concept known to the ancient world and one we can understand."

"Interesting," Kirsten said.

"No, it is true," the bishop said. "Intellectual matters are interesting and so are odd factual things, such as the amount of salt produced by a single mine. This that I speak of is a topic that determines not what we know but what we are. We have our life through Jesus Christ. 'He is the image of the unseen God and the first-born of all creation, for in him were created all things in heaven and on earth, everything visible and everything invisible, Thrones, Dominations, Sovereignties, Powers — all things were created through him and for him. Before anything was created, he existed, and he holds all things in unity.'" The bishop's voice was low and intense; he spoke evenly, and as he spoke he gazed directly at Kirsten, and I saw her return his gaze, in almost a stricken way, as if she both wanted to hear and did not want to hear, fearing and fascinated. Many times I had heard Tim preach at Grace Cathedral and he now addressed her, one person, with the same intensity that he brought to bear on great masses of people. And yet it was all for her.

There was silence for a moment.

"A lot of the priests still say 'deaconess,'" Jeff said. He shuffled awkwardly. "When Tim isn't around."

I said to Kirsten, "Bishop Archer is probably the strongest supporter of women's rights in the Episcopal Church."

"Actually, I think I've heard that," Kirsten said. She turned to me and said calmly, "I wonder — do you suppose —"

"I'd be glad to address your organization," the bishop said. "That's why we're having lunch." Reaching into his coat pocket, he brought out his black notebook. "I'll take your phone number and I promise to call you within the next few days. I'll have to consult with Jonathan Graves, the bishop suffragan, but I'm sure I'll be able to find time for you."

"I'll give you both my number at FEM," Kirsten said, "and my home phone number. Do —" She hesitated. "Do you want me to tell you something about FEM, Bishop?"

"Tim," Bishop Archer said.

"We are not militant in the conventional sense of —"

"I'm quite familiar with your organization," Bishop Archer said. "I want you to consider this. 'If I have all the eloquence of men or of angels, but speak without love, I am simply a gong booming or a cymbal clashing. If I have the gift of prophecy, understanding all the mysteries there are, and knowing everything, and if I have faith in all its fullness, to move mountains, but without love, then I am nothing at all.' First Corinthians, chapter thirteen. As women, you find your place in the world out of love, not animosity. Love is not limited to the Christian, love is not just for the church. If you wish to conquer us, show us love and not scorn. Faith moves mountains, love moves human hearts. The people opposing you are people, not things. Your enemy is not men but ignorant men. Don't confuse the men with their ignorance. It has taken years; it will take years more. Don't be impatient and don't hate. What time is it?" He looked around, suddenly concerned. "Here." He passed a card to Kirsten. "You call me. I have to be going. It was nice meeting you."

He left us then. I realized after he had gone, very suddenly realized, that he had forgotten to pay the check.

# 3

THE BISHOP OF California spoke to the members of FEM and then talked their governing board out of two thousand dollars as a contribution to the church's fund for world famine, really a nominal sum and for a meritorious cause. It took a while for the news that Tim was seeing Kirsten socially to percolate down to Jeff and me. Jeff was simply amazed. I thought it was funny.

It did not even strike Jeff as funny that his father had shaken two thousand dollars loose from FEM. He had seen a free speech looming up; that hadn't come to pass. He had anticipated friction and dislike between his father and my friend Kirsten. That had not come to pass either. Jeff did not understand his own father.

The way I found out was through Kirsten, not Tim. I got a phone call the week following Tim's speech. Kirsten wanted to go shopping with me in San Francisco.

When you're dating a bishop you do not tell everybody in town. Kirsten spent hours fussing with dresses and blouses and tops and skirts, at store after store before even hinting at what was going on. My promised silence was secured in advance by means of oaths more elaborate than those of the Rosicrucians. Telling me was ten percent of the fun; she strung the revelation out, seemingly forever. We were, in fact, all the way down at the Marina before I fathomed what she had been hinting at.

"If Jonathan Graves finds out," Kirsten said, "Tim will have to resign."

I could not even remember who Jonathan Graves was. The disclosure seemed irreal; I thought at first that she was joking and then I thought she was hallucinating.

"The *Chronicle* would put it on page one," Kirsten said, in a solemn tone. "And on top of the heresy trial—"

"Jesus Christ!" I said. "You can't sleep with a bishop!"

"I already have," Kirsten said.

"Who else have you told?"

"Nobody else. I'm not sure if you should tell Jeff. Tim and I talked it over. We couldn't decide."

We, I thought. You destructive bitch, I thought. To get laid you'd ruin a man's entire life, a man who knew Dr. King and Bobby Kennedy and determines the opinion of — *my* opinion, to name one person.

"Don't look so upset," Kirsten said.

"Whose idea was it?"

"Why should it make you angry?"

"Was it your idea?"

Kirsten said calmly, "We discussed it."

After a minute I began to laugh. Kirsten, annoyed at first, presently joined me; we stood on the grass by the edge of the bay, laughing and holding onto each other. Passing people regarded us with curiosity. "Was it any good?" I managed to say finally. "I mean, what was it like?"

"It was terrific. But now he has to confess."

"Does that mean you can't do it again?"

"It just means he has to confess again."

"Aren't you going to go to hell?"

Kirsten said, "He is. I'm not."

"Doesn't that bother you?"

"That I'm not going to hell?" She giggled.

"We have to be real adult about this," I said.

"Yes we do. We absolutely have to be totally adult. We have to walk around as if everything is normal. This is *not* normal. I mean, it isn't like I'm saying it's abnormal in the sense of—you know."

"Like making it with a goat."

Kirsten said, "I wonder if there's a word for it . . . making it with an Episcopal bishop. Bishopric. Tim told me that word."

"Bishop prick?"

"No, bishop *ric*. You're not pronouncing it right." We had to hold onto each other to keep from falling; neither of us could stop laughing. "It's the place he lives or something. Oh, God." She wiped the tears of laughter from her eyes. "Always be sure you pronounce it bishop *ric*. This is terrible. We really are going to go to hell, straight to hell. You know what he let me do?" Kirsten leaned close to me to whisper in my ear. "I tried on some of his robes and his miter; you know, the shovel hat. The first lady bishop."

"You may not be the first."

"I looked great. I looked better than he does. I want you to see. We're getting an apartment. For Christ's sake, don't say anything about this part especially, but he's paying for it out of his Discretionary Fund."

"Church money?" I stared at her.

"Listen." Kirsten looked solemn again, but she could not maintain her expression; she hid her face in her hands.

"Isn't that illegal?" I said.

"No, it's not illegal. That's why it's called the Bishop's Discretionary Fund; he gets to do with it what he wants. I'm going to go to work for him as—we haven't decided, but some kind of general secretary, like a booking agent or something, to handle all the speeches and traveling he does. His business affairs. I can still stay on with the organization . . . FEM, I mean." She was silent a moment and then she said, "The problem is going to be Bill. I can't tell him because he's nuts again. I shouldn't say that. Deep autistic fugal withdrawal with impaired ideation compounded with delusions of reference, plus alternating cata-tonic stupor and excitement. He's down at Hoover Pavilion, at Stanford. Mostly for diagnosis. In terms of diagnosis, they're the best on the West Coast. They use something like four psy-chiatrists for diagnosis, three from the hospital itself and one from outside."

"I'm sorry," I said.

"The Army thing did it. Anxiety about being drafted. They accused him of malingering. Well, I guess it's part of life. He had to drop out of school anyhow. He would have had to drop school anyhow, is what I'm trying to say. His episodes always begin the same way — he starts crying and he doesn't take out the trash. The crying part doesn't bother me; it's the goddamn trash. It just piles up, trash and garbage. And he doesn't bathe. And he stays in his apartment. And he doesn't pay his utility bills, so they cut off his gas and electricity. And he starts writing letters to the White House. This is one area Tim and I haven't discussed. I really don't discuss it with very many people. So I would esti-mate that I can keep our affair — my affair with Tim — secret be-cause I've had practice keeping things secret. No, pardon me; it doesn't begin with him crying — it begins with him not being able to drive his car. Driving phobia; he's afraid he'll veer off the road. First it has to do with the Eastshore Freeway and then it spreads to all the other streets, and then he winds up afraid to walk to the store, so as a result he can't shop for food. But that doesn't matter because by that time he isn't eating anything anyhow." She lapsed into silence. "There's a Bach cantata about it," she said finally, and I saw her try to smile. "A line in the 'Coffee Cantata.' About having trouble with your children. They're a hundred thousand miseries, something like that. Bill used to play the goddamn thing. Few people know Bach wrote a cantata about coffee, but he did."

We walked in silence.

"It sounds as if —" I said.

"It's schizophrenia. They use him to try out every new phenothiazine that comes along. He goes in cycles, but the cycles get worse. He's sick longer and he's more sick. I shouldn't have brought it up; it's not your problem."

"I don't mind."

Kirsten said, "Maybe Tim can effect a deep spiritual cure. Didn't Jesus cure mentally ill people?"

"He sent the evil spirits into a bunch of pigs," I said. "And they all rushed over a cliff."

"That seems like a waste," Kirsten said.

"They may have eaten them anyhow."

"Not if they were Jews. Anyhow, who would want to eat a pork chop that had an evil spirit in it? I shouldn't joke about this, but — I will talk to Tim about it. But not for a while. I think Bill got it from me. I'm screwed up, God knows. I'm screwed up and I screwed him up. I keep looking at Jeff and noticing the difference between them; they're about the same age and Jeff has such a good grip on reality."

"Don't bet on it," I said.

Kirsten said, "When Bill gets out of the hospital, I'd like him to meet Tim. I'd like him to meet your husband, in fact; they never have met, have they?"

"No," I said. "But if you think Jeff can serve as a role-model, I'm really not —"

"Bill has very few friends. He's not outgoing. I've talked about you and your husband; you're both his age."

Thinking about it, I perceived down the pipe of time Kirsten's lunatic son messing up our lives. That thought surprised me. It was utterly devoid of charity and it had in it an essence of fear. I knew my husband and I knew myself. Neither of us was ready to take on the job of amateur therapy. Kirsten, however, was an organizer. She organized people into doing things, good things but things not necessarily to their own benefit.

I had, at that instant, a keen intuition that I was being hustled. At the Bad Luck, I had essentially witnessed Bishop Archer and Kirsten Lundborg hustle each other in an intricate transaction, but it was, apparently, a transaction that benefited them both, or anyhow they both thought so. This, with her son Bill, looked to me like a purely one-way matter. I didn't see what we had to gain.

"Let me know when he's out," I said. "But I think that Tim, because of his professional training, would be a better —"

"But there's the age difference. And you get the element of the father-figure."

"Maybe that would be good. Maybe that's what your son needs."

Glaring at me, Kirsten said, "I've done an excellent job of raising Bill. His father walked out of our lives and never looked back."

"I didn't mean —"

"I know what you meant." Kirsten stared at me, and now, really, she had changed; she was angry and I could see hatred on her face. It made her look older. It made her look, in fact, physically ill. She had a bloated quality and I felt uncomfortable. I thought, then, of the pigs that Jesus had cast the evil spirits into, the pigs that rushed over the cliff. This is what you do when an evil spirit inhabits you, I thought. This is the sign, this look: the stigma. Maybe your son did inherit it from you.

But now we had an altered situation. Now she was my father-in-law's *pro tem* lover, potentially his mistress. I couldn't tell Kirsten to go fuck herself. She was family — in an illegal and unethical way. I was stuck with her. All of the curses of family, I thought, and none of the blessings. And I arranged it. The idea of introducing her and Tim had been mine. Bad karma, I thought, come back from the other side of the barn. As my father used to say.

Standing there in the grass near the San Francisco Bay, in the midafternoon sunlight, I felt uncomfortable. This is really in some respects a reckless and savage person, I said to myself. She dabbles in the life of a famous and respected man; she has a psychotic son; pins bristle from her as from an animal. Bishop Archer's future depends on Kirsten not flying into a rage one day and phoning up the *Chronicle* — his future depends on her unending goodwill.

"Let's go back to Berkeley," I said.

"No." Kirsten shook her head. "I have yet to find a dress I can wear. I came to the City to shop. Clothes are very important to me. They have to be; I'm seen in public a lot and I expect to be seen much more, now that I'm with Tim." Rage still showed on her face.

I said, "I'll go back by BART." I walked away.

"She's a very attractive woman," Jeff said that night when I told him. "Considering her age."

"Kirsten is on reds," I said.

"You don't know that."

"I suspect it. Her mood-changes. I've seen her take them. Yellow jackets. You know. Barbiturates. Sleeping pills."

"Everybody takes something. You smoke grass."

I said, "But I'm sane."

"You may not be when you get to be her age. It's too bad about her son."

"It's too bad about your father."

"Tim can manage her."

"He may have to have her killed."

Eying me, Jeff said, "What a strange thing to say."

"She's out of control. And what happens when Bounding Bill the Dingaling finds out?"

"I thought you said—"

"He'll be out. It costs thousands of dollars to be in Hoover Pavilion. You stay about four days. I've known people who passed in their front door and out the back. Even with all the financial resources of the Episcopal Diocese of California, Kirsten can't keep him in there. He'll bound out on kangaroo-spring shoes one of these days, his eyes rolling around in their sockets—that's all Tim needs. First she has me introduce her to Tim; *then* she tells me about her son the madman. Tim'll be preaching a sermon some Sunday morning at Grace Cathedral, and all of a sudden this lunatic will stand up and God will grant him the gift of tongues and that'll be the end of the most famous bishop in America."

"Life is a risk."

I said, "That's probably what Dr. King said that last morning of his life. They're all dead but Tim anyhow; Dr. King is dead; Bobby Kennedy and Jack Kennedy are dead—I've set up your father." I knew it that evening as I sat with my husband in our little living room. "He stops bathing; he stops taking out the garbage; he writes letters; what more do you need to know? He's probably writing a letter to the pope right now. Martians probably walked through the wall of his room and told him about his mother and your father. Christ. And I did it." I reached around under the couch for my beer can of grass.

"Don't get loaded. Please."

You worry about me, I thought, when madness rules our friends. "One joint," I said. "Half a joint. I'll toke up. A puff. I'll look at the joint. I'll pretend to look at the joint." I fished the empty beer can out. I guess I moved my stash, I said to my-self. To a safer place. I remember; in the middle of the night, I decided that monsters were going to rip me off. Mad Marga-ret from *Ruddigore* enters, the picture of theatrical madness, or however Gilbert put it. "Maybe I smoked it all up," I said. And I don't remember, I thought, because that's what mary jane does to you: fucks up your short-term memory. Probably I smoked it up five minutes ago and already I've forgotten.

"You're borrowing trouble," Jeff said. "I like Kirsten. I think it'll work out. Tim misses my mother."

Tim misses getting his rocks off, I said to myself. "That is a truly kinky lady," I said. "I had to come home by snail train. It took two hours. I'm going to talk to your father."

"No you're not."

"I will. I'm responsible. My stash is behind the stereo tuner. I'm going to get totally wasted and phone Tim and tell him that—" I hesitated, and then futility crushed me; I felt like cry-ing. Seating myself, I got out a Kleenex. "Goddamn it," I said. "Fry the bacon is not a game bishops are supposed to play. If I had known he felt that way—"

"'Fry the bacon'?" Jeff said wonderingly.

"Pathology frightens me. I sense pathology. I sense highly professional, responsible people wrecking their lives in ex-change for a warm body, a temporarily warm body. I don't even sense the bodies staying warm, for that matter. I sense every-thing getting cold. You're only supposed to get into such limited time-binding if you're on junk and think in hours; these peo-ple are supposed to think in terms of decades. Lifetimes. They meet in a restaurant run by Fred the Hatchetman, which is ill-omen incarnate, the ghost of Berkeley coming back to get us all, and when they leave they have each other's phone number and it's all accomplished. What I wanted to do was help a women's lib group, but then everyone queeged out on me, you included.

You were there; you watched it happen. *I* watched it happen. I was as crazy as the rest of you; I suggested that Fred the Soviet narc get photographed with the Bishop of the Diocese of California — they should have been in drag, according to my logic. The trouble with seeing ruin coming is that —" I wiped at my eyes. "Please, God, let me locate my mary jane. Jeff, look behind the tuner. It's in a Carl's Junior bag, a white bag. Okay?"

"Okay." Obligingly, Jeff rummaged behind the tuner. "I found it. Calm down."

"You can see ruin but you can't see what direction it's coming from. It just sort of hangs there, like a cloud. Who was that character in *Li'l Abner* who had the cloud following him around? You know, this was the stuff the FBI was trying to hang on Martin Luther King. Nixon loves this shit. Maybe Kirsten is a government agent. Maybe I am. Maybe we're programmed. Pardon me for playing Cassandra in our collective movie, but I see death. I thought Tim Archer, your father, was a spiritual person. Does he dive into —" I broke off. "My metaphor is offensive. Forget it. Does he go after women like this normally? I mean, is this just merely the fact that I know about it and arranged it? Remind me not to go to Mass, not that I ever do. There's no telling where the hands that hold out the chalice —"

"That's enough."

"No, I get to be crazy along with Bong-Bong-Bill and Creepy Kirsten and Tim the No-Longer-Torpid. And Jeff the Jerk, you jerk. Is there a joint already rolled, or do I have to chew up grass like a cow? I can't roll a joint right now; look." I held out my hands; they shook. "This is called a *grand mal* seizure. Get somebody in here. Get up to the Avenue and score me some tranks. I will tell you what is coming: somebody's life is going to get destroyed because of all this, not 'this' that I'm doing right now but 'this' that I did at the Bad Luck, appropriately named. When I die, I will have a choice: head up in shit or head down in shit. Shit is the word for it, what I did." I had begun to gasp. Crying and gasping, I reached for the joint my husband held. "Light it for me," I said, "you fool. I really can't chew it up; it's a waste. You have to chew up half a lid to get off, or at least I do. God knows about the rest of the world; maybe they can get off anyhow, any time. Head down in shit and never able to get loaded again — exactly what I deserve. And if I could call it all back, if I knew any way to call it back, I would. I am cursed with total insight. I see and —"

"You want to go to Kaiser?"

"The hospital?" I stared at him.

"I mean, you're out of control."

"That's what total insight does for you. Thanks." I took the joint, which he had lit, and inhaled. At least now I could no longer talk. And pretty soon I would no longer know or think. Or even remember. Put on *Sticky Fingers,* I said to myself. The Stones. "Sister Morphine." Hearing about all those bloody sheets calms me. I wish there was a comforting hand placed on my head, I thought. I'm not the one who's going to be dead tomorrow, although I should be. Let us by all means name the most innocent person possible. That will be the one. "The bitch made me walk home. From San Francisco."

"You took —"

"That's walking."

Jeff said, "I like her. I think she's a good friend. I think she will be — and probably is already — good for Dad. Has it occurred to you that you're jealous?"

"What?" I said.

"That's right. I said jealous. You're jealous of the relationship. You wish you were part of it. I see your reaction as an insult to me. I should be — our relationship should be — enough for you."

"I'm going for a walk."

"Suit yourself."

"If you had eyes in the front of your head — let me finish. I'll be calm. I'll say it calmly. Tim is not just a religious figure; he speaks for thousands in the church and outside the church, maybe more so outside. Do you grasp it? If he tumbles, we all take a fall. We all are doomed. He is almost the last one left; the others are dead. The thing about this is, it isn't necessary. It's like he decided. He saw it and he walked right at it; he didn't duck and he didn't fight — he embraced it. You think this — what I feel — is because I had to come home on the train? One by one, they got every public figure and now Tim hands over the keys, hands them over under his own power, without a fight."

"And *you* want to fight. Me, if necessary."

I said, "I see you as stupid. I see everyone as dumb. I see stupidity winning. This is not something the Pentagon is doing. This is dumb. This is walking right at it and saying, 'Take me, I'm —'"

"Jealousy," Jeff said. "Your psychological motivation is all over this house."

"I have no 'psychological motivation.' I just want to see someone there when the firing ends, someone who isn't —" I broke off. "Don't come around later and say this was done to us, because it wasn't. And don't tell me it was a complete surprise. A bishop who has an affair with a woman he meets in a restaurant — this *is* a man who just finished backing over a gasoline pump and drove happily away. And the pump came after him. That's how it works: you flatten some joker's pump and he runs until he catches up with you. You're in a car and he's on foot, but he seeks you out and then, all of a sudden, there he is. This is that; this is someone chasing us down and he will catch up; he always does. I saw that pump jockey; he was mad. He was going to keep running. They never give up."

"And you see that now. Due to one of your best friends."

"That's the worst kind."

Grinning, Jeff said, "I know that story. It's a W. C. Fields story. There's this director—"

"And she isn't running any more," I said. "She caught up with him. They're renting an apartment. All it takes is one nosy neighbor. What about this redneck bishop prosecuting Tim for heresy? What would he do with this? If someone is after you for heresy, do you bang the next broad you meet for lunch? And then go shopping for an apartment? Look." I walked over to my husband. "Where do you go after being a bishop? Is Tim tired of that already? He got tired of everything else he ever did. He even got tired of being an alcoholic; he's the only hopeless drunk who sobered himself up out of boredom, out of a short attention span. People generally will their own misfortune. I see us doing that now. I see him getting bored and subconsciously saying, 'What the hell; it's dull putting on these funny clothes every day; let's stir up some human misery and see what comes out of it.'"

Laughing, Jeff said, "You know what—who—you remind me of? The witch in Purcell's *Dido and Aeneas*."

"What do you mean?"

"'Who, like dismal ravens crying, Beat the windows of the dying.' I'm sorry but—"

"You fool Berkeley intellectual," I said. "What horse's ass world do you inhabit? Not the same as me, I hope. Quoting some old verse—that's what did us in. They will report when they dig up our bones—your dad quoted the Bible in the restaurant the same way you're doing now. You ought to hit me or me you. I'll be glad when civilization ends. People babble out bits of books. Put on *Sticky Fingers*—put on 'Sister Morphine.' I can't be trusted with the stereo at this moment. You do it for me. Thanks for the joint."

"When you've calmed down—"

"When you've woken up," I said, "it'll all be over."

Jeff bent to search for the record I wanted to hear. He said nothing. Finally he had become angry. A dollar short and a day late, I thought, and at the wrong person. Like with me. Destroyed by our giant intellects: reasoning and pondering and doing nothing. Nitwits rule. We squabble. The sorceress in *Dido;* you are right. *"Thy hand, Belinda, darkness shades me; on thy bosom let me rest: more I would, but Death invades me —"* And what else does she say? *"Death is now a welcome guest."* Shit, I thought. It is relevant. He's right. Absolutely right.

Fiddling with the stereo, Jeff put the Stones' record on.

The music calmed me. A little. But I still cried, thinking about Tim. And all because they are stupid. It goes no deeper than that. And that is the worst of it all, that it is that simple. That there is no more.

A few days later, after thinking about it and making up my mind, I phoned Grace Cathedral and got an appointment to see Tim. He met me in his office, which was large and beautiful, in a building separate from the cathedral itself. After greeting me with a hug and kiss, he showed me two ancient clay vessels which, he explained, had been used as oil lamps in the Near East over four thousand years ago. As I watched him handling them, the thought came to me that the lamps probably — in fact, certainly — did not belong to him; they belonged to the Diocese. I wondered what they were worth. It was amazing that they had survived all these years.

"It's nice of you to give me some of your time," I said. "I know how busy you are."

The expression on Tim's face told me that he knew why I had shown up in his office. He nodded absently, as if, in fact, giving me as little of his attention as he could manage. I had seen him tune out that way several times; a part of his brain listened, but the greater part had sealed itself off already.

When I had finished delivering my set little speech, Tim said gravely, "Paul, you know, had been a Pharisee. For them a strict observance of the minutiae of the Torah — the Law — was everything. That particularly involved ritual purity. But later — after his conversion — he saw salvation not in the Law but in *zadiqah,* which is the state of righteousness that Jesus Christ brings. I want you to sit down with me here." He beckoned me over, opening a very large leatherbound Bible. "You're familiar with Romans, four through eight?"

"No, I'm not," I said. But I sat down beside him. I could see it coming, the lecture. The sermon. Tim had met me prepared.

"Romans five states Paul's basic premise, that we are saved through grace and not by works." He read, then, from the Bible he held open on his lap. "'So far then we have seen that, through our Lord Jesus Christ, by faith we are judged righteous and at peace with God —'" He glanced up at me; his gaze was keen and sharp. This was Timothy Archer the lawyer. "'— since it is by faith and through Jesus that we have entered this state of grace in which we can boast about looking forward to God's glory.' Let's see." He ran his fingers down the page, his lips moving. "'If it is certain that through one man's fall so many died, it is even more certain that divine grace, coming through the one man, Jesus Christ, came to so many as an abundant free gift.' He looked further on, turning pages. "Yes; ah. Here. 'But now we are rid of the Law, freed by death from our imprisonment, free to serve in the new spiritual way and not the old way of a written law.'" Again he looked further along. "'The reason, therefore, why those who are in Christ Jesus are not condemned, is that the law of the spirit of life in Christ Jesus has set you free from the law of sin and death.'" He glanced up at me. "This goes to the heart of Paul's perception. What 'sin' really refers to is hostility toward God. Literally, it means 'missing the mark,' as if, for example, you shot an arrow and it fell short, too low, or went too high. What mankind needs, what it requires, is righteousness. Only God has that and only God can provide it to men . . . men and women; I don't mean —"

"I understand," I said.

"Paul's perception is that faith, *pistis,* has the power, the absolute power, to kill sin. Out of this comes freedom from the Law; one is not required to believe that by following a formal stipulated code — code-ethics, it's called — one is saved. That position, that one is saved by following a very intricate, complex system of code-ethics, is what Paul rebelled against; that was the position of the Pharisees and that's what he turned from. This really is what Christianity, faith in our Lord Jesus Christ, is all about; righteousness through grace, and grace coming through faith. I'm going to have you read —"

"Yes," I said, "but the Bible says you're not supposed to commit adultery."

Instantly, Tim said, "Adultery is sexual unfaithfulness on the part of a married person. I am no longer married; Kirsten is no longer married."

"Oh," I said, nodding.

"The Seventh Commandment. Which pertains to the sanctity of marriage." Tim set down his Bible and crossed the room to the vast bookshelves; he lifted down a blue-backed volume. As he returned, he opened the book and searched its pages. "Let me quote to you what Dr. Hertz said, the late Chief Rabbi of the British Empire. In connection with the Seventh Commandment. Exodus, twenty thirteen. 'Adultery. Is an execrable and god-detested wrong-doing.' Philo. This Commandment against infidelity warns husband and wife alike against profaning the sacred Covenant of Marriage.'" He read further silently, then shut the book. "I think you have enough common sense, Angel, to understand that Kirsten and I are —"

"But it's risky," I said.

"Driving on the Golden Gate Bridge is risky. Do you know that Yellow Cabs are not allowed — I mean, not allowed by Yellow Cab, not the police — to drive in the fast lane on the Golden Gate Bridge? What they call 'suicide lane.' If a driver is caught driving in that lane he is fired. But people drive in the fast lane on the Golden Gate Bridge constantly. Maybe that's a poor analogy."

"No, it's a good one," I said.

"Do you drive in the fast lane on the Golden Gate Bridge?"

After a pause I said, "Sometimes."

"What if I came to you and sat you down and started lecturing you about it? Wouldn't you think I was treating you as a child, not an adult? Do you follow what I'm saying? When an adult does something you don't approve of, you discuss the matter with him or her. I'm willing to discuss my relationship with Kirsten with you because, for one thing, you're my daughter-in-law, but much more important, you're someone I know and care about and love. I think that's the salient term, here; it's the key to Paul's thinking. *Agape* in the Greek. Translated into Latin, it's *caritas,* from which we get the word 'caring,' to be concerned about someone. As you're concerned about me now, myself and your friend Kirsten. You care about us."

"That's right," I said. "That's why I'm here."

"Then for you, caring is important."

"Yes," I said. "Obviously."

"You can call it *agape* or you can call it *caritas* or love or caring about another person, but whatever you call it — let me read from Paul. Bishop Archer again opened his big Bible; he flipped through the pages rapidly, knowing exactly where he was going. "First Corinthians, chapter thirteen. 'If I have the gift of prophecy, understanding—'"

"Yes, you quoted that at the Bad Luck," I interrupted.

"And I will quote it again." His voice was brisk. "'If I give away all that I possess, piece by piece, and if I even let them take my body to burn it, but am without love, it will do me no good whatever.' Now listen to this. 'Love does not come to an end. But if there are gifts of prophecy, the time will come when they must fail; or the gift of languages, it will not continue for ever; and knowledge—for this, too, the time will come when it must fail. For our knowledge is imperfect and our prophesying is imperfect, but once perfection comes, all imperfect things will disappear. When I was a child, I used to talk like a child, and think like a child, and argue like a child, but now I am a man, all childish ways are put behind me.'"

The phone on his big desk rang, then.

Looking annoyed, Bishop Archer set down his Bible, open. "Excuse me." He went to get the phone.

As I sat, waiting for him to finish his phone conversation, I looked over the passage he had been reading. It was a passage familiar to me, but in the King James translation. This Bible, I saw, was the Jerusalem Bible. I had never seen it before. I read on past the point at which he had stopped.

His phone conversation finished, Bishop Archer returned. "I have to be off. There's an African bishop waiting to see me; they just brought him here from the airport."

"It says," I said, putting my finger on the passage in his big Bible, "that all we see is a dim reflection."

"It also says, 'In short there are three things that last: faith, hope and love; and the greatest of these is love.' I would point out to you that that sums up the *kerygma* of our Lord."

"What if Kirsten tells people?"

"I think she can be counted on to be discreet." He had already reached the door of his office; reflexively, I rose to my feet and followed after him.

"She told me."

"You're my son's wife."

"Yeah, well —"

"I'm sorry I have to run off like this." Bishop Archer shut and locked his office door behind us. "God bless." He kissed me on the forehead. "We want to have you over when we're set up. Kirsten found an apartment today, in the Tenderloin. I haven't seen it. I'm leaving that up to her." And off he strode, leaving me standing there. He got me on a technicality, I realized. I had adultery confused with fornication. I keep forgetting he was a lawyer. I entered his large office with something to say and never said it; I went in smart and came out stupid. With nothing in between.

Maybe if I didn't smoke dope I could argue better. He won; I lost. No: he lost; I lost; we both lost. Shit.

I never said love was bad. I never knocked *agape*. That was not the point, the fucking point. Not getting caught is the point. Bolting your feet down to the floor is the point, the floor we call reality.

As I started toward the street, I thought: I am passing judgment on one of the most successful men in the world. I will never be known as he is known; I will never influence opinion. I did not put away my pectoral cross for the duration of the Vietnam War as Tim did. Who the fuck am I?

# 4

NOT LONG THEREAFTER, Jeff and I received an invitation to visit the Bishop of California and his mistress at their hideout in the Tenderloin. It turned out to *be* a sort of party. Kirsten had fixed canapés and hors d'oeuvres; we could smell food cooking in the kitchen . . . Tim had me drive him to a nearby liquor store to get wine; they had forgotten. I chose the wine. Tim stood blankly, as if abstracted, while I paid the clerk. I guess when you've been a member of AA, you learn to phase out in a liquor store.

Back at the apartment, in the medicine cabinet of the bathroom, I found a vast bottle of Dexamyl, the size bottle they give you when you're going on a long trip. Kirsten doing speed? I asked myself. Making no noise, I took down the bottle. The bishop's name was on the prescription label. Well, I thought. Off booze and onto speed. Aren't they supposed to warn you about that in AA? I flushed the toilet—so as to create some sound—and while the water gurgled I opened the bottle and stuck a few of the Dex tablets in my pocket. This is something you automatically do if you live in Berkeley; no one thinks anything about it. On the other hand, no one in Berkeley leaves their dope in the bathroom.

Presently, the four of us sat around the modest living room, relaxing. Everyone but Tim held a drink. Tim wore a red shirt and permapress slacks. He did not look like a bishop. He looked like Kirsten Lundborg's lover.

"This is a really nice place," I said.

On the way home from the liquor store, Tim had talked about private detectives and how they go about finding you. They sneak into your apartment while you're gone and go through all the dresser drawers. The way you catch on to this is by taping a human hair to every outer door. I think Tim had seen that in a movie.

"If you come back and find the hair gone or broken," he informed me as we walked from the car to the apartment, "you know you're being watched." He narrated, then, the history of the FBI in regard to Dr. King. It was a story everyone in Berkeley knew. I listened politely.

In the living room of their hideout that evening, I first heard about the Zadokite Documents. Now, of course, you can buy the Doubleday Anchor book, the Patton, Myers and Abré translation, which is complete. With the Helen James introduction dealing with mysticism, comparing and contrasting the Zadokites with, for example, the Qumran people, who presumably were Essenes, although that has really never been established,

"I feel," Tim said, "that this may prove more important than even the Nag Hammadi Library. We already have a fair working knowledge of Gnosticism, but we know nothing about the Zadokites, except for the fact that they were Jews."

"What is the approximate date on the Zadokite scrolls?" Jeff asked.

"They have made a preliminary estimate of about two hundred B.C.E.," Tim said.

"Then they could have influenced Jesus," Jeff said.

"It's not likely," Tim said. "I'll be flying over there to London in March; I'll have a chance to talk to the translators. I wish

John Allegro were involved, but he's not." He talked for a while about Allegro's work in connection with the Qumran scrolls, the so-called Dead Sea Scrolls.

"Wouldn't it be interesting," Kirsten said, "if the —" She hesitated. "Zadokite Documents turned out to contain Christian material."

"Christianity is, after all, based on Judaism," Tim said.

"I mean specific sayings attributed to Jesus," Kirsten said.

"There is not that clear a break in the rabbinical tradition," Tim said. "You find Hillel expressing some of the ideas we consider basic to the New Testament. And of course Matthew understood everything that Jesus did and said as a fulfillment of Old Testament prophecies. Matthew wrote to Jews and for Jews and, essentially, as a Jew. God's plan set forth in the Old Testament is brought to completion by Jesus. The term 'Christianity' was not in use at his time; by and large, apostolic Christians simply spoke of 'the Way.' Thus they stressed its naturalness and universality." After a pause he added, "And you find the expression 'the word of the Lord.' That appears in Acts, six. 'The word of the Lord continued to spread; the number of disciples in Jerusalem was greatly increased.'"

"What does 'Zadokite' derive from?" Kirsten asked.

"Zadok, a priest of Israel, about the time of David," Tim said. "He founded a priestly house, the Zadokites. They were of the house of Eleazar. There is mention of Zadok in the Qumran scrolls. Let me check." He rose to go get a book from a still-unpacked carton. "First Chronicles, chapter twenty-four. 'These also, side by side with their kinsmen the sons of Aaron, cast lots in the presence of Kind David, Zadok —' There he is mentioned." Tim shut the book. It was another Bible.

"But I guess now we're going to find out a lot more," Jeff said.

"Yes, I hope so," Tim said. "When I'm in London." He now, as was his custom, abruptly shifted mental gears. "I'm commissioning a rock mass to be given at Grace this Christmas." Scrutinizing me he said, "What is your opinion about Frank Zappa?"

I was at a loss for an answer.

"We would arrange for the actual service to be recorded," Tim continued. "So it could be released as an album. Captain Beefheart has also been recommended to me. And there were several other names offered. Where could I get a Frank Zappa album to listen to?"

"At a record store," Jeff said.

"Is Frank Zappa black?" Tim asked.

"I don't see that that matters," Kirsten said. "To me, that is inverse prejudice."

Tim said, "I was just curious. This is an area I know nothing about. Does any of you have an opinion about Marc Bolan?"

"He's dead," I said. "You're talking about T. Rex."

"Marc Bolan is dead?" Jeff said. He looked amazed.

"I could be wrong," I said. "I suggest Ray Davies. He writes the Kinks' stuff. He's very good."

"Would you look into it for me?" Tim said, speaking both to Jeff and me.

"I wouldn't know how to go about doing that," I said.

Kirsten said quietly, "I'll take care of it."

"You could get Paul Kantner and Gracie Slick," I said. "They just live over at Bolinas in Marin County."

"I know," Kirsten said, nodding placidly and with the air of total confidence.

Bullshit, I thought. You don't even know who I'm talking about. Already you're in charge, just from being set up in this apartment. It isn't even that much of an apartment.

Tim said, "I would like Janis Joplin to sing at Grace."

"She died in 1970," I said.

"Then whom do you recommend in her place?" Tim asked. He waited expectantly.

"'In Janis Joplin's place,'" I said. "'In Janis Joplin's place.' I'll have to think that over. I really can't come up with a name off the top of my head. That will take some time."

Kirsten regarded me with a mixture of expressions. Mostly disapproval. "I think what she's trying to say," Kirsten said, "is that no one can or ever will take Joplin's place."

"Where would I get one of her records?" Tim said.

"At a record store," Jeff said.

"Would you do that for me?" his father said.

"Jeff and I have all her records," I said. "There aren't that many. We'll bring them over."

"Ralph McTell," Kirsten said.

"I want all these suggestions written down," Tim said. "A rock mass at Grace Cathedral is going to attract a good deal of attention."

I thought: There is no such person as Ralph McTell. From across the room Kirsten smiled at me, a complicated smile. She had me; I couldn't be sure one way or another.

"He's on the Paramount label," Kirsten said. Her smile increased.

"I had really hoped to get Janis Joplin," Tim said, half to himself. He seemed puzzled. "They were playing a song with her — perhaps she didn't write it — on the car radio this morning. She's black, isn't she?"

"She is white," Jeff said, "and she is dead."

"I hope somebody is writing this down," Tim said.

My husband's emotional involvement with Kirsten Lundborg did not begin at one particular moment on a certain day, at least so far as I could discern. Initially, he maintained that Kirsten was good for the bishop; she had enough practical realism to keep both of them anchored, not floating endlessly upward. It is necessary, in evaluating these things, to distinguish your awareness from that of which you are aware. I can say when I noticed it but that is all I can say.

Considering her age, Kirsten still managed to emit tolerable amounts of sexually stimulating waves. That was how Jeff saw her. From my standpoint she remained an older female friend who now, by virtue of her relationship with Bishop Archer, out-ranked me. The degree of erotic provocativeness in a woman has no interest for me; I do not swing both ways, as the expression goes. Nor for me is it a threat. Until, of course, my own husband is involved. But the problem is with him, then.

While I worked at the law office and candle shop, seeing to it that drug dealers got out of trouble as fast as they got in, Jeff bothered his head with a series of extension courses at the University of California. We in Northern California had not quite reached the point of offering survey courses in how to compose your own mantras; that belonged to the Southland, totally despised by everyone in the Bay Area. Jeff had enrolled in a serious project: tracing the ills of modern Europe back to the Thirty Years War which had devastated Germany (circa 1648), caused the collapse of the Holy Roman Empire, and culminated in the rise of Nazism and Hitler's Third Reich. Above and beyond the courses pertaining to this, Jeff now advanced his own theory as to the root of it all. Upon reading Schiller's *Wallenstein Trilogy*, Jeff leaped to the intuitive insight that had the great general not gotten involved with astrology the imperial cause would have triumphed, and, as a result, World War Two would never have come into being.

The third play in Schiller's trilogy, *The Death of Wallenstein*, profoundly affected my husband. He regarded the play as equal to any of Shakespeare's and a whole lot better than most. Moreover, no one had read it — at least insofar as he could tell — except himself. To him, Wallenstein loomed as one of the ultimate enigmas of Western history. Jeff noted that Hitler, like Wallenstein, relied in times of crisis on the occult rather than on reason. In Jeff's view this all added up to something significant, but he could not fathom just what. Hitler and Wallenstein had had so many traits in common — Jeff maintained — that the resemblance bordered on the uncanny. Both were great but eccentric generals and both had utterly wrecked Germany. Jeff hoped to do a paper on the coincidences, extracting from the evidence the conclusion that the abandoning of Christianity for the occult opened the door to universal ruin. Jesus and Simon Magus (as Jeff saw it) stood as the bipolarities, absolute and distinct.

I couldn't have cared less.

You see, this is what going to school forever and ever does to you. While I slaved away at the law office and candle shop, Jeff read everything in the U.C. Berkeley Library on, for instance, the Battle of Lützen (November 16, 1632) at which time and place Wallenstein's fortunes were decided. Gustavus II Adolphus, king of Sweden, died at Lützen, but the Swedes won anyhow. The real significance of this victory lay, of course, in the fact that at no time again would the Catholic powers be in a position to crush the Protestant cause. Jeff, however, viewed it all in terms of Wallenstein. He reread and reread Schiller's trilogy and tried to reconstruct from it — and from more accurate historical accounts — the precise moment when Wallenstein lost touch with reality.

"It's like with Hitler," Jeff said to me. "Can you say he was always crazy? Can you say he was crazy at all? And if he was crazy but not always crazy, when did he become crazy and what caused him to become crazy? Why should a successful man who holds really an enormous amount of power, a staggering amount of power, power to determine human history — why should he drift off like that? Okay; with Hitler it was probably paranoid schizophrenia and those injections that quack doctor was giving him. But neither factor was involved in Wallen-stein's case."

Kirsten, being Norwegian, took a sympathetic interest in Jeff's preoccupation with Gustavus Adolphus' campaign into Central Europe. In between telling Swede jokes she revealed great pride in the role that the great Protestant King had played in the Thirty Years War. Also, she knew something about all this, which I did not. Both she and Jeff agreed that the Thirty Years War had been, up until World War One, the most dreadful war since the Huns sacked Rome. Germany had been reduced to cannibalism. Soldiers on both sides had regularly skewered bodies and roasted them. Jeff's reference books hinted at even more abominations too dreadful to detail. Everything con-nected with that period in time and place had been dreadful.

"We are still paying the price today," Jeff said, "for that war."

"Yeah, I guess it really was dreadful," I said, seated by myself in a corner of our living room reading a current issue of *Howard the Duck*.

Jeff said, "I don't think you're particularly interested."

Glancing up, I said, "I get tired from bailing out heroin deal-ers. I'm always the one they send over to the bail bondsman. I'm sorry if I don't take the Thirty Years War as seriously as you and Kirsten do."

"Everything hinges on the Thirty Years War. And the Thirty Years War hinged on Wallenstein."

"What are you going to do when they go to England? Your fa-ther and Kirsten."

He stared at me.

"She's going, too. She told me. They've got that agency set up, Focus Center, where she's his agent or whatever."

"Jesus Christ," Jeff said bitterly.

I went back to reading *Howard the Duck*. It was the episode where space people turn Howard the Duck into Richard Nixon.

Reciprocally, Richard Nixon grows feathers while addressing the nation on network TV. Likewise the top brass at the Pentagon.

"And they're going to be gone how long?" Jeff said.

"Until Tim figures out the meaning of the Zadokite Documents and how they pertain to Christianity."

"Shit," Jeff said.

"What's 'Q'?" I said.

"'Q.'" Jeff echoed.

"Tim said that preliminary reports, based on fragmentary translations of some documents —"

"'Q' is the hypothetical source for the Synoptics." His voice was brutal and rough.

"What are the Synoptics?"

"The first three Gospels. Matthew, Mark and Luke. They supposedly come from one source, probably Aramaic. Nobody's ever been able to prove it."

"Well," I said, "Tim told me on the phone the other night while you were in class that the translators in London think that the Zadokite Documents contain — not just Q — but the material Q is based on. They're not sure. Tim sounded more excited than I ever heard him sound before."

"But the Zadokite Documents date from two hundred years before Christ."

"That's probably why he was so excited."

Jeff said, "I want to go along."

"You can't," I said.

"Why not?" Raising his voice, he said, "Why don't I get to go if she gets to go? I'm his son!"

"He's straining the Bishop's Discretionary Fund as it is. They're going to be staying several months; it's going to cost a whole lot."

Jeff walked out of the living room. I continued reading. After a time, I realized I was hearing a strange sound; I lowered my copy of *Howard the Duck* and listened.

In the kitchen, in the darkness, by himself, my husband was crying.

One of the strangest and most perplexing accounts I ever read concerning my husband's suicide was that he, Jeff Archer, Bishop Timothy Archer's son, killed himself because he was afraid he was a homosexual. Some book written a number of years after his death — after all three of them had died — mangled the facts so thoroughly that, when you had finished reading it (I don't even remember the title or who wrote it) you knew less about Jeff and Bishop Archer and Kirsten Lundborg than before you started. It is like information theory; it is noise driving out signal. But it is noise posing as signal so you do not even recognize it as noise. The intelligence agencies call it disinformation, something the Soviet Bloc relies on heavily. If you can float enough disinformation into circulation you will totally abolish everyone's contact with reality, probably your own included.

Jeff held two mutually exclusive views toward his father's mistress. On the one hand she sexually stimulated him, so he felt strongly but wickedly attracted to her. On the other hand he loathed her and hated her and resented her for — he supposed — replacing him in terms of Tim's interest and affections.

But it did not end even there . . . although I didn't discern the rest until years had passed. Beyond and above being jealous of Kirsten, he was jealous of — well, Jeff had it all screwed up; I can't really untangle it. One has to bear in mind the special problems in being the son of a man whose picture has appeared on the cover of *Time* and *Newsweek* and who gets interviewed by David Frost, shows up on the Johnny Carson program, gets political cartoons in major newspapers devoted to him — what in Christ's name do *you* do, as the son?

For one week Jeff joined them in England, and regarding that week I know little; Jeff came back mute and withdrawn, and that was when he headed for the hotel room in which he shot himself in the face one late night. I am not going to go into my feelings about that as a way of killing yourself. It did bring the bishop back from London within a matter of hours, which, in a certain sense, the suicide was all about.

In a very real sense, it also had to do with Q, or rather the source of Q, now referred to in the newspaper articles as U.Q., which is *Ur-Quelle* in German: Original Source. Behind Q lay the *Ur-Quelle*, and this is what led Timothy Archer to London and several months in a hotel with his mistress, ostensibly his business agent and general secretary.

No one had ever expected the documents behind Q to reappear in the world; no one had known that U.Q. existed. Since I am not a Christian — and never will be, after the deaths of the people I loved — I am not now and was not then particularly interested, but I suppose it is theologically important, especially so inasmuch as the date assigned to U.Q. is two hundred years before the time of Jesus.

# 5

WHAT I REMEMBER most, in the first newspaper articles to come out, the first intimation we had, anybody beyond the translators had, that this was an even more important find than the Qumran scrolls, was (the articles said) a particular Hebrew noun. They spell it two different ways; sometimes it showed up as *anokhi* and sometimes *anochi*.

The word shows up in Exodus, chapter twenty, verse two. This is a terribly moving and important section of the Torah, for here God Himself speaks, and he says:

> *"I am the Lord thy God, who brought thee out of the land of Egypt, out of the house of bondage."*

The first Hebrew word is *anokhi* or *anochi* and it means "I" — as in "I am the Lord thy God." Jeff showed me what the official Jewish commentary is on this part of the Torah:

> "The God adored by Judaism is not an impersonal Force, an It, whether spoken of as 'Nature' or 'World-Reason.' The God of Israel is the Source not only of power and life, but of consciousness, personality, moral purpose and ethical action."

Even for me, a non-Christian — or I should say a non-Jew, I guess — this shakes me; I am touched and changed; I am not the same. What is expressed here, Jeff explained to me, is, in this single word, one letter of the English alphabet, the unique self-consciousness of God:

> "As man towers above all the other creatures by his will and self-conscious action, so God 'rules over all as the one completely self-conscious Mind and Will. In both the visible and the invisible realms, He manifests Himself as the absolutely free personality, moral and spiritual, who allots to everything its existence, form and purpose.'"

That was written by Samuel M. Cohon, quoting Kaufmann Kohler. Another Jewish writer, Hermann Cohen, wrote:

> "God answered him thus: 'I am that which I am. So shalt thou say to the children of Israel: *"I am"* has sent me to you.' There is probably no greater miracle in the history of the spirit than that revealed in this verse. For here, a primeval language which is as yet without any philosophy, emerges and haltingly pronounces the most profound word of all philosophy. The name of God is 'I am that which I am.' This signifies that God is Being, that God is the I, which denotes the Existing One."

And this is what turned up at the *wadi* in Israel, dating from 200 B.C.E., the *wadi* not far from Qumran; this word lay at the heart of the Zadokite Documents, and every Hebrew scholar knows this word, and every Christian and Jew should know it, but there at that *wadi* the word *anokhi* was used in a different way, a way no living person had ever seen it employed before. And so Tim and Kirsten stayed in London twice as long as they had intended to stay, because the very core of something had been located, the core in fact, of the Decalogue, as if the Lord had left tracings in his own autograph, which is to say, his own hand.

While these discoveries took place — in the translating stage — Jeff wandered around the U.C. Berkeley campus learning about the Thirty Years War and Wallenstein, who had cut himself off progressively from reality during the worst war, perhaps, of all wars, except for the total wars of this century; I am not going to say that I have ascertained which particular drive killed my husband, which thrust from the mix got to him, but one did or they all did in chorus — he is dead and I wasn't even there at the time, nor did I expect it. My expectation came initially when I learned that Kirsten and Tim had gotten involved in an invisible affair. I said what I had to say then; I took my best shot — I visited the bishop at Grace Cathedral and found myself outargued with little effort on his part: little effort and professional skill. It was an easy verbal victory for Tim Archer. So much for that.

If you intend to kill yourself you don't require a reason, in the usual sense of the term; just as, to the contrary, when you intend to stay alive, no verbal, articulated, formal reason is necessary, one you can seize on if the issue comes up. Jeff had been left out. I could see that his interest in the Thirty Years War really had. to do with Kirsten; his mind, or some portion of it, had noted her Scandinavian origin, and another part of his mind had perceived and recorded the fact that the Swedish army was the victor and heroic power of that war; his emotional pursuits and his intellectual pursuits wove together, which was, for a time, to his advantage, and then when Kirsten flew to England he found himself wrecked by his own cleverness. Now he had to confront the fact that he didn't really give a good goddamn about Tilly and Wallenstein and the Holy Roman Empire; he was in love with a woman his mother's age who was sleeping with his father — and doing that eight thousand miles away, and above and beyond everything else the two of them, to his exclusion, participated in one of the most exhilarating archeological theology discoveries in history, on a day-to-day basis as the translations became available, as the documents got patched and pasted together and the words emerged, one by one, and again and again the Hebrew word *anokhi* manifested itself, in unusual contexts, baffling contexts: new contexts. The documents spoke as if *anokhi* were present at the *wadi*. It or he was referred to as *here*, not there, *now*, not then. *Anokhi* was not something the Zadokites thought about or knew about; *it was something they possessed.*

It is very hard to read your library books and listen to a Donovan record, no matter how good, when a discovery of that magnitude is going on in another part of the world, and if your father and his mistress, both of whom you love and at the same time furiously hate, are involved in that unfolding discovery — what drove me frantic was Jeff playing and replaying Paul McCartney's first solo album; he liked "Teddy Boy" in particular. When he left me to go live alone in the hotel room — the room where he shot himself — he took the album with him, although he had, it turned out, nothing to play it on. He wrote me a number of times, telling me that he was still active in antiwar happenings. Probably he was. I think, though, by and large he just sat alone in the hotel room trying to figure out how he felt about his father and, even more important, how he felt about Kirsten. So that would be 1971, since the McCartney album came out in 1970. But see, that left me alone, too, in our house. I got the house; Jeff died. I told you not to live alone but I am speaking, really, to myself. You can do any goddamn thing you want but I am never going to live alone again. I'll take in street people before I let that happen to me, that isolation.

Just don't play any Beatles albums around me. That's the main thing I ask. I can take Joplin, because I still think it's funny that Tim thought Joplin was alive and black instead of dead and white, but I do not want to hear the Beatles because they are linked to too much pain in me, inside me, in my life, in what happened.

I am not quite rational myself when it comes down to it, to, specifically, my husband's suicide. I hear in my mind a mélange of John and Paul and George — with Ringo thumping away in the rear somewhere — with fragments of tunes and their words, critical terms pertaining to souls suffering a great deal, although not in a way I can pin down except, of course, for my husband's death and then Kirsten's death, and finally, Tim Archer's death — but I suppose that is enough. Now, with John Lennon shot, everyone is pierced as I have been, so I can fucking well stop feeling sorry for myself and join the rest of the world, no better off than they are, no worse off either.

Often, when I look back to Jeff's suicide, I discover that I rearrange dates and events in sequences more syntonic to my mind; that is, I edit. I condense, cut bits out, do a fast number myself so that — for example — I no longer recall viewing Jeff's body and identifying it. I have managed to forget the name of the hotel where he stayed. I don't know how long he stayed there. As near as I can make out, he didn't hang around the house very long after Tim and Kirsten flew to London; one early letter came from them, typed: signed by both of them but almost certainly written by Kirsten. Possibly Tim dictated it. The first hint of the magnitude of the find showed up in that letter. I didn't recognize what the news implied but Jeff did. So, perhaps, he left right after that.

What surprised me the most was to grasp, all at once, that Jeff had wanted to go into the priesthood, but what point was there, in view of his father's role? But this left a vacuum. Jeff did not want to do anything else either. He *could* not become a priest; he did not care about any other profession. So he remained what we in Berkeley called a "professional student"; he never stopped going to Cal. Maybe he left and came back. Our marriage hadn't been working for some time; I have blank spots back to 1968, perhaps a full year missing in all. Jeff had emotional problems that I later repressed any knowledge of. We both repressed it. There is always free psychotherapy in the Bay Area and we took advantage of it.

I don't think Jeff could be called — could have been called — mentally ill; he simply wasn't terribly happy. Sometimes it is not a drive to die but a failure of a subtle kind, a failing of the sense of joy. He fell out of life by degrees. When he came across someone he genuinely wanted she became his father's mistress, whereupon they both flew to England, leaving him to study a war he didn't care about, leaving him stranded back where he had started from. He started out not caring; he wound up not caring. One of the doctors did say he believed that Jeff started taking LSD during that period after he left me and before he shot himself. That is only a theory. However, unlike the homosexual theory, it may have been true.

Thousands of young people kill themselves in America each year, but it remains the custom, by and large, to list their deaths as accidental. This is to spare the family the shame attached to suicide. There is, indeed, something shameful about a young man or woman, maybe an adolescent, wanting to die and achieving that goal, dead before in a certain sense they ever lived, ever were born. Wives get beaten by their husbands; cops kill blacks and Latinos; old people rummage in garbage cans or eat dog food — shame rules, calling the shots. Suicide is only one shameful event out of a plethora. There are black teenagers who will never get a job as long as they live, not because they are lazy but because there are no jobs — because, too, these ghetto kids possess no skills they can sell. Children run away, find the strip in New York or Hollywood; they become prostitutes and wind up with their bodies hacked apart. If the impulse to slay the Spartan runners reporting the battle results, the outcome at Thermopylae, rises in you, by all means slay them. I am those runners and I report what you do not want, most likely, to hear. Personally, I report only three deaths, but three more than were necessary. This is the day John Lennon died; you wish to slay those who report that, too? As Sri Krishna says when he assumes his true form, his universal form, that of time:

> *"All these hosts must die; strike, stay*
> *your hand — no matter.*
> *Seem to slay. By me these men are slain already."*

It is an awful sight. Arjuna has seen what he cannot believe exists.

> *"Licking with your burning tongues,*
> *Devouring all the worlds,*
> *You probe the heights of heaven*
> *With intolerable beams, O Vishnu."*

What Arjuna sees was once his friend and charioteer. A man like himself. That was only an aspect, a kindly disguise. Sri Krishna wished to spare him, to hide the truth. Arjuna asked to see Sri Krishna's true form and he got to see it. He will not now be as he was. The spectacle has changed him, changed him forever. This is the true forbidden fruit, this kind of knowledge. Sri Krishna waited a long time before he showed Arjuna his actual shape. He wanted to spare him. The true shape, that of the universal destroyer, emerged at last.

I would not want to make you unhappy by detailing pain, but there is a crucial sort of difference between pain and the nar-

ration of pain. I am telling you what happened. If there is vi-
carious pain in knowing, there is actual peril in not knowing. In
aversion lies a colossal risk.

When Kirsten and the bishop had returned to the Bay Area — not
permanently but, rather, to deal with Jeff's death and the problems raised by it — I could upon seeing them again notice a
change in both of them. Kirsten looked worn and wretched,
and this did not seem to me to emanate from the shock of Jeff's
death alone. Obviously she was in ill health in purely physical
terms. On the other hand, Bishop Archer seemed even more an-
imated than when I had last seen him. He took complete charge
of the situation regarding Jeff; he selected the burial spot, the
kind of gravestone; he delivered the eulogy and all other rites,
wearing full robes, and he paid for everything. The inscription
on the gravestone came as a result of his inspiration. He chose
a phrase which I found quite acceptable; it is the motto or basic statement of the school of Heraclitus: NO SINGLE THING
ABIDES; BUT ALL THINGS FLOW. I had been taught in philosophy class that Heraclitus himself invented that, but Tim explained that this summation came after Heraclitus, by those
of his school who followed him. They believed that only flux,
which is to say change, is real. They may have been right.

The three of us joined together after the graveside service;
we returned to the Tenderloin apartment and tried to make ourselves comfortable. It took a while for any of us to say anything.

Tim talked about Satan, for some reason. Tim had a new theory about Satan's rise and fall that he apparently wanted to try
out on us, since we — Kirsten and I — were the closest people at
hand. I presumed at the time that Tim intended to include his
theory in the book he had begun working on.

"I see the legend of Satan in a new way. Satan desired to
know God as fully as possible. The fullest knowledge would

come if he became God, was himself God. He strove for this and achieved it, knowing that the punishment would be permanent exile from God. But he did it anyhow, because the memory of knowing God, really knowing him as no one else ever had or would, justified to him his eternal punishment. Now, who would you say truly loved God out of everyone who ever existed? Satan willingly accepted eternal punishment and exile just to know God — by becoming God — for an instant. Further, it occurs to me, Satan truly knew God, but perhaps God did not know or understand Satan; had He understood him, He would not have punished him. That is why it is said that Satan rebelled — which means Satan was outside of God's control, outside God's domain, as if in another universe. But Satan did I think welcome his punishment, for it was his proof to himself that he knew and loved God. Otherwise he might have done what he did for the reward . . . had there been a reward. 'Better to rule in hell than to serve in heaven' *is* an issue, here, but not the true one: which is the ultimate goal and search to know and be: fully and really to know God, in comparison to which all else is really very little."

"Prometheus," Kirsten said absently. She sat smoking and gazing.

Tim said, "Prometheus means 'Forethinker.' He was involved in the creating of man. He was also the supreme trickster among the gods. Pandora was sent down to Earth by Zeus as a punishment to Prometheus for stealing fire and bringing it to man. In addition, Pandora punished the whole human race. Epimetheus married her, he was Hindsight. Prometheus warned him not to marry Pandora, since Prometheus could foresee the consequences. This same kind of absolute foreknowledge is or was considered by the Zoroastrians to be an attribute of God, the Wise Mind."

"An eagle ate his liver," Kirsten said remotely.

Nodding, Tim said, "Zeus punished Prometheus by chaining him and sending an eagle to eat his liver, which regenerated itself endlessly. However, Hercules released him. Prometheus was a friend to mankind beyond any doubt. He was a master craftsman. There is an affinity to the legend of Satan, certainly. As I see it, Satan could be said to have stolen — not fire — but true knowledge of God. However, he did not bring it to man, as Prometheus did with fire. Perhaps Satan's real sin was that upon acquiring that knowledge he kept it to himself; he did *not* share it with mankind. That's interesting . . . by that line of reasoning, one could argue that we could acquire a knowledge of God by way of Satan. I've never heard that theory put forth before." He became silent, apparently pondering. "Would you write this down?" he said to Kirsten.

"I'll remember." Her tone was listless and drab.

"Man must assault Satan and seize this knowledge," Tim said, "and take it from him. Satan does not want to yield it up. For concealing it — not for taking it in the first place — he was punished. Then, in a sense, human beings can redeem Satan by wresting this knowledge from him."

I said, "And then go off and study astrology."

Glancing at me, Tim said, "Pardon?"

"Wallenstein," I said. "Off casting horoscopes."

"The Greek words which our word 'horoscope' is based on," Tim said, "are *hora,* which means 'hour,' and *scopos,* which means 'one who watches.' So 'horoscope' literally means 'one who watches the hours.'" He lit a cigarette; both he and Kirsten, since their return from England, seemed to smoke constantly. "Wallenstein was a fascinating person."

"So Jeff says," I said. "Said, I mean."

Cocking his head alertly, Tim said, "Was Jeff interested in Wallenstein? Because I have —"

"You didn't know?" I said.

Looking puzzled, Tim said, "I don't think so."

Kirsten regarded him steadily, with an inscrutable expression.

"I have a number of very good books on Wallenstein," Tim said. "You know, in many ways Wallenstein resembled Hitler."

Both Kirsten and I remained silent.

"Wallenstein contributed to the ruin of Germany," Tim said. "He was a great general. Friedrich von Schiller, as you may know, wrote three plays about Wallenstein, whose titles are: *Wallenstein's Camp, The Piccolominis* and *The Death of Wallenstein*. They are profoundly moving plays. This brings up, of course, the role of Schiller himself in the development of Western thought. Let me read you something." Setting his cigarette down, Tim went over to the bookcase for a book; he found it after a few minutes of hunting. "This may shed some light on the subject. In writing to his friend — let me see; I have the name here — in writing to Wilhelm von Humboldt, this was toward the very end of Schiller's life, Schiller said, 'After all, we are both idealists, and should be ashamed to have it said that the material world formed us, instead of being formed by us.' The essence of Schiller's vision was, of course, freedom. He was naturally absorbed in the great drama of the revolt of the Lowlands — by that I mean Holland — and —" Tim paused, thinking, his lips moving; he gazed absently off into space. On the couch, Kirsten sat in silence, smoking and staring. "Well," Tim said finally, leafing through the book he held, "let me read you this. Schiller wrote this when he was thirty-four years old. Perhaps it sums up much of our aspirations, our most noble ones." Peering at the book, Tim read aloud. "'Now that I have begun to know and to employ my spiritual powers properly, an illness unfortunately threatens to undermine my physical ones. However,

I shall do what I can, and when in the end the edifice comes crashing down, I shall have salvaged what was worth preserving.'" Tim shut the book and returned it to the shelf.

We said nothing. I did not even think; I merely sat.

"Schiller is very important to the twentieth century," Tim said; he returned to his cigarette, stubbed it out. For a long time, he stared down at the ashtray.

"I'm going to send out for a pizza," Kirsten said. "I'm not up to fixing dinner."

"That's fine," Tim said. "Ask them to put Canadian bacon on it. And if they have soft drinks —"

"I can fix dinner," I said.

Kirsten rose, made her way to the phone, leaving Tim and me alone together.

Earnestly, Tim said to me, "It is really a matter of great importance to know God, to discern the Absolute Essence, which is the way Heidegger puts it. *Sein* is his term: Being. What we have uncovered at the Zadokite *Wadi* simply beggars description."

I nodded.

"How are you fixed for money?" Tim said, reaching into his coat pocket.

"I'm fine," I said.

"You're working, still? At the real estate —" He corrected himself. "You're a legal secretary; you're still with them, then?"

"Yes," I said. "But I'm just a clerk-typist."

"I found my career as a lawyer taxing," Tim said, "but rewarding. I'd advise you to become a legal secretary and then perhaps you can use that as a jumping-off platform and go into law, become an attorney. It might even be possible for you to be a judge, someday."

"I guess so," I said.

Tim said, "Did Jeff discuss the *anokhi* with you?"

"Well, you wrote to us. And we saw newspaper and magazine articles."

"They used the term in a special sense, a technical sense — the Zadokites. It could not have meant the Divine Intelligence because they speak of having it, literally. There is one line from Document Six: '*Anokhi* dies and is reborn each year, and upon each following year *anokhi* is more.' Or greater; more or greater, it could be either, perhaps lofty. It's extremely puzzling but the translators are working on it and we hope to have it during the next six months . . . and, of course, they're still piecing together the fragments, the scrolls that became mutilated. I have no knowledge of Aramaic, as you probably realize. I studied both Greek and Latin — you know, 'God is the final bulwark against non-Being.'"

"Tillich," I said.

"Beg pardon?" Tim said.

"Paul Tillich said that," I said.

"I'm not sure about that," Tim said. "It was certainly one of the Protestant existential theologians; it may have been Reinhold Niebuhr. You know, Niebuhr is an American, or rather was; he died quite recently. One thing that interests me about Niebuhr —" Tim paused a moment. "Niemöller served in the German navy in World War One. He worked actively against the Nazis and continued to preach until 1938. The Gestapo arrested him and he was sent to Dachau. Niebuhr had been a pacifist originally, but urged Christians to support the war against Hitler. I feel that one of the significant differences between Wallenstein and Hitler — actually it is a very great similarity — lies in the loyalty oaths that Wallenstein —"

"Excuse me," I said. I went into the bathroom, opened the medicine cabinet to see if the bottle of Dexamyls was still there. It was not; all the medicine bottles were gone. Taken to England, I realized. Now in Kirsten's and Tim's luggage. Fuck.

When I came out, I found Kirsten standing alone in the living room. "I'm terribly, terribly tired," she said in a faint voice.

"I can see that," I said.

"There is no way I am going to be able to keep down *pizza*. Could you go to the store for me? I made a list. I want boned chicken, the kind that comes in a jar, and rice or noodles. Here; this is the list." She handed it to me. "Tim'll give you the money."

"I have money." I returned to the bedroom, where I had put my coat and purse. As I was putting on my coat, Tim appeared from behind me, anxious to say something more.

"What Schiller saw in Wallenstein was a man who colluded with fate to bring on his own demise. This would be for the German Romantics the greatest sin of all, to collude with fate, fate regarded as doom." He followed me from the bedroom, down the hall. "The whole spirit of Goethe and Schiller and — the others, their whole orientation was that the human will could overcome fate. Fate would not be regarded as inevitable but as something a person allowed. Do you see my point? To the Greeks, fate was *ananke*, a force absolutely predetermined and impersonal; they equated it with Nemesis, which is retributive, punishing fate."

"I'm sorry," I said. "I have to go to the store."

"Aren't they bringing the pizza?"

"Kirsten's not feeling well."

Standing close to me and speaking in a low voice, Tim said, "Angel, I'm very concerned about her. I can't get her to go to a doctor. Her stomach — either that or her gall bladder. Maybe you can convince her to undergo a multiphasic. She's afraid of what they'll find. You know, don't you, that she had cervical cancer a number of years ago."

"Yes," I said.

"And a hysterocleisis."

"What is that?"

"A surgical procedure; the mouth of the uterus is closed. She has so many anxieties in this area, that is, pertaining to this topic; it's impossible for me to discuss it with her."

"I'll talk to her," I said.

"Kirsten blames herself for Jeff's death."

"Shit," I said. "I was afraid of that."

Coming from the living room, Kirsten said to me, "Add ginger ale to the list I gave you. Please."

"Okay," I said. "Is the store —"

"Turn right," Kirsten said. "It's four blocks straight and then one block left. It's a Chinese-run little grocery store but they have what I want."

"Do you need any more cigarettes?" Tim said.

"Yes, you might pick up a carton," Kirsten said. "Any of the low-tar brands; they all taste the same."

"Okay," I said.

Opening the door for me, Tim said, "I'll drive you." The two of us made our way down the sidewalk to his rented car, but, as we stood, he discovered that he did not have the keys. "We'll have to walk," he said. So we walked together, saying nothing for a time.

"It's a nice night," I said finally.

"There's something I've been meaning to discuss with you," Tim said. "Although technically it's not within your province."

"I didn't know I had a province," I said.

"It's not an area of expertise for you. I'm not sure who I should talk to about it. These Zadokite Documents are in some respects —" He hesitated. "I would have to say distressing. To me personally, is what I mean. What the translators have come across is many of the Logia — the sayings — of Jesus predating Jesus by almost two hundred years."

"I realize that," I said.

"But that means," Tim said, "that he was not the Son of God. Was not, in fact, God, as the Trinitarian doctrine requires us to believe. That may pose no problem for you, Angel."

"No, not really," I agreed.

"The Logia are essential to our understanding and apperception of Jesus as the Christ; that is, the Messiah or Anointed One. If, as would now seem to be the case, the Logia can be severed from the person Jesus, then we must reevaluate the four Gospels — not just the Synoptics but all four . . . we must ask ourselves what, then, we indeed do know about Jesus, if indeed we know anything at all."

"Can't you just assume Jesus was a Zadokite?" I said. That was the impression I had gotten from the newspaper and magazine articles. Upon the discovery of the Qumran Scrolls, the Dead Sea Scrolls, there had been an enormous flurry of speculation that Jesus came from or was in some way connected with the Essenes. I saw no problem. I could not see what Tim was concerned about, as the two of us walked slowly along the sidewalk.

"There is a mysterious figure," Tim said, "mentioned in a number of the Zadokite Documents. He's referred to by a Hebrew word best translated as 'Expositor.' It is this shadowy personage to whom many of the Logia are attributed."

"Well, then Jesus learned from him, or anyhow they were derived from him," I said.

"But then Jesus is not the Son of God. He is not God Incarnate, God as a human being."

I said, "Maybe God revealed the Logia to the Expositor."

"But then the Expositor is the Son of God."

"Okay," I said.

"These are problems over which I've agonized — although that is rather a strong term. But it bothers me. And it should bother me. Here we have many of the parables related in the Gospels now extant in scrolls predating Jesus by two hundred years. Not all the Logia are represented, admittedly, but many are, many crucial ones. Certain cardinal doctrines of resurrection are also present, those being expressed in the well-known 'I am' utterances by Jesus. 'I am the bread of life.' 'I am the Way.' 'I am the narrow gate.' These simply cannot be separated from Jesus Christ. Just take that first one: 'I am the bread of life. Anyone who does eat my flesh and drink my blood has eternal life, and I shall raise him up on the last day. For my flesh is real food and my blood is real drink. He who eats my flesh and drinks my blood lives in me and I live in him.' Do you see my point?"

"Sure," I said. "The Zadokite Expositor said it first."

"Then the Zadokite Expositor conferred eternal life, and specifically through the Eucharist."

"I think that's wonderful," I said.

Tim said, "It was always the hope, but never the expectation, that we would someday unearth Q, or unearth something that would permit us to reconstruct Q, or parts of Q; but no one ever dreamed that an *Ur-Quelle* would manifest itself predating Jesus, and by two centuries. Also, there are peculiar other—" He paused. "I want to obtain your promise not to discuss what I'm going to say; not to talk about it with anyone. This part hasn't been released to the media."

"May I die horribly."

"Associated with the 'I am' statements are certain very peculiar additions not found in the Gospels and apparently not known to the early Christians. At least, no written record of their knowing these things, believing these things, has passed down to us. I—" He broke off. "The term 'bread' and the term used for 'blood' suggest literal bread and literal blood. As if the Zadokites had a specific bread and a specific drink that they prepared and had that constituted in essence the body and blood of what they call the *anokhi,* for whom the Expositor spoke and whom the Expositor represented."

"Well," I said. I nodded.

"Where is this store?" Tim looked around.

"Another block or so," I said. "I guess."

Tim said earnestly, "Something they drank; something they ate. As in the Messianic banquet. It made them immortal, they believed; it gave them eternal life, this combination of what they ate and what they drank. Obviously, this prefigures the Eucharist. Obviously it's related to the Messianic banquet. *Anokhi.* Always that word. They ate *anokhi* and they drank *anokhi* and, as a result, they became *anokhi.* They became God Himself."

"Which is what Christianity teaches," I said, "regarding the Mass."

"There are parallels found in Zoroastrianism," Tim said. "The Zoroastrians sacrificed cattle and combined this with an intoxicating drink called *haoma.* But there is no reason to assume that this resulted in a homologizing with the Deity. That, you see, is what the Sacraments achieve for the Christian communicant: he — or she — is homologized to God as represented in and by Christ. Becomes God or becomes one with God, unified with, assimilated to, God. An apotheosis, is what I'm saying. But here, with the Zadokites, you get precisely this with the bread and the drink derived from *anokhi,* and of course the term '*anokhi*' itself refers to the Pure Self-Awareness, which is to say, Pure Consciousness of Yahweh, the God of the Hebrew people."

"Brahman is that," I said.

"I beg your pardon? 'Brahman'?"

"In India. Brahmanism. Brahman possesses absolute, pure consciousness. Pure consciousness, pure being, pure bliss. As I recall."

"But what," Tim said, "is this *anokhi* that they ate and drank?"

"The body and blood of the Lord," I said.

"But what *is* it?" He gestured. "It's one thing to say glibly, 'It's the Lord,' because, Angel, that is what in logic is called a *hysteron proteron* fallacy: what you are trying to prove is assumed in your premise. Obviously, it's the body and blood of the Lord; the word '*anokhi*' makes that clear; but it doesn't —"

"Oh, I see," I said, then. "It's circular reasoning. In other words, you're saying that this *anokhi* actually exists."

Tim stopped and stood, gazing at me. "Of course."

"I understand. You mean it's real."

"God is real."

"Not really real," I said. "God is a matter of belief. It isn't real in the sense that that car —" I pointed to a parked Trans-Am — "is real."

"You couldn't be more wrong."

I started to laugh.

"Where did you ever get an idea like that?" Tim said. "That God isn't real?"

"God is a —" I hesitated. "A way of looking at things. An interpretation. I mean, He doesn't exist. Not the way objects exist. You couldn't, say, bump into Him, like you can bump into a wall."

"Does a magnetic field exist?"

"Sure," I said.

"You can't bump into it."

I said, "But it'll show up if you spread iron filings across a piece of paper."

"The hieroglyphs of God lie all about you," Tim said. "As the world and in the world."

"That's just an opinion. It's not my opinion."

"But you can see the world."

"I see the world," I said, "but I don't see any sign of God."

"But there cannot be a creation without a creator."

"Who says it's a creation?"

"My point," Tim said, "is that if the Logia predate Jesus by two hundred years, then the Gospels are suspect, and if the Gospels are suspect, we have no evidence that Jesus was God, very God, God Incarnate, and therefore the basis of our religion is gone. Jesus simply becomes a teacher representing a particular Jewish sect that ate and drank some kind of — well, whatever it was, the *anokhi,* and it made them immortal."

"They believed it made them immortal," I corrected him. "That's not the same thing. People believe that herbal remedies can cure cancer, but that doesn't make it true."

We arrived at the little grocery store and stood momentarily.

"I take it you're not a Christian," Tim said.

"Tim," I said, "you've known that for years. I'm your daughter-in-law."

"I'm not sure I'm a Christian. I'm now not sure there in fact is such a thing as Christianity. And I've got to get up and tell people — I have to go on with my ministerial and pastoral duties. Knowing what I know. Knowing that Jesus was a teacher and not God, and not even an original teacher; what he taught was the aggregate belief-system of an entire sect. A group product."

I said, "It could still have come from God. God could have revealed it to the Zadokites. What else does it say about the Expositor?"

"He returns in the Final Days and acts as Eschatological Judge."

"That's fine," I said.

"That's found in Zoroastrianism also," Tim said. "So much seems to go back to the Iranian religions . . . the Jews developed a distinct Iranian quality to their religion during the time . . ." He broke off; he had turned inward, mentally, oblivious, now, to me, to the store, our errand.

I said, trying to cheer him up. "Maybe the scholars and translators will find some of this *anokhi*."

"Find God," he echoed, to himself.

"Find it growing. A root or a tree."

"Why do you say that?" He seemed angry. "What would make you say that?"

"Bread has to be made out of something. You can't eat bread unless it's made from something."

"Jesus was speaking metaphorically. He did not mean literal bread."

"Maybe he didn't, but the Zadokites apparently did."

"That thought crossed my mind. Some of the translators are proposing that. That a literal bread and a literal drink is signified. 'I am the gate of the sheepfold.' Jesus certainly did not mean he was made of wood. 'I am the true vine, and my father is the vinedresser. Every branch in me that bears no fruit he cuts away, and every branch that does bear fruit he prunes to make it bear even more.'"

"Well, it's a vine, then," I said. "Look for a vine."

"That's absurd and carnal."

"Why?" I said.

Tim said savagely, "'I am the vine, you are the branches.' Are we to assume that a literal plant is referred to? That this is a physical, not a spiritual, matter? Something growing in the Dead Sea Desert?" He gestured. "'I am the light of the world.' Are we to assume you could read a newspaper by holding it up to him? Like this streetlight?"

"Maybe so," I said. "Dionysos was a vine, in a manner of speaking. His worshippers got drunk and then Dionysos possessed them, and they ran over the hills and fields and bit cows to death. Devoured whole animals alive."

"There are certain resemblances," Tim said.

Together, we continued on into the little grocery store.

# 6

BEFORE TIM AND Kirsten could return to England, the Episcopal Synod of Bishops convened to look into the matter of his possible heresies. The jerk-off — I should say, I suppose, conservative; that is the more polite term — bishops who stood as his accusers proved themselves idiots in terms of their ability to mount a successful attack on him. Tim emerged from the Synod officially vindicated. It made the newspapers and magazines, of course. Never at any time had this subject worried him. Anyhow, due to Jeff's suicide, Tim had plenty of public sympathy. He had always had that, but now, because of the tragedy in his personal life, he had it even more.

Somewhere Plato says that if you are going to shoot at a king you must be sure you kill him. The conservative bishops, in failing to destroy Tim, left him as a result even stronger than ever, which is the way with defeat; we say about such a turn of events that it has backfired. Tim knew now that no one within the Episcopal Church of the United States of America could bring him down. If he were to be destroyed, he would have to do it himself.

As for myself, in regard to my own life, I owned the house that Jeff and I had been buying. Jeff had made out a will, due to his father's insistence. I did not acquire much, but I acquired what there was. Since I had supported Jeff and myself, no financial problems confronted me. I continued to work at the law office and candle shop. For a time I believed that, with Jeff dead, I would gradually lose touch with Tim and Kirsten. That did not turn out to be the case. Tim seemed to find in me someone he could talk to. After all, I was one of the few people who knew the story about his relationship with his general secretary and business agent. And, of course, I had brought him and Kirsten together.

Beyond that, Tim did not jettison people who had become his friends. I amounted to much more than that anyhow; a great deal of love existed between the two of us, and out of that had come an understanding. We were, literally, good friends, in a sort of traditional way. The Bishop of California who held so many radical views and advanced such wild theories was, in his immediate life, an old-fashioned human being, in the best sense of the term. If you were his friend, he became loyal to you and stayed loyal to you, as I informed Ms. Marion years later, long after Kirsten and Tim were, like my husband, dead. It is a forgotten matter about Bishop Archer, that he loved his friends and stuck with them, even if he had nothing to gain in the sense that they had, or did not have, some power to advance his career, to enhance his station or advantage him in the practical world. All I amounted to in that world was a young woman working as a clerical secretary in a law office, and not an important law office. Tim had nothing to gain strategically by maintaining our relationship, but he maintained it up until his death.

Kirsten, during this period following Jeff's death, showed progressive symptoms of a deteriorating physical condition which, finally, the doctors diagnosed correctly as peritonitis, from which you can die. The bishop paid all her medical expenses, which came to a staggering sum; for ten days she languished in the intensive care unit of one of the best hospitals in San Francisco, complaining bitterly that no one visited her or gave a good goddamn. Tim, who flew all around the United States lecturing, saw her as often as he could, but it was not nearly often enough to suit her. I came over to the city to see her as frequently as possible. With me, as with Tim, it was (in her opinion) far too inadequate a response to her illness. Most of the time I spent with her amounted to a one-way diatribe in which she complained about him and about all else in life. She had aged.

It strikes me as semi-meaningless to say, "You are only as old as you feel" because, in point of fact, age and illness are going to win out, and this stupid statement only resonates with people in good health who have not undergone the sort of traumas that Kirsten Lundborg had. Her son Bill had disclosed an infinite capacity to be crazy and for this Kirsten felt responsible; she knew, too, that a major factor in Jeff's suicide had been her relationship with his father. That made her bitterly severe toward me, as if guilt — her guilt — goaded her into chronically abusing me, the chief victim of Jeff's death.

We really did not have much of a friendship left, she and I. Nevertheless, I visited her in the hospital, and I always dressed up so that I looked great, and I always brought her something she could not eat, if it was food, or could not wear or use.

"They won't let me smoke," she said to me one time, by way of a greeting.

"Of course not," I said. "You'll set your bed on fire again. Like you did that time." She had almost suffocated herself, a few weeks before going into the hospital.

Kirsten said, "Get me some yarn."

"'Yarn,'" I said.

"I'm going to knit a sweater. For the bishop." Her tone withered the word; Kirsten managed to convey through words a kind of antagonism one rarely encountered. "The bishop," she said, "needs a sweater."

Her animosity centered on the fact that Tim had proved able to handle his affairs quite well in her absence; at the moment, he was all the way up in Canada somewhere, delivering a speech. It had been Kirsten's contention for some time that Tim could not survive a week without her. Her confinement in the hospital had proven her wrong.

"Why don't Mexicans want their children to marry blacks?" Kirsten said.

"Because their kids would be too lazy to steal," I said.

"When does a black man become a nigger?"

"When he leaves the room." I seated myself in a plastic chair facing her bed. "What's the safest time to drive your car?" I said.

Kirsten gave me a hostile glance.

"You'll be out of here soon," I said, to help her cheer up.

"I'll never be out of here. The bishop is probably — never mind. Grabbing ass in Montreal. Or wherever he is. You know, he had me in bed the second time we met. And the first time was at a restaurant in Berkeley."

"I was there."

"So he couldn't do it the first time. If he could have, he would have. Doesn't that surprise you about a bishop? There are a few things I could tell you . . . but I won't." She ceased speaking, then, and glowered.

"Good," I said.

"Good what? That I'm not going to tell you?"

"If you start telling me," I said, "I will get up and leave. My therapist told me to set clear limits with you."

"Oh, that's right; you're another of them. Who's in therapy. You and my son. You two ought to get together. You could make clay snakes in occupational therapy."

"I am leaving," I said; I stood up.

"Oh Christ," Kirsten said irritably. "Sit down."

I said, "What became of the Swedish mongoloid cretin who escaped from the asylum in Stockholm?"

"I don't know."

"They found him teaching school in Norway."

Laughing, Kirsten said, "Go fuck yourself."

"I don't have to. I'm doing fine."

"Probably so." She nodded. "I wish I was back in London. You've never been to London."

"There wasn't enough money," I said. "In the Bishop's Discretionary Fund. For Jeff and me."

"Oh, that's right; I used it all up."

"Most of it."

Kirsten said, "I got to go nowhere. While Tim hung around those old faggot translators. Did he tell you that Jesus is a fake? Amazing. Here we find out two thousand years later that somebody else entirely made up all those Logia and all those 'I am' statements. I never saw Tim so downcast; he just sat and stared at the floor, in our flat, day after day."

To that I said nothing.

"Do you think it matters?" Kirsten said. "That Jesus was a fake?"

"Not to me it doesn't," I said.

"They haven't really published the important part. About the mushroom. They're keeping that secret for as long as they can. However —"

"What mushroom?"

"The *anokhi*."

I said, incredulous, "The *anokhi* is a mushroom?"

"It's a mushroom. It was a mushroom back then. They grew it in caves, the Zadokites."

"Jesus Christ," I said.

"They made mushroom bread out of it. They made a broth from it and drank the broth; ate the bread, drank the broth. That's where the two species of the Host come from, the body and the blood. Apparently the *anokhi* mushroom was toxic but the Zadokites found a way to detoxify it, at least somewhat, enough so it didn't kill them. It made them hallucinate."

I started laughing. "Then they were a—"

"Yes, they turned on." Kirsten, too, now laughed, in spite of herself. "And Tim has to get up every Sunday at Grace and give Communion knowing that, knowing they were simply getting off on a psychedelic trip, like the kids in the Haight-Ashbury. I thought it was going to kill him when he found out."

"So then Jesus was in effect a dope dealer," I said.

She nodded. "The Twelve, the disciples, were—this is the theory—smuggling the *anokhi* into Jerusalem and they got caught. This just confirms what John Allegro figured out . . . if you happened to see his book. He's one of the greatest scholars *vis-à-vis* Near Eastern languages . . . he was the official translator of the Qumran scrolls."

"I didn't see his book," I said, "but I know who he is. Jeff used to talk about him."

"Allegro figured out that the early Christians were a secret mushroom cult; he deduced it from internal evidence in the New Testament. And he found a fresco or wall-painting . . . anyhow, a picture of early Christians with a huge *amania muscaria* mushroom—"

"*Amanita muscaria,*" I corrected. "It's the red one. They are terribly toxic. So the early Christians found a way to detoxify it, then."

"That's Allegro's contention. And they saw cartoons." She began to giggle.

"Is there actually an *anokhi* mushroom?" I said. I knew something about mushrooms; before I married Jeff, I had gone with an amateur mycologist.

"Well, there probably was, but nobody today knows what it would be. So far, in the Zadokite Documents, there's no description. No way to tell which one it was or if it still exists."

I said, "Maybe it did more than cause hallucinations."

"Like what?"

A nurse came over to me, at that point. "You'll have to leave, now."

"Okay." I rose, gathered up my coat and purse.

Kirsten said, "Bend over." She waved me toward her; in a whisper directly into my ear she said, "Orgies."

After kissing her good-bye, I left the hospital.

When I arrived back in Berkeley and had made my way by bus to the little old farmhouse that Jeff and I had been living in, I saw, as I walked up the path, a young man crouched over in the corner of the porch; I halted warily, wondering who he was.

Pudgy, with light-colored hair, he bent stroking my cat Magnificat, who had curled up happily against the front door of the house. I watched for a time, thinking: Is this a salesman or something? The young man wore trousers too large for him, and a brightly colored shirt. On his face, as he petted Magnificat, was the most gentle expression I had ever seen on a human face; this kid, who obviously had never encountered my cat before, radiated a kind of fondness, a kind of palpable love, that in fact was something new to me. Some of the very early statues of the god Apollo reveal that sweet smile. Totally absorbed in petting Magnificat, the kid remained oblivious to me, to my nearby presence; I watched, fascinated, because for one thing Magnificat was a rough-and-tumble old tomcat who normally did not allow strangers to get near him.

All at once the kid glanced up. He smiled shyly and rose awkwardly to his feet. "Hi."

"Hi." I walked toward him, carefully, very slowly.

"I found this cat." The kid blinked, still smiling; he had guileless blue eyes, absent of any cunning.

"It's my cat," I said.

"What's her name?"

"It's a tomcat," I said, "and he's named Magnificat."

"He's very beautiful," the kid said.

"Who are you?" I said.

"I'm Kirsten's son. I'm Bill."

That explained the blue eyes and the blond hair. "I'm Angel Archer," I said.

"I know. We've met. But it was —" He hesitated. "I'm not sure how long ago. They gave me electroshock . . . my memory isn't very good."

"Yes," I said. "I guess we did meet. I just came from the hospital visiting your mom."

"Can I use your bathroom?"

"Sure," I said. I got my keys from my purse and unlocked the front door. "Excuse the mess. I work; I'm not home enough to keep it neat. The bathroom is off the kitchen, in the back. Just keep on going."

Bill Lundborg did not close the bathroom door behind him; I could hear him urinating loudly. I filled the tea kettle and put it on the burner. Strange, I thought. This is the son she derides. As she derides us all.

Reappearing, Bill Lundborg stood self-consciously, smiling at me anxiously, quite obviously ill at ease. He had not flushed the toilet. I thought, then, very suddenly: He has just come out of the hospital, the mental hospital; I can tell.

"Would you like coffee?" I said.

"Sure."

Magnificat entered the kitchen.

"How old is she?" Bill asked.

"I have no idea how old he is. I rescued him from a dog. After he had grown, I mean, not as a kitten. He probably lived somewhere in the neighborhood."

"How is Kirsten?"

"Doing really well," I said. I pointed to a chair. "Sit down."

"Thanks." He seated himself; placing his arms on the kitchen table, he interlocked his fingers. His skin was so pale. Kept indoors, I thought. Caged up. "I like your cat."

"You can feed him," I said; I opened the refrigerator and got out the can of cat food.

As Bill fed Magnificat, I watched the two of them. The care he took in spooning out the food . . . systematically, his attention deeply fixed, as if it were very important, what he had become involved in; he kept his gaze intent on Magnificat, and as he scrutinized the old cat he smiled again, that smile that so touched me, so made me start.

Batter me, oh God, I thought, remembering for some strange reason. Batter and kill me; they have injured this sweet kind baby until there is almost nothing left. Burned his circuits out as a pretense of healing him. The fucking sadists, I thought, in their sterile coats. What do they know about the human heart? I felt like crying.

And he will be back in, I thought, as Kirsten says. In and out of the hospital the rest of his life. The fucking sons of bitches.

> Batter my heart, three person'd God; for, you
> As yet but knocke, breathe, shine, and seeke to mend;
> That I may rise, and stand, o'erthrow mee, and bend
> Your force, to breake, blowe, burn and make me new.
> I, like an usurpt towne, to'another due,
> Labour to'admit you, but Oh, to no end,

*Reason your viceroy in mee, mee should defend,*
*But is captiv'd, and proves weake or untrue.*
*Yet dearely' I love you, and would be loved faine,*
*But am betroth'd unto your enemie:*
*Divorce mee, untie, or breake that knot againe,*
*Take mee to you, imprison mee, for I*
*Except you enthrall mee, never shall be free,*
*Nor ever chaste, except you ravish mee.*

My favorite poem of John Donne's; it came up into me, into my mind, as I watched Bill Lundborg feed my worn old cat.

And I laugh at God, I thought; I make no sense out of what Tim teaches and believes, and the torment he feels over these various issues. I am fooling myself; in my own labored way, I do understand. Look at him serve that ignorant cat. He — this child — would have been a veterinarian, if they hadn't maimed him, shredded up his mind. What had Kirsten told me? He is afraid to drive; he stops taking out the garbage; he will not bathe and then he cries. I cry, too, I thought, and sometimes I let the trash pile up, and one time I nearly got sideswiped on Hoffman and had to pull over. Lock me up, I thought; lock up us all. This, then, is Kirsten's affliction, having this boy for her son?

Bill said, "Is there anything else I can feed her? She's still hungry."

"Anything you see in the fridge," I said. "Would you like something to eat?"

"No thanks." Again he stroked the awful old cat — a cat who never gave the time of day to any person. He has made this animal tame, I thought, as he himself is: tame.

"Did you come here on the bus?" I said.

"Yes." He nodded. "I had to surrender my driver's license. I used to drive, but —" He became silent.

"I take the bus," I said.

"I had a real great car," Bill said "A '56 Chevy. A stick shift with an eight, the big eight they made; it was only the second year Chevrolet made an eight; the first year was '55."

"Those are very valuable cars," I said.

"Yes; Chevrolet had changed to that new body-style. After the old higher, shorter body-style they used so long. The difference between a '55 and a '56 Chevy is in the front grille; if the grille includes the turn-signal lights, you can tell it's a '56."

"Where are you living?" I said. "In the City?"

"I'm not living anywhere. I got out of Napa last week. They let me out because Kirsten is sick. I hitched down here. A man gave me a ride in his Stingray." He smiled. "You have to take those 'Vettes out on the freeway every week or they build up carbon deposits in the mill. He was blowing carbon out the whole way. What I don't like about a 'Vette is the fiberglass body; you can't really repair it." He added, "But they certainly are good-looking. His was white. I forget the year, although he told me. We got it up to a hundred, but the cops pace you a lot when you're in a 'Vette, hoping you'll exceed the limit. We had a Highway Patrol after us part of the way but he had to turn his siren on and take off; an emergency of some kind, somewhere. We flipped him off as he went by. He was real disgusted but he couldn't cite us; he was in too much of a hurry."

I asked him, then, as tactfully as I could, why he had come to see me.

"I wanted to ask you something," Bill said. "I met your husband one time. You weren't home; you were working or something. He was here alone. Was his name Jeff?"

"Yes," I said.

"What I wanted to know is —" Bill hesitated. "Could you tell me why he killed himself?"

"There are a lot of factors involved in something like that." I seated myself at the kitchen table, facing him.

"I know he was in love with my mother."

"Oh," I said. "You do know that."

"Yes, Kirsten told me. Was that the main reason?"

"Perhaps," I said.

"What were the other reasons?"

I was silent.

"Would you tell me one thing," Bill said, "one particular thing? Was he mentally disturbed?"

"He had been in therapy. But not intensive therapy."

"I've been thinking about it," Bill said. "He was mad at his father because of Kirsten. A lot of it had to do with that. See, when you're in the hospital — a mental hospital — you know a lot of people who've tried suicide. Their wrists are all sawed on. That's always the way you can tell. The best way, when you do that, is up the arm in the direction the veins run." He showed me his bare arm, pointing. "The mistake most people make is cutting at right angles to the vein, down at the wrist. We had this one guy, he laid open his arm for like about seven inches and —" He paused, calculating. "Maybe as much as a quarter inch wide. But they still were able to sew it up. He had been in for months. He said one time in group therapy that all he wanted to be was a pair of eyes bugging out from the wall, so he could see everyone but no one could see him. Just an observer, not a part of what was going on, ever. Just watching and listening. He would have to be a pair of ears, too, to do that."

For the life of me I could think of nothing to say.

"Paranoids have a fear of being looked at," Bill said. "So invisibility would be important to them. There was this one lady, she couldn't eat in front of anyone. She always took her tray off to her room. I guess she thought eating was dirty." He smiled. I managed to smile back.

How strange this is, I thought. An eerie conversation, as if it is not actually taking place.

"Jeff was real hostile," Bill said. "Toward his father and toward Kirsten both, and maybe toward you, but I don't think as much; toward you, I mean. We talked about you that day I came over. I forget when that was. I had a two-day pass. I hitched down then, too. It's not that hard to hitch. A truck picked me up, even though it had a NO RIDERS sign posted. It was carrying some kind of chemicals, but not the toxic kind. If they're carrying flammable material or toxic material they know not to give you a ride, because if there is an accident and you're killed or poisoned then sometimes it voids their insurance."

Again I could think of nothing to say; I nodded.

"The law," Bill said, "in case of an accident where a hitch-hiker is injured or killed, is that it's presumed he rode at his own risk. He took the chance. So because of that when you hitch if something happens you can't sue. That's California law. I don't know how it is in other states."

"Yes," I said. "Jeff felt a lot of anger toward Tim."

"Do you feel animosity toward my mother?"

After a pause, after I had thought it over, I said, "Yes. I really do."

"Why? It wasn't her fault. Any time a person kills himself, he has to take full responsibility. We learned that. You learn a lot in the hospital. You know a whole bunch of things that people on the outside never find out. It's a crash course in reality, which is the ultimate—" He gestured. "Paradox. Because the people there are there because, presumably, they don't face reality, and then they wind up in the hospital, the mental hospital, a state hospital like Napa, and have to face a whole lot more reality all of a sudden than other people ever have to do. And they face it very well. I've seen things I have been very proud of, patients helping other patients. One time this lady—she was like about in her fifties—said to me, 'Can I confide in you?' She swore me to secrecy. I promised not to say anything. She said, 'I'm going to kill myself tonight.' She told me how she was going to do it. This was not a locked ward. She had her car parked out in the lot and she had an ignition key they didn't know she had; they — the staff — thought they had all her keys but she kept this one back. So I thought it over, about what I should do. Should I tell Dr. Gutman? He was in charge of the ward. What I did was, I sneaked outside onto the lot — I knew which car was hers — and I removed the coil wire that runs — well, you wouldn't know. It runs between the coil and the distributor. There's no way you can start an engine with that wire missing. It's easy to do. When you park your car in a really rough neighborhood and you're afraid someone will steal it, you can pull out that wire; it comes out real easy. She cranked it until the battery ran down and then she came back in. She was furious but later on she thanked me." He pondered and then said, half to himself, "She was going to ram an ongoing car on the Bay Bridge. So I saved him, too; the other car. It might have been like a station wagon full of kids."

"My God," I said faintly.

"It was a decision I had to make in a hurry." Bill said. "Once I knew she had that key, I had to do something. It was a big Merc. Silver-colored. Almost new. She had a lot of money. In a situation like that if you don't act, it's the same as helping them."

I said, "It might have been better to tell the doctor."

"No." He shook his head. "Then she would have — well, it's hard to explain. She knew that I did it to save her life, not to get her in trouble. If I had told the staff — especially if I had told Dr. Gutman — she would have interpreted that as me just trying to get her kept there another couple of months. But this way they never knew, so they didn't hold her any longer than they originally intended to. When I got out — she got out before I did — one time she came by my apartment . . . I gave her my address; anyhow, she came by — she was driving that same Merc; I recognized it when she pulled up — and she wanted to know how I was getting along."

"How were you getting along?" I said.

"Not good at all. I didn't have money to pay my rent; they were going to evict me. She had a whole lot of money; her husband was rich. They owned a bunch of apartment buildings up and down California, as far down as San Diego. She went back to her car and came back and handed me a roll of what I thought were nickels. You know; a roll of coins. After she left, I opened the roll at one end and they were gold coins. She told me later she kept a lot of her money in the form of gold. It was from some British colony. She told me when I sold them to a coin dealer to specify that they were 'B.U.' That stands for 'bright uncirculated.' It's a dealers' term. A bright uncirculated coin is worth more than whatever the opposite would be. I got about twelve dollars a coin, when I sold them. I kept one, but I lost it. I got something like six hundred dollars for the roll, with that one coin missing." Turning, he scrutinized the stove. "Your water's boiling."

I poured the water into the Silex coffee pot.

"Unboiled coffee," Bill said, "filtered coffee, is a lot better for you than the percolated kind, where it shoots back up to the top and starts all over again."

"That's true," I said.

Bill said, "I've been thinking a lot about your husband's death. He seemed like a really nice person. Sometimes that's a problem."

"Why?" I said.

"Much mental illness stems from people repressing their hostility and trying to be nice, too nice. The hostility can't be repressed forever. Everybody has it; it has to come out."

"Jeff was very calm," I said. "It was hard to get him to fight. Marital quarrels; I was usually the one who got mad."

"Kirsten says he had been dropping acid."

"I don't think that's true," I said. "That he dropped acid."

"A lot of people who get messed up get messed up from drugs. You see a lot of them in the hospital. They don't always stay that way, contrary to what you hear. Most of it is due to malnutrition; people on drugs forget to eat and, when they do eat, they eat junk food. The munchies. Everyone who does drugs gets the munchies, unless, of course, they're taking amphetamines, in which case they don't eat at all. Much of what looks like toxic brain psychosis in speed freaks is in fact a deficiency in their galvanic electrolytes. Which are easily replaced."

"What sort of work do you do?" I said. He seemed less ill at ease, now. More confident in what he was saying.

"I'm a painter," Bill said.

"What artist is your work —"

"Car painting." He smiled gently. "Spray painting. At Leo Shine's. In San Mateo. 'I'll spray your car any color you want it for forty-nine-fifty and give you a written six-month guarantee.'" He laughed and I laughed, too; I had seen Leo Shine's commercials on TV.

"I loved my husband very much," I said.

"Was he going to be a minister?"

"No. I don't know what he was going to be."

"Maybe he wasn't going to be anything. I'm taking a course in computer programming. Right now I'm studying algorithms. An algorithm is nothing but a recipe, like when you bake a cake. It is a sequence of incremental steps sometimes utilizing built-in repeats; certain steps have to be reiterated. One primary aspect of an algorithm is that it be meaningful; it's very easy to unintentionally ask a computer a question it can't answer, not because it's dumb but because the question really has no answer."

"I see," I said.

"Would you consider this a meaningful question," Bill said. "Give me the highest number short of two."

"Yes," I said. "That's meaningful."

"It's not." He shook his head. "There is no such number."

"I know the number," I said. "It's one-point-nine-plus—" I broke off.

"You would have to carry the sequence of digits into infinity. The question is not intelligible. So the algorithm is faulty. You're asking the computer to do something that can't be done. Unless your algorithm is intelligible, the computer can't respond, but it will attempt to respond, by and large."

"Garbage in," I said, "garbage out."

"Right." He nodded.

"I'm going to ask you a question," I said. "In return. I'm going to give you a proverb, a common proverb. If you are not familiar with the proverb—"

"How much time will I have?"

"This isn't timed. Just tell me what the proverb means. 'A new broom sweeps clean.' What does that mean?"

After a pause, Bill said, "It means that old brooms wear out and you have to throw them away."

I said, "'The burnt child is afraid of fire.'"

Again he was silent a moment, his forehead wrinkling. "Children easily get hurt, especially around a stove. Like this stove here." He indicated my kitchen stove.

"'It never rains but it pours.'" But I could tell already. Bill Lundborg had a thinking impairment; he could not explain the proverb: instead he repeated it back in concrete terms, the terms in which it itself had been phrased.

"Sometimes," he said haltingly, "there's a lot of rain. Especially when you don't expect it."

"'Vanity, thy name is woman.'"

"Women are vain. That's not a proverb. It's a quotation from something."

"You're right," I said. "You did fine." But in truth, in very truth, as Tim would say, as Jesus used to say, or the Zadokites said, this person was totally schizophrenic, according to the Benjamin Proverb Test. I felt a vague, haunting ache, realizing this, seeing him sit there so young and physically healthy, and so unable to desymbolize, to think abstractly. He had the classic schizophrenic cognitive impairment; his ratiocination was limited to the concrete.

You can forget about being a computer programmer, I said to myself. You will be spray-painting low-rider cars until the Eschatological Judge arrives, and frees us, one and all, from our cares. Frees you and frees me; frees everyone. And then your damaged mind will, presumably, be healed. Cast into a passing pig, to be run over the edge of a cliff, to doom. Where it belongs.

"Excuse me," I said. I walked from the kitchen, through the house, to the farthest point from Bill Lundborg possible, leaned against the wall with my face pressed into my arm. I could feel my tears against my skin — warm tears — but I made no sound.

# 7

I VIEWED MYSELF AS Jeff, weeping off by myself in the margins of the house, weeping over someone I cared about. Where is this going to end? I wondered. It has to end. And it seems not to have an end; it just goes on: a sequence of explosions, like Bill Lundborg's computer trying to figure out what the highest number less than an integer is, a hopeless task.

Not long thereafter, Kirsten came out of the hospital; she gradually recovered from her digestive ailment, upon which cure having happened, she and Tim returned to England. Before they left the United States, I found out from her that her son Bill had gone to jail. The U.S. Postal Service had hired him and then fired him; his response to being fired had been to smash the plate glass windows of the San Mateo substation. He smashed them with his bare knuckles. Obviously he was crazy again. If it could be said at any time that he was ever not.

So I lost track of everyone: I did not see Bill again after that day he visited me; I saw Kirsten and Tim a number of times—Kirsten more often than Tim—and then I found myself alone, and not very happy, and wondering and speculating about the sense underlying the world, assuming that any sense existed. Like Bill Lundborg's periods of sanity, it was a dubitable thing.

The law office and candle shop, one day, ceased to be in business. My two employers got busted on drug charges. I had foreseen it. More money could be made in the sale of cocaine than in the sale of candles. Cocaine at that time did not enjoy the fad popularity that it enjoys now, but the demand even so amounted to an inducement that my employers could not refuse. The authorities managed to accommodate them in their inability to say no to big bucks: each man got a five-year prison term. I drifted for a few months, drawing unemployment compensation, and then I squeezed in as a retail record clerk at the Musik Shop on Telegraph Avenue near Channing Way, which is where I work now.

Psychosis takes many forms. You can be psychotic about everything or you can concentrate on one particular topic. Bill represented ubiquitous dementia; madness had infiltrated every part of his life, or so I presume.

The fixed idea kind of madness is fascinating, if you are inclined toward viewing with interest something that is palpably impossible and yet nonetheless exists. *Over-valence* is a notion about possibilities in the human mind, possibilities of something going wrong, that did it not exist it could not be supposed. I mean by this simply that you have to see an over-valent idea at work fully to appreciate it. The older term is *idée fixe*. Over-valent idea expresses it better, because this is a term derived from mechanics and chemistry and biology; it is a graphic term and it involves the notion of *power*. The essence of valence is power and that is what I am talking about; I speak of an idea that once it comes into the human mind, the mind, I mean, of a given human being, it not only never goes away, it also consumes everything else in the mind so that, finally, the person is gone, the mind as such is gone, and only the over-valent idea remains.

How does such a thing begin? When does it begin? Jung speaks somewhere — I forget which of his books it is mentioned in — but anyhow he speaks in one place of a person, a normal person, into whose mind one day a certain idea comes, and that idea never goes away. Moreover, Jung says, upon the entering of that idea into the person's mind, nothing new ever happens to that mind or in that mind; time stops for that mind and it is dead. The mind, as a living, growing entity has died. And yet the person, in a sense, continues on.

Sometimes, I guess, an over-valent idea enters the mind as a problem, or imaginary problem. This is not so rare. You are getting ready for bed, late at night, and all of a sudden the idea comes into your mind that you did not shut off your car lights. You look out the window at your car — which is parked in your driveway in plain sight — and you can see that it shows no lights. But then you think: Maybe I left the lights on and they stayed on so long that they ran the battery down. So to be sure, I must go out and check. You put on your robe and go out, unlock the car door, get in and pull on the headlight switch. The lights come on. You turn them off, get out, lock up the car and return to the house. What has happened is that you have gone crazy; you have become psychotic. Because you have discounted the testimony of your senses; you could see out the window that the car lights were not on, yet you went out to check anyhow. This is the cardinal factor: you saw but you did not believe. Or, conversely, you did not see something but you believed it anyhow. Theoretically, you could travel between your bedroom and the car forever, trapped in an eternal closed loop of unlocking the car, trying the light-switch, returning to the house — in this regard you herewith are a machine. You are no longer human.

Also, the over-valent idea can arise — not as a problem or imaginary problem — but as a solution.

If it arises as a problem, your mind will fight it off, because no one really wants or enjoys problems; but if it arises as a solution, a spurious solution, of course, then you will not fight it off because it has a high utility value; it is something you need and you have conjured it up to fill this need.

There exists very little likelihood that you will travel in a loop between your parked car and your bedroom for the rest of your life, but there is a very great possibility that if you are tormented by guilt and pain and self-doubt — and vast floods of self-accusations that hit every day without fail — that a fixed idea as solution will, once it is happened upon, remain. This is what I next saw with Kirsten and with Tim, upon their return to the United States from England, their second return, after Kirsten got out of the hospital. During the period that they lived in London that second time, an idea, an over-valent idea, one day came into their minds, and that was that.

Kirsten flew back several days before Tim. I did not meet her at the airport; I met her at her room on the top floor of the St. Francis, on the same noble hill of San Francisco that Grace Cathedral itself enjoys. I found her busily unpacking her many bags, and I thought: My God, how young she looks! In contrast to the last time I saw her . . . she glows. What has happened? Fewer lines marred her face; she moved with deft flexibility, and, when I entered the room, she glanced up and smiled at me, with none of the sour overtones, the various latent accusations I had become familiar with.

"Hi," she said.

"Boy, do you look great," I said.

She nodded. "I quit smoking." She lifted a wrapped package from a suitcase open before her on the bed. "I brought you a couple of things. More are on the way by surface mail; I could only fit these in. Do you want to open them now?"

"I can't get over how good you look," I said.

"Don't you think I've lost weight?" She went over to stand before one of the suite's mirrors.

"Something like that," I said.

"I have a huge steamer trunk coming by ship. Oh, you've seen it. You helped me pack. I've got a lot to tell you."

"On the phone, you hinted—"

"Yes," Kirsten said. She seated herself on the bed, reached for her purse, opened it and took out a package of Player's Cigarettes; smiling at me, she lit a cigarette.

"I thought you quit," I said.

Reflexively, she put out the cigarette. "I still do it now and then, out of habit." She continued to smile at me, in a wild, yet veiled, mysterious way.

"Well, what is it?" I said.

"Look over there on the table."

I looked. A large notebook lay on the table.

"Open it," Kirsten said.

"Okay." I picked the notebook up and opened it. Some of the pages showed nothing but most of them had been scribbled on, in Kirsten's handwriting.

Kirsten said, "Jeff has come back to us. From the other world."

Had I said, then, at that moment: Lady, you are totally crazy—it would have made no difference, and I do not castigate myself because I failed to say it. "Oh," I said, nodding. "Well; what do you know." I tried to read her handwriting but I could not. "What do you mean?" I said.

"Phenomena," Kirsten said. "That's what Tim and I call them. He sticks needles under my fingernails at night and he sets all the clocks to six-thirty, which was the exact moment he died."

"Gee," I said.

"We've kept a record," Kirsten said. "We didn't want to tell you in a letter or over the phone; we wanted to tell you face-to-face. So I waited until now." She raised her arms in excitement. "Angel, he came back to us!"

"Well, I'll be fucked," I said mechanically.

"Hundreds of incidents. Hundreds of the phenomena. Let's go down to the bar. It started right away after we got back to England. Tim went to a medium. The medium said it was true. We knew it was true; nobody had to tell us but we wanted to be really certain because we thought possibly — just possibly — it was only a poltergeist. But it isn't! It's Jeff!"

"Hot damn," I said.

"Do you think I'm joking?"

"No," I said, with sincerity.

"Because we both witnessed it. And the Winchells saw it, too; our friends in London. And now that we're back in the United States, we want you to witness it and record it, for Tim's new book. He's writing a book about it, because this has meaning not just for us but for everyone, because it proves that man exists in the other world after he dies here."

"Yes," I said. "Let's go down to the bar."

"Tim's book is called *From the Other World*. He's already gotten a ten-thousand-dollar advance on it; his editor thinks it'll be his bestselling book by far."

"I stand before you amazed," I said.

"I know you don't believe me." Her tone, now, had become wooden, and edged with anger.

"Why would it enter my head not to believe you?" I said.

"Because people don't have faith."

"Maybe after I read the notebook."

"He — Jeff — set fire to my hair sixteen times."

"Wow."

"And he shattered all the mirrors in our flat. Not once but several times. We would get up and find them broken but we didn't hear it; neither of us heard anything. Dr. Mason — he's the medium we went to — said that Jeff wants us to understand that he forgives us. And he forgives you, too."

"Oh," I said.

"Don't be sarcastic with me," Kirsten said.

"I'll really truly try not to be sarcastic," I said. "It is as you can see a great surprise to me. I am left without words. I'll certainly recover, later on." I moved toward the door.

Edgar Barefoot, in one of his lectures on KPFA, discussed a form of inferential logic developed in India by the Hindu school. It is very old and has been much studied, not just in India but also in the West. It is the second means of knowledge by which man obtains accurate cognition and is called *anumana,* which is Sanskrit for: "Measuring along some other thing, inference." It has five stages and I will not go into it because it is difficult, but what is important about it is that if these five stages are correctly carried out — and the system contains safeguards by which one can determine precisely whether he has indeed carried them out — one is assured of going from premise to correct conclusion.

What especially dignifies *anumana* is step three, the illustration *(udaharana);* it requires what is called an invariable concomitance *(vyapti,* literally "pervasion"). The *anumana* form of inferential reasoning will only work if you can be absolutely certain that you indeed possess a *vyapti;* not a concomitance but an invariable concomitance (for example, late at night you hear a loud, sharp, echoing popping sound; you say to yourself, "That must be an auto backfiring because when an auto backfires, such a sound is created." This precisely is where inferential reasoning — reasoning, that is, from effect back to cause — breaks down. This is why in the West many logicians feel that inductive reasoning as such is suspect, that only deductive reasoning can be relied on. The Indian *anumana* strives for what is called a sufficient ground; the illustration requires an actual — not assumed — observation at all times, holding that no concomitance can be assumed *which fails to be exemplified*). We in the West have no syllogism exactly equal to the *anumana* and it is a shame that we do not, because had we such a rigorous form by which to check our inductive reasoning, Bishop Timothy Archer might well know of it, and had he known of it he would have known that his mistress waking up to find her hair singed does not, in fact, prove that the spirit of his dead son has returned from the other world, from, in essence, beyond the grave. Bishop Archer could and did fling around such terms as *hysteron proteron* because that logical fallacy is known in Greek — which is to say, Western — thought. But the *anumana* is from India. The Hindu logicians distinguished a typical fallacious ground that wrecked the *anumana;* they called it *hetvabhasa* ("merely the appearance of a ground") and this deals with only one step in the *anumana* out of five. They found all sorts of ways to fuck up this five-stage structure, any one of which a man with Bishop Archer's intelligence and education would have — or should have — been able to follow. That he could believe that a few weird unexplained events proved that Jeff was not only still alive (somewhere) but communicating with the living (somehow) shows that, like Wallenstein with his astrological charts during the Thirty Years War, the faculty of accurate cognition is variable and depends, in the final analysis, on what you want to believe, not what is so. A Hindu logician living centuries ago could have seen at a glance the basic fallacy in the reasoning that argued for Jeff's immortality. Thus the will to believe chases out the rational mind, whenever and wherever the two come into conflict. This is all I can assume, based on what I now was seeing.

I suppose we all do it, and do it often; but this was too glaring, too basic, to ignore. Kirsten's lunatic son, palpably schizophrenic, could show why asking a computer for the largest number short of two is an unintelligible request, but Bishop Timothy Archer, a lawyer, a scholar, a sane adult, could see a pin on the bedsheet beside his mistress and leap to the conclusion that his dead son was communicating with him from another world; moreover, Tim was writing it all up in a book, a book that would first be published and then read; he not only believed nonsense, he believed it in a public way.

"Wait'll the world hears about this," Bishop Archer and his mistress declared. Winning the heresy confrontation perhaps had convinced the bishop that he could not err; or, if he erred, no one could pull him down. He was wrong in both respects: he could err and there were people who could pull him down. He could pull himself down, for that matter.

I saw all this clearly as I sat with Kirsten at one of the bars in the St. Francis Hotel that day. And there was nothing I could do. Their fixed idea, being not a problem but a solution, could not be reasoned away, even though, finally, it amounted to a further problem on its own. They had tried to solve one problem with yet another. That is not how you do it; you do not solve one problem with another, greater problem. This is how Hitler, who uncannily resembled Wallenstein, had tried to win World War Two. Tim could admonish me about *hysteron proteron* reasoning to his heart's content — and then fall victim to the merely occult nonsense-stuff of popular paperback books. He might as well have believed that Jeff had been brought back by ancient astronauts from another star system.

I hurt, thinking about this. I hurt in my legs; I hurt throughout. Bishop Archer, who *hysteron-proteron*ed me up and down the street, he being a bishop, I being a young woman with a B.A. from Cal in liberal arts — I had one night heard Edgar Barefoot talk about this *anumana* Hindu thing and I knew more or could do more than the Bishop of California; and it didn't matter because the Bishop of California was not going to listen to me any more than he was going to listen to anybody else, over and beyond his mistress, who, like himself, was so steeped in guilt and so messed up by intrigue and deceit — emanating from their invisible relationship — that they had long since ceased to be able to reason properly. Bill Lundborg, shut up in jail now, could have set them straight. A taxi driver picked at random could have told them they were calculatedly destroying their lives — not just by believing this, although that alone was sufficiently destructive, but by deciding to publish it. Fine. Do it. Wreck your goddamn life. Cast charts of the stars, cast horoscopes while the most destructive war in modern times is raging. It will earn you a place in the history books — as a dunce. You get to sit on the tall stool in the comer; you get to wear the conical cap; you get to undo all the social activist shit you ever engineered in concert with some of the finest minds of the century. For this, Dr. Martin Luther King, Jr., died. For this you marched at Selma: to believe — and to say publicly that you believe — that the ghost of your dead son is pushing pins under the fingernails of your mistress while she is asleep. By all means publish it. Be my guest.

The logical error, of course, is that Kirsten and Tim reasoned backward from effect to cause; they did not see the cause — they saw only what they called "phenomena" — and from these phenomena they inferred Jeff as the secret cause operating in or from "the other world." The *anumana* structure shows that this inductive reasoning is not reasoning at all; with the *anumana* you begin with a premise and work through the five steps to your conclusion, and each step is airtight in relation to the step before it and the step after it, but there is no airtight logic involved in inferring that broken mirrors and singed hair and stopped clocks and all that other crap reveals and, in fact, proves another reality in which the dead are not dead; what it proves is that you are credulous and you are operating at a six-year-old level mentally: you are not reality-testing, you are lost in wish fulfillment, in autism. But it is an eerie kind of autism because it revolves around a single idea; it does not invade your general field, your total attention. Outside of this one spurious premise, this one faulty induction, you are clear-headed and sane. It is a localized madness, allowing you to speak and act normally the rest of the time. Therefore no one locks you up because you can still earn a living, take baths, drive a car, take out the trash. You are not crazy in the manner that Bill Lundborg is crazy, and in a certain sense (depending on how you define "crazy") you are not crazy at all.

Bishop Archer could still perform his pastoral chores. Kirsten could still buy clothes at the best stores in San Francisco. Neither of them would smash the windows of a U.S. Postal Service substation with their bare fists, You cannot arrest someone for believing that his son is communicating to this world from the next, or believing, for that matter, that there *is* a next world. Here the fixed idea shades off into religion generally; it becomes part of the other-worldly orientation of the revealed religions of the world. What is the difference between believing in a God you can't see and your dead son whom you can't see? What distinguishes one invisibility from another invisibility? Nonetheless, there is a difference, but it is tricky. It has to do with the general opinion, a slippery area; many people believe in God but few people believe that Jeff Archer sticks pins under Kirsten Lundborg's fingernails while she is asleep — that is the difference, and when put that way the subjectivity of it is plain. After all, Kirsten and Tim have the goddamn pins, and the burned hair, and the broken mirrors, not to mention the stopped clocks. But the two of them are making a logical error, for all that. Whether the people who believe in God are making an error I don't know, since their belief-system cannot be tested one way or another. It simply is faith.

Now I had been formally asked to sit in as a hopeful spectator to further "phenomena," and were they to occur I could, along with Tim and Kirsten, vouch for what I witnessed and add my name to Tim's forthcoming book — a book that, his editor had said, would undoubtedly outsell all his previous books based on less sensational material. But I could not be disinterested. Jeff had been my husband. I loved him. I wanted to believe. Worse, I sensed the psychological motor driving Kirsten and Tim to believe; I did not want to shoot their faith — or credulity — down because I could see what cynicism would do to them: it would leave them with nothing — leave them, once more, with staggering guilt, a guilt neither could cope with. I found myself, then, in a position where I had to comply, at least *pro forma*. I had to allege belief, allege interest, allege excitement. Neutrality would not be enough: enthusiasm was required. The damage had been done in England, before I was brought in on this. The decision was already made. If I said, "It's bullshit," they would continue on anyhow, but bitterly. Fuck the cynicism, I thought to myself as I sat with Kirsten that day at the St. Francis bar. There is nothing to be gained and a lot to lose, and anyhow it doesn't matter; Tim's book is going to get written and published — with or without me.

That is bad reasoning. Just because something bears the aspect of the inevitable one should not, therefore, go along willingly with it. But that was my reasoning. I saw this: if I told Kirsten and Tim how I felt, I could look forward never to seeing either of them again; they would cut me off, lop me away and discard me, and I would have my job at the record shop — my friendship with Bishop Archer would be a thing of the past. It meant too much to me; I could not let it go.

That was *my* faulty motivation, my wish. I wanted to keep on seeing them. And so I arranged to collude and *knew* that I was colluding. I decided that day in the St. Francis; I kept my mouth shut and my opinions to myself and I agreed to log the expected phenomena, and so I came to be a part of something that I knew was silly. Bishop Archer wrecked his career and not once did I try to talk him out of it. After all, I had tried to talk him out of his affair with Kirsten, to no avail. This time, he would not merely out-argue me; he would drop me. The cost, to me, would be too great.

I did not share their fixed idea. But I did as they did and talked as they talked. I'm mentioned in Bishop Archer's book; he gives me credit for "invaluable assistance" in "noting and recording the day-to-day manifestations of Jeff," of which there were none. I guess this is how the world is run: by weakness. It all goes back to Yeats' poem where he speaks of "the best lack all conviction" or however he phrases it. You know the poem; I don't have to quote it to you.

"When you shoot at a king you must kill him." When you plan to tell a world-famous man that he is a fool, you must face the fact that you will lose what you cannot bring yourself to lose. So I kept my fucking mouth shut, drank my drink, paid for my drink and Kirsten's, accepted the presents she had brought me from London, and promised to watch for fast-breaking phenomena, for all new developments.

And I would do it again, if I had the opportunity, because I loved the two of them very much, both Kirsten and Tim. I loved them far more than I cared about my own probity. Friendship loomed large; the importance of probity—hence, probity itself—dwindled and at last vanished entirely. I said good-bye to my integrity and kept my friendships alive. Somebody else will have to judge if I did the right thing, for I am still not disinterested; I still see only two friends, just returned from months abroad, friends I had longed for, especially with Jeff dead . . . friends I could not survive without, and, deep inside me, a subtle factor urged me on, a factor I did not admit to that day; I took pride in the fact that I knew a man who had marched with Dr. King at Selma, a famous man whom David Frost interviewed, whose opinions helped shape the modern intellectual world. There you have it, the essence of it. I defined myself to myself — my identity — in terms of being Bishop Archer's daughter-in-law and friend.

This is an evil motivation and it pinned me; it had me caught fast. "I know Bishop Timothy Archer," my mind uttered to itself in the darkness of the night. It whispered these words to me, bolstering my self-esteem; I, too, felt guilt over Jeff's suicide, and by participating in the life and times, the customs and habits of Bishop Archer, I lost my own self-doubts — or, at least, felt them diminish.

But there is a logical error in *my* reasoning — as well as an ethical one — and I had not perceived it; through his credulity and superstitious folly, the Bishop of California intended to barter away his influence, his power to control public opinion, the very power that drew me to him. Had I been able to timebind adequately that day at the St. Francis, I would have foreseen this — and done differently. He would not long be a great man; he connived to transform himself from authority to crank. Thus, much of what drew me to him would soon vanish. So, in this respect, I stood in as deluded a state as he. This failed to register on my mind that day. I saw him only as he was then, not as he would be in a few years. I, too, was operating at a six-year-old level. I did not do any real harm, but I did not do any real good, and I debased myself really for nothing; no good came out of it, and when I look back I long bitterly for the insight I have now, long to have had it then. Bishop Archer swept us along with him because we loved him and believed in him, even when we knew he was wrong, and this is a terrible realization, a matter that should incite moral and spiritual dread. It does that, in me, now; but it did not then; my dread came too late; it came as hindsight.

This may be tiresome prattle to you, but it is something else to me: it is my heart's despair.

# 8

THE AUTHORITIES DID not keep Bill Lundborg in jail long. Bishop Archer arranged for his release — based on Bill's history of chronic mental illness — and presently a day came when the boy showed up at their apartment in the Tenderloin, wearing a wool sweater Kirsten had knitted for him, and his baggy pants, his pudgy face bland.

It personally gladdened me to see him. I had thought about him a number of times, wondering how he was doing. Jail did not seem to have done him any harm. Perhaps he did not distinguish it from his periodic confinements in the hospital. For all I knew, not that much difference existed; I had been confined in neither.

"Hi, Angel," he said to me as I entered the apartment; I had been forced to move my new Honda to keep from getting a ticket. "What is that you're driving?"

"A Honda Civic," I said.

"That's a good engine in that," Bill said. "It doesn't over-rev like most mills that small. And it's sprung well. Do you have the four-speed or the five?"

"Four." I took off my coat and hung it in the hall closet.

"For that short a wheel-base, it rides really good," Bill said.

"But on impact—if an American car hits you—you'd be wiped out. You'd probably roll."

He told me, then, the statistics on fatalities in single-car accidents. It presented a gloomy picture insofar as small foreign cars were concerned. My chances were nothing like, say, with a Mustang. Bill spoke with enthusiasm about the new front-wheel drive Oldsmobile, which he depicted as a major engineering advance in terms of traction and road-handling. It was evident that he believed I should get a larger car; he exhibited concern for my safety. I found this touching, and, moreover, he knew what he was talking about. I had lost two friends to a single-car accident involving a VW Beetle, the rear wheels of which had cambered in, causing the car to roll. Bill explained that that design had been successfully modified, starting in 1965; after that, VW utilized a fixed rather than swing axle. It limited toe-in.

I think I have these terms right. I am dependent on Bill for this kind of information about cars. Kirsten listened with apathy; Bishop Archer revealed at least simulated attention, although I had the impression that this was a pose. It seemed impossible to me that he either cared or understood; for the bishop such matters as toe-in were as metaphysical matters are to the rest of us: mere speculation, and a frivolous one at that.

When Bill disappeared into the kitchen for a can of Coors, Kirsten's lips formed into a word directed at me.

"What?" I said, cupping my ear.

"Obsession." She nodded solemnly and with distaste.

Returning with the beer, Bill said, "Your life depends on the suspension of your car. A transversal torsion-bar suspension provides—"

"If I hear anything more about cars," Kirsten interrupted, "I am going to begin shrieking."

"Sorry," Bill said.

"Bill," Bishop Archer said, "if I were to buy a new car, what car should I get?"

"How much money —"

"I have the money," the bishop said.

"A BMW," Bill said. "Or a Mercedes-Benz. One advantage with a Mercedes-Benz is that nobody can steal it." He explained, then, about the astoundingly sophisticated locks on the Mercedes-Benz. "Even car repossessors have trouble getting into them," he finished. "A thief can rip off six Caddies and three Porsches in the time it takes to get into a Mercedes-Benz. So they tend to leave them alone; that way, you can leave your stereo in the car. Otherwise, with any other car, you have to lug it around with you." He told us, then, that it had been Carl Benz who had engineered and built the first practical automobile propelled by an internal combustion engine. In 1926 Benz had merged his company with Daimler-Motoren-Gesellschaft to form Daimler-Benz from which had come the Mercedes-Benz cars. The name "Mercedes" was that of a little girl whom Carl Benz had known, but Bill could not remember if Mercedes had been Benz's daughter, grandchild or what.

"So 'Mercedes' was not the name of an auto designer or engineer," Tim said, "but, rather, the name of a child. And now that child's name is associated with some of the finest automobiles in the world."

"That's true," Bill said. He told us another story about automobiles that few people knew. Dr. Porsche, who had designed both the VW and, of course, the Porsche, had not invented the rear-engine, air-cooled design; he had encountered it in Czechoslovakia in an auto firm there when the Germans took over that country in 1938. Bill could not remember the name of the Czech car, but it had been eight-cylinder, not four, a high-powered, very fast car that rolled so readily that German officers were finally forbidden to drive them. Dr. Porsche had modified the eight-cylinder high-performance design at Hitler's personal order. "Hitler wanted an air-cooled engine utilized," Bill said, "because he expected to use the VWs on *autobahns* in the Soviet Union after Germany took it over, and because of the weather, because of the cold —"

"I think you should get a Jaguar," Kirsten interrupted, speaking to Tim.

"Oh, no," Bill said. "The Jaguar is one of the most unstable, trouble-prone cars in the world; it's far too complex and requires you to have it in the shop all the time. However, their terrific double-overhead cam engine is maybe the finest high-performance mill ever built, excepting the sixteen-cylinder touring cars of the Thirties."

"Sixteen cylinders?" I said, amazed.

"They were very smooth," Bill said. "There was a huge gap between the flivvers of the Thirties and the expensive touring cars; we don't have that gap now . . . there is a complete spread from, say, your Honda Civic — which is basic transportation — up to the Rolls. Price and quality go in small increments, now, which is a good thing. It's a measure of the change in society between then and now." He started to tell us about steam cars and why that design had failed; Kirsten, however, rose to her feet and glared at him severely.

"I think I'll go to bed," Kirsten said.

Tim said to her, "What time am I speaking at the Lions' Club tomorrow?"

"Oh God, I don't have that speech finished," Kirsten said.

"I can improvise," Tim said.

"It's on the tape. All I have to do is transcribe it."

"You can do that in the morning."

She stared at him.

"As I say," Tim said, "I can improvise."

To Bill and me, Kirsten said, "'He can improvise.'" She continued to stare at the bishop, who shifted about uncomfortably. "Christ," she said.

"What's wrong?" Tim said.

"Nothing." She walked toward the bedroom. "I'll finish transcribing it. It wouldn't be a good idea if you — I don't know why we have to keep going into this. Promise me you won't launch into one of your tirades about the Zoroastrians."

Faintly but firmly, Tim said, "If I'm to trace the origins of Patristic thought —"

"I don't think the Lions want to hear about the desert fathers and the monastic life in the second century."

"Then that is exactly what I should talk about," Tim said. To Bill and me he said, "A monk was dispatched to a city carrying with him medicine for an ailing saint . . . the names are not necessary. What must be understood is that the ailing saint was a very great saint, one of the most beloved and revered in the north of Africa. When the monk reached the city, after a long journey across the desert, he —"

"Good night," Kirsten said, and disappeared into the bedroom.

"Good night," we all said.

After a pause, Tim continued, speaking in a low voice to Bill and me. "When he entered the city, the monk did not know where to go. Stumbling about in the darkness — it was night — he came across a beggar lying in the gutter, quite ill. The monk, after pondering the spiritual aspects of the issue, ministered to the beggar, applying the medication to him, with the result that the beggar soon showed signs of mending. However, now the monk had nothing to take to the great ailing saint. He therefore returned to the monastery from which he had come, dreadfully afraid of what his abbot would say. When he had told the abbot what he had done, the abbot said, 'You did the right thing.'" Tim fell silent, then. The three of us sat, none of us speaking.

"Is that it?" Bill said.

Tim said, "In Christianity no distinction is made between the humble and the great, the poor and the not-so-poor. The monk, by giving the medication to the first sick man he saw, instead of saving it for the great and famous saint, had seen into the heart of his Savior. There was a term of contempt used in Jesus' time for the ordinary people . . . they were dismissed as the *Am ha-aretz*, a Hebrew term meaning, simply, 'the people of the land,' meaning that they had no importance. It was to these people, the *Am ha-aretz*, that Jesus spoke, and with whom he mingled, ate and slept, that is, slept in their houses — although he did sleep occasionally in the houses of the rich, for even the rich are not excluded." Tim seemed somewhat downcast, I noticed.

"'The bish,'" Bill said, smiling. "That's what Kirsten calls you behind your back."

Tim said nothing to that. We could hear Kirsten moving about in the other room; something fell and she cursed.

"What makes you think there's a God?" Bill said to Tim.

For a time Tim said nothing. He seemed quite tired, and yet I sensed him trying to summon a response. Wearily, he rubbed his eyes. "There is the ontological proof . . ." he murmured. "St. Anselm's ontological argument, that if a Being can be imagined —" He broke off, lifted his head, blinked.

"I can type up your speech," I said to him. "That was my job at the law office; I'm good at that." I rose. "I'll go tell Kirsten."

"There is no problem," Tim said.

"Wouldn't it be better if you were speaking from a written transcript?" I said.

Tim said, "I want to tell them about the —" He ceased speaking. "You know, Angel," he said to me, "I really love her. She has done so much for me. And if she hadn't been with me after Jeff's death . . . I don't know what I would have done; I'm sure you understand." To Bill, he said, "I am terribly fond of your mother. She is the person closest to me in all the world."

"Is there any proof of God's existence?" Bill said.

After a pause, Tim said, "A number of arguments are given. Perhaps the best is the argument from biology, advanced for instance by Teilhard de Chardin. Evolution — the existence of evolution — seems to point to a designer. Also there is Morrison's argument that our planet shows a remarkable hospitality toward complex forms of life. The chance of this happening on a random basis is very small. I'm sorry." He shook his head. "I'm not feeling well. We'll discuss it some other time. I would say, however, in brief, that the teleological argument, the argument from design in nature, from purpose in nature, is the strongest argument."

"Bill," I said, "the bishop is tired."

Opening the bedroom door, Kirsten, who now had on her robe and slippers, said, "The bishop is tired. The bishop is always tired. The bishop is too tired to answer the question, 'Is there any proof of the existence of God?' No; there is no proof. Where is the Alka-Seltzer?"

"I took the last packet," Tim said, remotely.

"I have some in my purse," I said.

Kirsten closed the bedroom door. Loudly.

"There are proofs," Tim said.

"But God doesn't talk to anybody," Bill said.

"No," Tim said. He rallied, then; I saw him draw himself up. "However, the Old Testament gives us many instances of Yahweh addressing his people through the prophets. This fountain of revelation dried up, finally. God no longer speaks to man. It is called 'the long silence.' It has lasted two thousand years."

"I realize God talked to people in the Bible," Bill said, "in the olden days, but why doesn't he talk to them now? Why did he stop?"

"I don't know," Tim said. He said no more; there he ceased. I thought: You should not stop there. That is not the place to come to the end.

"Please go on," I said.

"What time is it?" Tim said; he looked around the living room. "I don't have my watch."

Bill said, "What's this nonsense about Jeff coming back from the next world?"

Oh God, I said to myself; I shut my eyes.

"I really wish you would explain it to me," Bill said to Tim. "Because it's impossible. It's not just unlikely; it's impossible." He waited. "Kirsten has been telling me about it," he said. "It's the stupidest thing I ever heard of."

"Jeff has communicated with the two of us," Tim said. "Through intermediary phenomena. Many times, in many ways." All at once, he reddened; he drew himself up and the authority that lay deep in him rose to the surface: he changed as he sat there from a tired, middle-aged man with personal problems into force itself, the force of conviction contrived into, formed into, words. "It is God Himself working on us and through us to bring forth a brighter day. My son is with us now; he is with us in this room. He never left us. What died was a material body. Every material thing perishes. Whole planets perish. The physical universe itself will perish. Are you going to argue, then, that nothing exists? Because that is where your logic will carry you. It isn't possible right now to prove that external reality exists. Descartes discovered that; it's the basis of modern philosophy. All you can know for sure is that your own mind, your own consciousness, exists. You can say, 'I am' and that's all. And that is what Yahweh tells Moses to say when the people ask who he has talked to. 'I am,' Yahweh says. *Ehyeh,* in Hebrew. You also can say that and that is all you can say; that exhausts it. What you see is not world but a representation formed in and by your own mind. Everything that you experience you know by faith. Also, you may be dreaming. Had you thought of that? Plato relates that a wise old man, probably an Orphic, said to him, 'Now we are dead and in a kind of prison.' Plato did not consider that an absurd statement; he tells us that it is weighty and something to think about. 'Now we are dead.' We may have no world at all. I have enough evidence — your mother and I — for Jeff returning to us as I have that the world itself exists. We do not suppose he has come back; we experience him as coming back. We have lived and are living through it. So it is not our opinion. It is real."

"Real for you," Bill said.

"What more can reality give?"

"Well, I mean," Bill said, "I don't believe it."

"The problem does not lie with our experience in this matter," Tim said. "It lies with your belief-system. Within the confines of your belief-system, such a thing is impossible. Who can say, truly say, what is possible? We have no knowledge of what is and isn't possible; we do not set the limits — God sets the limits." Tim pointed at Bill; his finger was steady. "What one believes and what one knows depend, in the final analysis, on God: you can't will your own consent or refusal to consent; it is a gift from God, an instance of our dependence. God grants us a world and compels our assent to that world; he makes it real for us: this is one of his powers. Do you believe that Jesus was the Son of God, was God Himself? You don't believe that, either. So how can I prove to you that Jeff returned to us from the other world? I can't even demonstrate that the Son of Man walked this Earth two thousand years ago for us and lived for us and died for us, for our sins, and rose in glory on the third day. Am I not right about that? Do you not deny that also? What do you believe, then? In objects you get into and drive around the block. There may be no objects and no block; someone pointed out to Descartes that a malicious demon may cause our assent to a world that is not there, may impress a forgery onto us as an ostensible representation of the world. If that happened, we would not know. We must trust; we must trust God. I trust in God that he would not deceive me; I deem the Lord faithful and true and incapable of deceit. For you that question does not even exist, for you will not grant that He exists in the first place. You ask for proof. If I told you this minute that I have heard God's voice speaking to me — would you believe that? Of course not. We call people who speak to God pious and we call people to whom God speaks lunatics. This is an age where there is little faith. It is not God who is dead; it is our faith that has died."

"But —" Bill gestured. "It doesn't make any sense. Why would he come back?"

"Tell me why Jeff lived in the first place," Tim said. "Then perhaps I can tell you why he came back. Why do you live? For what purpose were you created? You do not know who created you — assuming anyone did — and you do not know why, assuming there is a why. Perhaps no one created you and perhaps there is no purpose to your life. No world, no purpose, no Creator, and Jeff has not come back to us. Is that your logic? Is that how you live out your life? Is that what Being, in Heidegger's sense, is to you? That is an impoverished kind of inauthentic Being. It strikes me as weak and barren and, in the end, futile. There must be something you can believe, Bill. Do you believe in yourself? Will you grant that you, Bill Lundborg, exist? You will grant that; fine. Good enough. We have a start. Examine your body. Do you have sense organs? Eyes, ears, taste, touch and smell? Then, probably, this percept-system was designed to receive information. If that is so, it is reasonable to assume that information exists. If information exists, it probably pertains to something. Probably, there is a world — not certainly but probably, and you are linked to that world through your sense organs. Do you create your own food? Do you out of yourself, out of your own body, generate the food that you need in order to live? You do not. Therefore it is logical to assume that you are dependent on this outer world, of whose existence you possess only probable knowledge, not necessary knowledge; world is for us only a contingent truth, not an ineluctable one. What does this world consist of? What is out there? Do your senses lie? If they lie, why were they caused to come into being? Did you create your own sense organs? No, you did not. Someone or something else did. Who is that someone who is not you? Apparently you are not alone, the sole existent reality; apparently there are others, and one of them or several of them designed and built you and your body the way Carl Benz designed and built the first motorcar. How do I know there was a Carl Benz? Because you told me? I told you about my son Jeff returning—"

"Kirsten told me," Bill corrected him.

"Does Kirsten normally lie to you?" Tim said.

"No," Bill said.

"What do she and I gain by saying that Jeff has returned to us from the other world? Many people will not believe us. You yourself do not believe us. We say it because we believe it is true. And we have reasons to believe it is true. We have both seen things, witnessed things. I don't see Carl Benz in this room but I believe he once existed. I believe that the Mercedes-Benz is named after a little girl and a man. I am a lawyer; I am a person familiar with the criteria by which data is scrutinized. We—Kirsten and I—have the evidence of Jeff, the phenomena."

"Yeah, but that phenomena you have, all of them—they don't prove anything. You're just assuming Jeff caused it, caused those things. You don't know."

Tim said, "Let me give you an example. You look under your parked car and you find a pool of water. Now, you don't *know* that—the water—came from your motor; that is something you have to assume. You have evidence. As an attorney, I understand what constitutes evidence. You as an auto-mechanic —"

"Is the car parked in your own parking slot?" Bill said. "Or is it in a public parking lot, like at the supermarket."

Slightly taken aback, Tim paused. "I don't follow you."

"If it's your own garage or parking slot," Bill said, "where only you park, then it's probably from your car. Anyhow, it wouldn't be from the motor; it'd be from the radiator or the water pump or one of the hoses."

"But this is something you assume," Tim said. "Based on the evidence."

"It could be power-steering fluid. That looks a lot like water. It's sort of pinkish. Also, your transmission, if you have an automatic transmission, uses the same kind of fluid. Do you have power steering?"

"On what?" Tim said.

"On your car."

"I don't know. I'm speaking about a hypothetical car."

"Or it could be engine oil," Bill said, "in which case, it wouldn't be pink. You have to distinguish whether it's water or whether it's oil, if it's from the power-steering or the transmission; it could be several things. If you're in a public place and you see a puddle under your car, it probably doesn't mean anything because a lot of people park where you're parked; it could have come from the car parked there before you. The best thing to do is —"

"But you're only able to make an assumption," Tim said. "You can't know it came from your car."

"You can't know right away, but you can find out. Okay; let's say it's your own garage and no one else parks there. The first thing to figure out is what kind of fluid it is. So you reach under the car — you may have to back it out first — and dip your finger in the fluid. Now, is it pink? Or brown? Is it oil? Is it water?

Let's say it's water. Well, it could be normal; it could be overflow from the relief system of your radiator; after you turn off an engine, the water gets hotter sometimes and blows out through the relief pipe."

"Even if you can determine that it is water," Tim said, doggedly, "you can't be sure it came from your car."

"Where else would it come from?"

"That's an unknown factor. You're acting on indirect evidence; you didn't see the water come from your car."

"Okay — turn the engine on, let it run, and watch. See if it drips."

"Wouldn't that take a long time?" Tim said.

"Well, you have to know. You should check the level in the power-steering system; you should check your transmission level, your radiator, your motor oil; you should routinely check all those things. While you're standing there, you can check them. Some of them, like the level of fluid in the transmission, have to be checked while the motor's running. Meanwhile, you can also check your tire pressure. What pressure do you carry?"

"In what?" Tim said.

"Your tires." Bill smiled. "There're five of them. One in your trunk; your spare. You probably forget to check that when you check the others. You won't find out you've got no air in your spare until you get a blowout someday and then you'll find out if you have air in your spare. Do you have a bumper jack or an axle jack? What kind of car are you driving?"

"I think it's a Buick," Tim said.

"It's a Chrysler," I said quietly.

"Oh," Tim said.

After Bill departed for his trip back to the East Bay, Tim and I sat together in the living room of the Tenderloin apartment, and Tim talked openly and candidly to me. "Kirsten and I," he said, "have been having a few difficulties." He sat beside me on the couch, speaking in a low voice so that Kirsten, in the bedroom, would not hear.

"How many downers is she taking?" I said.

"You mean barbiturates?"

"Yes, I mean barbiturates," I said.

"I really don't know. She has a doctor who gives her all she wants . . . she gets a hundred at one time. Seconal. And also she has Amytal. I think the Amytal is from a different doctor."

"You better find out how many she's taking."

Tim said, "Why would Bill resist the realization that Jeff has come back to us?"

"Lord only knows," I said.

"The purpose of my book is to provide comfort to heart-broken people who have lost loved ones. What could be more reassuring than the knowledge that there is a life beyond the trauma of death, just as there is life beyond the trauma of birth? We are assured by Jesus that an afterlife awaits us; on this the whole promise of salvation depends. 'I am the Resurrection. If anyone believes in me, even though he dies he will live, and whoever lives and believes in me will never die.' And then Jesus says to Martha, 'Do you believe in this?' to which Martha responds, 'Yes, Lord. I believe that you are the Christ, the Son of God, the one who was to come into this world.' Later, Jesus says, 'For what I have spoken does not come from myself; no, what I was to say, what I had to speak, was commanded by the Father who sent me, and I know that his commands mean eternal life.' Let me get my Bible." Tim reached for a copy of the Bible which lay on the end table. "First Corinthians, fifteen, twelve. 'Now if Christ raised from the dead is what has been preached, how can some of you be saying that there is no resurrection of the dead? If there is no resurrection of the dead, Christ himself cannot have been raised, and if Christ has not been raised then our preaching is useless and your believing it is useless; indeed, we are shown up as witnesses who have committed perjury before God, because we swore in evidence before God that he had raised Christ to life. For if the dead are not raised, Christ has not been raised, and if Christ has not been raised, you are still in your sins. And what is more serious, all who have died in Christ have perished. If our hope in Christ has been for this life only, we are the most unfortunate of all people. But Christ has in fact been raised from the dead, the first-fruits of all who have fallen asleep.'" Tim closed his Bible. "That says it clearly and plainly. There can be no doubt whatsoever."

"Guess so," I said.

"So much evidence turned up at the Zadokite *Wadi*. So much that sheds light on the whole *kerygma* of early Christianity. We know so much, now. In no way was Paul speaking metaphorically; man literally rises from the dead. They had the techniques. It was a science. We would call it medicine today. They had the *anokhi*, there at the *wadi*."

"The mushroom," I said.

He eyed me. "Yes, the *anokhi* mushroom."

"Bread and broth," I said.

"Yes."

"But we don't have it now."

"We have the Eucharist."

I said, "But you know and I know that the substance is not there, in the Eucharist. It's like the cargo cults where the natives build fake airplanes."

"Not at all."

"How is it different?"

"The Holy Spirit —" He broke off.

"That's what I mean," I said.

Tim said, "I feel that the Holy Spirit is responsible for Jeff coming back."

"So then you reason that the Holy Spirit does still exist and always existed and is God, one of the forms of God."

"I do now," Tim said. "Now that I've seen evidence. I did not believe it until I saw the evidence, the clocks set at the time of Jeff's death, Kirsten's burned hair, the broken mirrors, the pins stuck under her fingernails. You saw her clothes all disarranged that time; we had you come in and see for yourself. We didn't do that. No living person did that; we wouldn't manufacture evidence. Do you believe we would do that, contrive a fraud?"

"No," I said.

"And the day that those books leaped out of the bookshelf and fell to the floor — no one was there. You saw that with your own eyes."

"Do you think the *anokhi* mushroom still exists?" I asked.

"I don't know. There is a *vita verna* mushroom mentioned in Pliny the Elder's *Historia Naturalis, Book Eight*. He lived in the first century . . . it would be about the right time. And this citation was not something he derived from Theophrastus; this was a mushroom he saw himself, from his direct knowledge of Roman gardens. It may be the *anokhi*. But that's only a guess. I wish we could be sure." He changed the subject, then, as was his custom; Tim Archer's mind never stayed on one topic for long. "It's schizophrenia that Bill has, isn't it?"

"Yep," I said.

"But he can earn a living."

"When he's not in the hospital," I said. "Or spiraling into himself and on the way to the hospital."

"He seems to be doing fine right now. But I note — an inability to theorize."

"He has trouble abstracting," I said.

"I wonder where and how he'll wind up," Tim said. "The prognosis . . . it's not good, Kirsten says."

"It's zero. For recovery. Zilch. Zip. But he's smart enough to stay off drugs."

"He does not have the advantage of an education."

"I'm not sure an education is an advantage. All I do is work in a record store. And I wasn't hired for that because of anything I learned in the English Department at Cal."

"I've been meaning to ask you which recording of Beethoven's *Fidelio* we should buy," Tim said.

"The Klemperer," I said. "On Angel. With Christa Ludwig as Leonora."

"I am very fond of her aria," Tim said.

"*'Abscheulicher! Wo Eilst Due Hin?'* She does it very well. But no one can match Frieda Leider's recording years ago. It's a collectors' item . . . it may have been dubbed onto an LP; if so, I've never seen it. I heard it once over KPFA, years ago. I never forgot it."

Tim said, "Beethoven was the greatest genius, the greatest creative artist the world has ever seen. He transformed man's conception of himself."

"Yes," I said. "The prisoners in *Fidelio* when they're let out into the light . . . it is one of the most beautiful passages in all music."

"It goes beyond beauty," Tim said. "It involves an apprehension of the nature of freedom itself. How can it be that purely abstract music, such as his late quartets, can without words change human beings in terms of their own awareness of themselves, in terms of their ontological nature? Schopenhauer believed that art, in particular music, had — has — the power to cause the will, the irrational, striving will, to somehow turn back onto and into itself and cease to strive. He considered this a religious experience, although temporary. Somehow art, somehow music especially, has the power to transform man from an irrational thing into some rational entity that is not driven by bio-logical impulses, impulses that cannot by definition ever be sat-isfied. I remember when I first heard the final movement of the Beethoven *Thirteenth Quartet*—not the 'Grosse Fuge' but the allegro that he added later in place of the 'Grosse Fuge.' It's such an odd little bit, that allegro ... so brisk and light, so sunny."

I said, "I've read that it was the last thing he wrote. That lit-tle allegro would have been the first work of Beethoven's fourth period, had he lived. It's not really a third-period piece."

"Where did Beethoven derive the concept, the entirely new and original concept of human freedom that his music ex-presses?" Tim asked. "Was he well-read?"

"He belonged to the period of Goethe and Schiller. The *Aufklärung,* the German Enlightenment."

"Always Schiller. It always comes back to that. And from Schiller to the rebellion of the Dutch against the Spanish, the War of the Lowlands. Which shows up in Goethe's *Faust, Part Two,* where Faust finally finds something that will satisfy him, and he bids the moment stay. Seeing the Dutch reclaiming land from the North Sea. I translated that passage, once, myself; I wasn't satisfied with any of the English translations available. I don't know what I did with it ... that was years ago. Do you know the Bayard Taylor translation?" He rose, approached a row of books, found the volume, brought it back, opening it as he walked.

> "'Below the hills, a marshy plain
> infects what I so long have been retrieving:
> that stagnant pool likewise to drain
> were now my latest and my best achieving.
> To many millions let me furnish soil,
> though not secure, let free for active toil:
> green, fertile fields, where men and herds go forth

> *at once, with comfort, on the newest earth, —*
> *all swiftly settled on the hill's firm base,*
> *raised by a bold, hard-working populace.*
> *In here, a land like Paradise about:*
> *up to the brink the tide may roar without,*
> *yet though it gnaw, to burst with force the limit,*
> *by common impulse all men seek to hem it.*
> *Yes! to this thought I hold with firm persistence,*
> *this wisdom's ultimate and true:*
> *he only earns his freedom and existence —'"*

I said, "'Who daily conquers them anew.'"

"Yes," Tim said; he closed the copy of *Faust, Part Two*. "I wish I hadn't lost the translation I made." He then opened the book again. "Do you mind if I read the rest?"

"Please do," I said.

> "'Thus here, by dangers girt, shall glide away*
> *of childhood, manhood, age, and vigorous day.*
> *And such a throng I fain would see, —*
> *stand on free soil among a people free!*
> *Then dared I hail the Moment fleeting,*
> *"Ah, linger still — thou art so fair!"'"*

"At that point God has won the bet in heaven," I said.

"Yes," Tim said, nodding.

> "'The traces cannot, of mine earthly being,*
> *in aeons perish: they are there! —*
> *Anticipating here such lofty bliss,*
> *I now enjoy the highest Moment, — this.'"*

"That's a very beautiful and clear translation," I said.

Tim said, "Goethe wrote *Part Two* just a year before his death. I remember only one German word from that passage:

*verdienen. Earns.* 'Earns his freedom.' I suppose that would be *Freiheit, freedom.* Perhaps it went, *'Verdient seine Freiheit —'"* He broke off. "That's the best I can do. 'Earns his freedom who daily conquers it — them, freedom and existence — anew.' The highest point in German Enlightenment. From which they so tragically fell. From Goethe, Schiller, Beethoven to the Third Reich and Hitler. It seems impossible."

"And yet it had been prefigured in Wallenstein," I said.

"Who picked his generals by means of astrological prognostications. How could an intelligent, educated man, a great man, really, one of the most powerful men of his times — how could he begin to believe in that?" Bishop Archer said. "It is a mystery to me. It is an enigma that perhaps will never be solved."

I saw how tired he was, so I got my coat and purse, said good night, and departed.

My car had been ticketed. Shit, I said to myself as I pulled the ticket from the wiper-blade and stuck it into my pocket. While we're reading Goethe, Lovely Rita Meter-Maid is ticketing my car. What a strange world, I thought; or, rather, strange worlds — plural. They do not come together.

# 9

BISHOP TIMOTHY ARCHER conceived in his mind after much prayer and pondering, after much application of his brilliant analytical faculties, the notion that he had no choice but to step down as Bishop of the Episcopal Diocese of California and go — as he phrased it — into the private sector. He discussed this matter with Kirsten and me at length.

"I have no faith in the reality of Christ," he informed us. "None whatsoever. I cannot in good conscience go on preaching the *kerygma* of the New Testament. Every time I get up in front of my congregation, I feel that I am deceiving them."

"You told Bill Lundborg that night that Christ's reality is proven by Jeff coming back," I said.

"It's not," Tim said. "It fails to. I have exhaustively scrutinized the situation and it fails to."

"What does it prove, then?" Kirsten said.

"Life after death," Tim said. "But not the reality of Christ. Jesus was a teacher whose teachings were not even original. I have the name of a medium, a Dr. Garret living in Santa Barbara. I will be flying down there to consult him, to try to talk to Jeff. Mr. Mason recommends him." He examined a slip of paper. "Oh," he said. "Dr. Garret is a woman. Rachel Garret. Hmmm . . . I was certain it was a man." He asked if the two of us wished to accompany him to Santa Barbara. It was his intention (he explained) to ask Jeff about Christ. Jeff could tell him, through the medium, Dr. Rachel Garret, if Christ were real or not, genuinely the Son of God and all the rest of that stuff that the churches teach. This would be an important trip; Tim's decision as to whether to resign his post as bishop hinged on this.

Moreover, Tim's faith was involved. He had spent decades rising within the Episcopal Church, but now he seriously doubted whether Christianity was valid. That was Tim's term: "valid." It struck me as a weak and trendy term, falling tragically short of the magnitude of the forces contending within Tim's heart and mind. However, it was the term he used; he spoke in a calm manner, devoid of any hysterical overtones. It was as if he were planning whether or not to buy a suit of clothes.

"Christ," he said, "is a role, not a person. It — the word — is a mistransliteration from the Hebrew 'Messiah,' which literally means the Anointed One, which is to say the Chosen One. The Messiah, of course, comes at the end of the world and ushers in the Age of Gold which replaces the Age of Iron, the age we now live in. This finds its most beautiful expression in the *Fourth Eclogue* of Virgil. Let me see . . . I have it here." He went to his books as he always did in time of gravity.

"We don't need to hear Virgil," Kirsten said in a biting tone.

"Here it is," Tim said, oblivious to her.

"'*Ultima Cumaei venit iam carminis aetas; magnus —*'"

"That's enough," Kirsten said sharply.

He glanced at her, puzzled.

Kirsten said, "I think it's insanely foolish and selfish of you to resign as bishop."

"Let me translate the eclogue for you, at least," Tim said. "Then you'll understand better."

"I understand that you're destroying your life and mine," Kirsten said. "What about me?"

He shook his head. "I'll be hired on at the Foundation for Free Institutions."

"What the hell is that?" Kirsten said.

"It's a think tank," I said. "In Santa Barbara."

"Then you're going to be talking with them while you're down there?" Kirsten said.

"Yes." He nodded. "I have an appointment with Pomeroy, who's in charge of it — Felton Pomeroy. I'd be their Consultant in Theological Matters."

"They're very highly thought of," I said.

Kirsten gave me a look that would have withered trees.

"There's been nothing decided," Tim said. "We are going to see Rachel Garret anyhow . . . I see no reason why I shouldn't combine the two in a single trip. That way, I'll have to fly down there only once."

"I'm supposed to set up your appointments," Kirsten said.

"Actually," Tim said, "this will be a purely informal discussion. We'll have lunch . . . I'll meet the other consultants. I'll see their buildings and gardens. They have very lovely gardens. I saw the Foundation's gardens several years ago and still remember them." To me he said, "You'll love them, Angel. Every kind of rose is represented, especially Peace. All the five-star patented roses are there, or however it is roses are rated. May I read the two of you the translation of Virgil's eclogue?

> "'Now comes the final age announced in the
> Cumaen Sibyl's chant; the great succession
> of epochs is born anew. Now the Virgin
> returns, the reign of Saturn returns; now
> a new race descends from heaven on high.

*O chaste Lucina, goddess of births! smile*
*upon the boy just born, in whose time the*
*race of iron shall first cease, and a race*
*of gold shall arise throughout the world.*
*Thine own Apollo is now king.'"*

Kirsten and I looked at each other. I saw Kirsten's lips move but I heard no sound. Heaven only knows what she was saying and thinking at that moment, as she witnessed Tim shoot down his career and life out of conviction — more properly, lack of conviction: faith in the Savior.

The problem for Kirsten was, simply, that she could not see the problem. To her, Tim's dilemma was a phantom dilemma, manufactured for bookish reasons. According to her reasoning, he had the option to shed the problem any time he saw fit; her analysis was, simply, that Tim had become restive in his job as bishop and wanted to move on; asserting a loss of faith in Christ was his way of justifying his career move. Since it was a stupid career move, she did not approve. After all, she gained so very much from his status; as she had said, Tim was not thinking about her: he thought only of himself.

"Dr. Garret is highly recommended," Tim said, almost in a plaintive voice, as if appealing to one or the other of us for support.

"Tim," I said, "I really think —"

"You think with your crotch," Kirsten said.

"What?" I said.

"You heard me. I know about your little conversations, that you two have, after I go to bed. When you're alone. And I know you've been meeting."

"Meeting what?" I said.

"Each other,"

"Christ," I said.

"'Christ,'" Kirsten echoed. "Always Christ. Always the sum-
moning of the Almighty Son of God to justify your selfishness
and what you're up to. I find it disgusting; I find both of you disgusting." To Tim she said, "I know you visited her goddamn record store last week."

"To buy an album," Tim said. "Of *Fidelio.*"

"You could have gotten it here in the City," Kirsten said. "Or I
could have picked it up for you."

Tim said, "I wanted to see what she had —"

"She doesn't have anything I don't have," Kirsten said.

"The *Missa Solemnis,*" Tim said faintly; he seemed dazed; appealing to me, he said, "Can you reason with her?"

"I can reason with myself," Kirsten said. "I can reason out exactly what's going on."

"You better knock off taking those downers, Kirsten," I said.

"And you better stop turning on five times a day." Her look
carried such furious hate that I could not credit my senses. "You
smoke enough grass to —" She broke off. "More than the San
Francisco Police Department uses in a month. I'm sorry; I'm
not feeling well. Excuse me." She walked into the bedroom; the
door shut silently after her. We could hear her stirring around.
Then we heard her go into the bathroom; water ran: she was
taking a pill, probably a barbiturate.

To Tim, who stood inert and amazed, I said, "Barbiturates
cause that kind of personality change. It's the pills talking, not
her."

"I think —" He rallied. "I really want to fly down to Santa
Barbara and see Dr. Garret. Do you think it's the fact that she's a
woman?"

"Kirsten?" I said. "Or Garret?"

"Garret. I could swear it was a man; I just now noticed the
first name. I may have gotten it wrong. Maybe that's what's up-
setting her. She'll calm down. We'll go together. Dr. Mason said

that Dr. Garret is elderly and infirm and semiretired, so she won't pose any threat to Kirsten, once she sees her."

To change the subject, I said, "Did you play the *Missa Solemnis* that I sold you?"

"No," Tim said vaguely. "I haven't had time."

"It's not the best recording," I said. "Columbia uses a peculiar microphone placement; they have microphones scattered around throughout the orchestra, with the idea of bringing out the individual instruments. The idea is good, but it does away with hall ambiance."

"It bothers her that I'm stepping down," Tim said. "As bishop."

"You should think about it longer," I said. "Before you do it. Are you sure it's this medium that you want to consult? Isn't there someone in the church you go to when you have a spiritual crisis?"

"I will be consulting Jeff. The medium acts as a passive agent, much in the fashion that a telephone acts." He went on, then, to explain how misunderstood mediums are; I half-listened, neither impressed nor caring. Kirsten's hostility had upset me, even though I had become used to it; this amounted to more than her chronic bitchiness. I can tell a red freak when I see one, I said to myself. The personality change, the hair-trigger response. The paranoia. She is crapping out on us, I said to myself. She is going down the drain. Worse, she is not going down the drain alone; her nails are dug deep in us and we go perforce along. Shit. This is just dreadful; a man like Tim Archer should not have to put up with this. *I* should not have to.

Kirsten opened the bedroom door. "Come in here," she said to Tim.

"I will in a minute," Tim said.

"You will come in here now."

I said, "I'll take off."

"No," Tim said, "you will not take off. I have further things to discuss with you. Is it your contention that I should not step down as bishop? When my book comes out about Jeff, I will have to step down. The church will not allow me to publish a controversial book of that sort. It is too radical for them; put another way, they are too reactionary for it. It is ahead of its time and they are behind the times. There is no difference between my stand on this issue and my stand on the Vietnam War; I bucked the Establishment on that, and I should — theoretically — be able to buck the Establishment on the issue of life beyond the grave, but with the war I have support from the youth of America. But in this matter, I have support from no one."

Kirsten said, "You have my support but that doesn't matter to you."

"I mean public support. The support of those in power, those who control human minds, unfortunately."

"My support means nothing to you," Kirsten repeated.

"It means everything to me," Tim said. "I could not — I would not — have dared to write the book without you; I would not even have *believed* without you. It is you who gives me my strength. My capacity to understand. And from Jeff, when we have contacted him, I will learn about Jesus Christ one way or another. I will learn if the Zadokite Documents do, in fact, indicate that Jesus spoke only secondhand of what he had been taught ... or possibly Jeff will tell me that Christ is with him, or he with Christ, in the other world, the upper realm, where we all go eventually, where he is now, reaching across to us as best he can, God bless him."

I said, "You see this business with Jeff, then, as a sort of opportunity. To clear up your doubts one way or another about the meaning of the Zadokite —"

"I think I have made that clear," Tim interrupted, peevishly. "That is why it is so crucial. To talk to him."

How strange, I thought. To use his son—make calculated use of his dead son—to determine an historical issue. But it is more than an historical issue: it is Tim Archer's entire corpus of faith, the summation, for him, of belief itself. Belief or the falling away of belief. What is at stake here is belief versus nihilism . . . for Tim to lose Christ is for Tim to lose everything. And he has lost Christ; his statements to Bill that night may have been Tim's last defense of the fortress before that fortress fell. It may have fallen then, or perhaps before then; Tim argued from memory, as if from a page. A written speech spread out before him, as when, in the celebration of the Last Supper, he reads from the Book of Common Prayer.

The son, his son, my husband, subordinated to an intellectual matter—I could never, myself, view it that way. This amounts to a depersonalization of Jeff Archer; he is converted into an instrument, a device for learning; why, he is converted into a talking book! Like all these books that Tim forever reaches for, especially in moments of crisis. Everything worth knowing can be found in a book; conversely, if Jeff is important he is important not as a person but as a book; it is books for books' sakes then, not knowledge, even, for the sake of knowledge. The book is the reality. For Tim to love and appreciate his son, he must—as impossible as this may seem—he must regard him as a kind of book. The universe to Tim Archer is one great set of reference books from which he picks and chooses as his restless mind veers on, always seeking the new, always turning away from the old; it is the very opposite of that passage from *Faust* that he read; Tim has not found the moment where he says, *"Stay"*; it is still fleeing from him, still in motion.

And I am not much different, I realized; I, who graduated from the English Department at U.C. Berkeley—Tim and I are of a kind. Had it not been the final canto of Dante's *Commedia* that struck off my identity when I first read it that day when I

was in school? Canto Thirty-three of *Paradiso,* for me the cul-
mination, where Dante says:

> *"I beheld leaves within the unfathomed blaze*
> *Into one volume bound by love, the same*
> *That the universe holds scattered through its maze.*
> *Substance and accidents, and their modes, became*
> *As if fused together, all in such wise*
> *That what I speak of is one simple flame."*

The superb Laurence Binyon translation; and then C. H.
Grandgent comments on this passage:

> *"God is the Book of the Universe."*

To which another commentator — I forget which one — said,
"This is a Platonist notion." Platonist or otherwise, this is the
sequences of words that framed me, that made me what I am:
this is *my* source, this vision and report, this view of final things.
I do not call myself a Christian but I cannot forget this view,
this wonder. I remember the night I read that final canto of *Paradiso,* read it — truly read it — for the first time; I had that infected tooth and I hurt hideously, unbearably, so I sat up all
night drinking bourbon — straight — and reading Dante, and at
nine A.M. the next day I drove to the dentist's without phoning,
without an appointment, showed up with tears dripping down
my face, demanding that Dr. Davidson do something for me . . .
which he did. So that final canto is deeply impressed onto and
into me; it is associated with terrible pain, and pain that went
on for hours, into the night, so there was no one to talk to; and
out of that I came to fathom the ultimate things in my own way,
not a formal or official way but a way nonetheless.

> *"He who learns must suffer. And even in our sleep pain that*
> *cannot forget falls drop by drop upon the heart, and in our*

*own despair, against our will, comes wisdom to us by the
awful grace of God."*

Or however it goes. Aeschylus? I forget, now. One of the three
of them who wrote the tragedies.

Which means that I can say with all truthfulness that for me
the moment of greatest understanding in which I knew spiritual reality at last came in connection with emergency root-canal irrigation, two hours in the dentist chair. And twelve hours
drinking bourbon — bad bourbon at that — and simply reading
Dante without listening to the stereo or eating — there was no
way I could eat — and suffering, and it was all worth it; I will
never forget it. *I am no different, then, from Timothy Archer.* To
me, too, books are real and alive; the voices of human beings issue forth from them and compel my assent, the way God compels our assent to the world, as Tim said. When you have been
in that much distress, you are not going to forget what you did
and saw and thought and read that night; I did nothing, saw
nothing, thought nothing; I read and I remember; I did not
read *Howard the Duck* or *The Fabulous Furry Freak Brothers* or
*Snatch Comix* that night; I read Dante's *Commedia,* from *Inferno*
through *Purgatorio,* until at last I arrived in the three colored
rings of light . . . and the time was nine A.M. and I could get into
my fucking car and shoot out into traffic and Dr. Davidson's office, crying and cursing the whole way, with no breakfast, not
even coffee, and stinking of sweat and bourbon, a sorry mess indeed, much gaped at by the dentist's receptionist.

So for me in a certain unusual way — for certain unusual reasons — books and reality are fused; they join through one incident, one night of my life: my intellectual life and my practical
life came together — nothing is more real than a badly infected
tooth — and having done so they never completely came apart
again. If I believed in God, I would say that he showed me

something that night; he showed me the totality: pain, physical pain, drop by drop, and then, this being his dreadful grace, there came understanding... and what did I understand? That it is *all* real; the abscessed tooth and the root-canal irrigation, and, no less and no more:

> *"Three circles from its substance now appeared,*
> *Of three colors, and each an equal whole."*

That was Dante's vision of God as the Trinity. Most people when they try to read the *Commedia* get bogged down in *Inferno* and suppose his vision to be that of a chamber of horrors: people head up in shit; people head down in shit; and a lake of ice (suggesting Arabic influences; that is the Muslim hell), but this is only the beginning of the journey; it is how it starts. I read the *Commedia* through to the end that night and then shot up the street for Dr. Davidson's office, and was never the same again. I never changed back into what I had previously been. So books are real to me, too; they link me not just with other minds but with the *vision* of other minds, what those minds understand and see. I see their worlds as well as I see my own. The pain and the crying and the sweating and stinking and cheap Jim Beam Bourbon was my *Inferno* and it wasn't imaginary; what I read bore the label "Paradiso" and *Paradiso* it was. This is the triumph of Dante's vision: that all the realms are real, none less than the others, none more than the others. And they blend into each other, by means of what Bill would call "gradual increments," which is indeed the proper term. There is a harmony in this because, like automobiles of today in contrast to autos of the Thirties, no sharp break exists.

God save me from another night like that. But goddamn it, had I not lived out that night, drinking and crying and reading and hurting, I would never have been born, truly born. That was the time of my birth into the real world; and the real world, for me, is a mixture of pain and beauty, and this is the correct view of it because these are the components that make up reality. And I had them all there that night, including a packet of pain-pills to carry home with me from the dentist's, after my ordeal had ended. I arrived home, took a pill, drank some coffee, and went to bed.

And yet — I feel that this was what Tim had not done; he had either not integrated the book and the pain, or, if he had, he had got it wrong. He had the tune but not the words. More correctly, he had the words but those words pertained not to world but to other words, which is termed by philosophy books and articles on logic "a vicious regress." It is sometimes said in such books and articles that "again a regress threatens," which means that the thinker has entered a loop and is in great danger. Usually he does not know it. A critical commentator with a mind that is keen and an eye that is keen comes along and points this out. Or doesn't. For Tim Archer I could not serve as that critical commentator. Who could? Dingaling Bill had taken a good shot at it and had been sent back to his East Bay apartment to think better of it.

"Jeff has the answers to my questions," Tim said. Yes, I should have said, but Jeff does not exist. And very likely the questions themselves are irreal as well.

That left only Tim. And he was busily preparing his book dealing with Jeff's return from the next world, the book that Tim knew would finish off his career in the Episcopal Church — and, moreover, deal him out of the game of influencing public opinion. That is a high price to pay; that is a very vicious regress. And indeed it threatened. It was, in fact, at hand; the time for the trip to Santa Barbara to visit Dr. Rachel Garret, the medium, had come.

. . .

Santa Barbara, California, strikes me as one of the most touchingly beautiful places in the country. Although technically
(which is to say, geographically) it is a portion of Southern California, spiritually it is not; either that or else we in the north su-
premely misunderstand the Southland. A few years ago, antiwar students from the University of California at Santa Barbara
burned down the Bank of America, to everyone's secret delight;
the town, then, is not cut off from time and world, not isolated,
although its lovely gardens suggest a tame persuasion rather
than a violent one.

The three of us flew from the San Francisco International
Airport to the small airport at Santa Barbara; we had to go by
two-motor prop plane, that airport being too short of runway
length to accommodate jets. Law requires that the city's adobe
character, which is to say, Spanish Colonial-style, be preserved.
As a cab took us to the house where we would stay, I noted the
overwhelmingly Spanish design of everything, including ar-
cade-type shopping centers; to myself I said, This is a place
where I reasonably might live. If I ever depart the Bay Area.

Tim's friends, with whom we stayed, made no impression on
me: they consisted of retractile, genteel, well-to-do people who
stayed out of our way. They had servants. Kirsten and Tim slept
in one bedroom; I had another, a rather small one, obviously
made use of only when the other rooms had filled up.

The next morning, Tim and Kirsten and I set forth by cab
to visit Dr. Rachel Garret, who would—no doubt—put us in
touch with the dead, the next world, heal the sick, turn water
into wine, and perform whatever other marvels were necessary.
Both Tim and Kirsten seemed excited; I felt nothing in particular, perhaps only a dim consciousness of what we planned, what
lay ahead; not even curiosity: only what a starfish living at the
bottom of a tidal pond might feel.

We found Dr. Garret to be a rather lively small elderly Irish lady wearing a red sweater over her blouse — even though the weather was warm — and low-heeled shoes, and the sort of utility skirt suggesting that she performed all her own chores.

"And who are you, again?" she said, cupping her ear. She could not even figure out who stood before her on her porch: Not an encouraging beginning, I said to myself.

Presently, the four of us sat in a darkened living room, drinking tea and hearing from Dr. Garret a narration, delivered with enthusiasm, of the heroism of the IRA to which — she told us proudly — she contributed all the money she took in via her séances. However, she informed us, "séance" was the wrong word; it suggests the occult. What Dr. Garret did belonged within the realm of the perfectly natural; one could rightly call it a science. I saw in a corner of the living room among the other archaic furniture a Magnavox radio-phonograph of the Forties, a large one, the kind with two identical twelve-inch speakers. On each side of the Magnavox, stacks of 78 records — albums of Bing Crosby and Nat Cole and all the other trash of that period could be discerned. I wondered if Dr. Garret still listened to them. I wondered if, in her supernatural fashion, she had learned about long-playing records and the artists of today. Probably not.

To me Dr. Garret said, "And you're their daughter?"

"No," I said.

"My daughter-in-law," Tim said.

"You have an Indian guide," Dr. Garret said to me brightly.

"Really," I murmured.

"He's standing just behind you, to your left. He has very long hair. And behind you on your right side stands your great-grandfather on your father's side. They are always with you."

"I had a feeling that was the case," I said.

Kirsten gave me one of her mixed looks; I said no more. I settled back against the couch with all its pillows, noted a fern

growing in a huge clay pot near the doors leading to the garden
. . . I noted assorted uninstructive pictures on the walls, including several famous loser pictures of the Twenties.

"Is it about the son?" Dr. Garret said.

"Yes," Tim said.

I felt as if I had found my way into Gian Carlo Menotti's opera *The Medium,* which Menotti describes in his album-liner
notes for Columbia Records as set in "Mme. Flora's weird
and shabby Parlor." That is the trouble with education, I realized; you have been everywhere before, seen everything, vi-
cariously; it has all already happened to you. We are Mr. and
Mrs. Gobineau visiting Mme. Flora, a fraud and lunatic. Mr. and
Mrs. Gobineau have been coming to Mme. Flora's séances — or,
rather, scientific sessions — every week for nearly two years, as
I recall. What a drag. Worst of all, the money Tim will be paying
her goes to kill British soldiers; this is a fund-raiser for terror-
ists. Great.

"What is your son's name?" Dr. Garret asked. She sat in an
ancient wicker chair, leaning back, her hands clasped together,
her eyes slowly shutting. She had begun to breathe through her
mouth, as the very ill do; her skin resembled that of a chicken,
with bits of hair here and there, little tufts like minor scarcely
watered plants. The whole room and everything in it now possessed a vegetable quality, totally lacking in vitality. I felt myself
drained and being drained, my own energy taken away. Perhaps
the light — or lack of light — gave me this impression. I did not
find it pleasant.

"Jeff," Tim said. He sat alert, his eyes fixed on Dr. Garret.
Kirsten had gotten a cigarette from her purse but did not light
it; she merely held it; she also scrutinized Dr. Garret, with evident expectations.

"Jeff has passed across to the distant shore," Dr. Garret said.

As the newspapers reported, I said to myself.

I had expected a lengthy preamble from Dr. Garret, to set up the scene. I was wrong. She launched into it at once.

"Jeff wants you to know that—" Dr. Garret paused as if listening. "You should feel no guilt. Jeff has been trying to reach you for some time. He wanted to tell you that he forgives you. He has tried one means after another to attract your attention. He has stuck pins into your fingers; he has broken things; he has left notes to you—" Dr. Garret opened her eyes wide. "Jeff is highly agitated. He—" She broke off. "He took his own life."

You are batting a thousand, I thought acridly.

"Yes, he did," Kirsten said, as if Dr. Garret's statement was a revelation or else confirmed in a startling way something up to now only suspected.

"And violently," Dr. Garret said. "I get the impression that he used a gun."

"That's correct," Tim said.

"Jeff wants you to know that he is no longer in pain," Dr. Garret said. "He was in a great deal of pain when he took his own life. He didn't want you to know. He suffered from great doubts about the worth of living."

"What does he say to me?" I said.

Dr. Garret opened her eyes long enough to fathom who had spoken.

"He was my husband," I said.

"Jeff says that he loves you and prays for you," Dr. Garret said. "He wants you to be happy."

That and fifty cents, I thought, will get you a cup of coffee.

"There is more," Dr. Garret declared. "A great deal more. It's all coming in a rush. Oh my. Jeff, what is it you're trying to tell us?" She listened silently for a time, her face showing agitation. "The man at the restaurant was a Soviet what?" Again she opened her eyes wide. "My goodness. A Soviet police agent."

Jesus, I thought.

"But there's nothing to worry about," Dr. Garret said, then, showing relief; she leaned back. "God will see that he is punished."

I glanced questioningly at Kirsten, trying to catch her eye; I wanted to know what — if anything — she had said to Dr. Garret; Kirsten, however, sat staring fixedly at the old lady, apparently dumbfounded. So it would seem I had my answer.

"Jeff says," Dr. Garret said, "that it is a matter of utmost joy to him that — that Kirsten and his father have each other. This is a great comfort to him. He wants you to know that. Who is 'Kirsten'?"

"I am," Kirsten said.

"He says," the old lady continued, "that he loves you."

Kirsten said nothing. But she listened with more intensity than I had ever seen her display before.

"He felt it was wrong," Dr. Garret said. "He says he's sorry . . . but he couldn't help it. He feels guilty about it and he would like your forgiveness."

"He has it," Tim said.

"Jeff says that he can't forgive himself," Dr. Garret said. "He also felt anger toward Kirsten for coming between him and his father. It made him feel cut off from his father. I get the impression that his father and Kirsten went on a long trip, a trip to England, and left him behind. He felt very badly about that." Again the old lady paused. "Angel is not to smoke any more drugs," Dr. Garret said, then. "She smokes too much . . . what is it, Jeff? I can't pick this up clearly. 'Too many numbers.' I don't know what that means."

I laughed. In spite of myself.

"Does that make any sense to you?" Dr. Garret said to me.

"In a way," I said, paying out as little line to her as possible.

"Jeff says he's glad about your job at the record store," Dr. Garret said. "But —" She laughed. "You're not being paid enough.

He liked it better when you worked at the — shop kind of shop. A bottle shop?"

"Law office and candle shop," I said.

"Strange," Dr. Garret said, puzzled. "'Law office and candle shop.'"

"It was in Berkeley," I said.

Dr. Garret said, "Jeff has something very important to say to Kirsten and his father." Her voice, now, had become faint, almost reduced to a rasping whisper. As if coming from a vast distance away. Traveling over invisible wires strung between stars. "Jeff has some dreadful news he wants to convey to the two of you. This is why he has been trying so badly to get through to you. This is why the pins and the burning and the breaking and the disordering and the smearing. He has a reason, a dreadful reason."

Silence, then.

Leaning toward Tim, I said, "This is a judgment call, but I want to leave."

"No," Tim said. He shook his head. His face showed unhappiness.

# 10

WHAT A PECULIAR mixture of nonsense and the uncanny, I thought as we waited for elderly Dr. Rachel Garret to go on. Mention of Fred Hill, the KGB agent . . . mention of Jeff disapproving of my turning on. Scraps derived obviously from newspapers: how Jeff had died and his probable motivations. *Lumpen* psychoanalysis and scandal-sheet garbage, and yet, stuck in here and there, a fragment like a tiny shard that could not be explained.

Beyond doubt Dr. Garret had easy access to most of the knowledge she had divulged, but there remained a creepy residuum: defined as, "That which remains after certain deductions are made," so this is the right term, and I have had a long time, many years, to mull over it. I have mulled and I can explain no part of it. How could Dr. Garret know about the Bad Luck Restaurant? And even if she knew that Kirsten and Tim had met originally at that place, how could she have known about Fred Hill or what we supposed was the case with Fred Hill?

It had been the joke passed endlessly between Jeff and me, that the owner of the Bad Luck Restaurant in Berkeley had been a KGB agent, but this fact wasn't printed anywhere; no one had ever written it down, except perhaps in the computers of the FBI and of course at KGB GHQ in Moscow, and it was only speculation anyhow. The issue of my turning on could be a shrewd guess, since I lived and worked in Berkeley, and, as everyone in the world knows, all the people in Berkeley do dope regularly — in fact, do it to excess. A medium is traditionally one who relies on a potpourri of hunches, common knowledge, clues unknowingly delivered by the audience itself, delivered unintentionally and then handed back . . . and, of course, the standard bullshit, such as "Jeff loves you" and "Jeff isn't in any more pain" and "Jeff felt a lot of doubt," generalizations available to anyone at any time, given the known facts.

Yet an eerie sensation held me, even though I knew that this old Irish lady who gave money — or said she gave money — to the Irish Republican Army was a fraud, that we three collectively were being fleeced out of our money, fleeced, too, in the sense that our credulity was being pandered to and manipulated — by someone in the business of doing this: a professional. The primary medium — it sounded like the medical term for cancer: "the primary cancer" — Dr. Mason had undoubtedly passed on everything *he* had learned and knew; this is how mediums work it, and we all know this.

The time to have left was before the revelation came, and now it was going to come, dumped on us by an unscrupulous old lady with dollar signs in her eyes and a clever ability to fathom the weak links in human psyches. But we didn't leave, and so it followed as the night the day that we got to hear from Dr. Garret what had so agitated Jeff, causing him to come back to Tim and Kirsten as the occult "phenomena" that they logged each day for Tim's forthcoming book.

It seemed to me as if Rachel Garret had become very old as she sat in her wicker chair, and I thought about the ancient sibyl — I could not remember which sibyl it had been, the one at Delphi or at Cumae — who had asked for immortality but had neglected

to stipulate that she remain young; whereupon she lived forever but got so old that eventually her friends hung her up on the
wall in a bag. Rachel Garret resembled that tattered wisp of skin
and fragile bones, whispering out of the bag nailed to the wall;
what wall in what city of the Empire I do not know — perhaps
the sibyl is still there; perhaps this being who faced us as Rachel
Garret was, in fact, that same sibyl; in any case, I did not want to
hear what she had to say: I wanted to leave.

"Sit down," Kirsten said.

I realized, then, that I had stood without intending to. Flight
reaction, I said to myself. Instinctive. Upon experiencing close
adversaries. The lizard part of the brain.

Rachel Garret whispered, "Kirsten." But now she pronounced it correctly: *Shishen,* which I did not do, nor had Jeff,
nor did Tim. But that was how she pronounced it herself, and
gave up on getting anyone else to, at least in the States.

At this, Kirsten gave a muffled gasp.

The old lady in the wicker chair said:

> "'*Ultima Cumaei venit iam carminis aetas; magnus ab inte-
> gro saeclorum nascitur ordo. Iam redit et Virgo, redeunt Sa-
> turnia régna; iam nova —*'"

"My God," Tim said. "It's the *Fourth Eclogue.* Of Virgil."

"That's enough," Kirsten said faintly.

I thought: The old lady is reading my mind. She knows I
thought about the sibyl.

Speaking to me, Rachel Garret said:

> "'*Dies irae, dies illa,
> Solvet saeclum in favilla:
> Teste David cum Sibylla.*'"

Yes, she is reading my mind, I realized. She even knows that
I know it; as I think she reads my thoughts back to me.

"*Mors Kirsten nunc carpit,*" Rachel Garret whispered. "*Hodie. Calamitas . . . timeo . . .*" She drew herself up in her wicker chair.

"What did she say?" Kirsten said to Tim.

"You are going to die very soon," Rachel Garret said to her, in a calm voice. "I thought today, but not today. I saw it here. But not quite yet. Jeff says so. This is why he came back: to warn you."

"Die how?" Tim said.

"He isn't sure," Rachel Garret said.

"Violently?" Tim said.

"He doesn't know," the old lady said. "But they are preparing a place for you, Kirsten." All her agitation had gone, now; she seemed completely composed. "This is awful news," she said. "I'm sorry, Kirsten. No wonder Jeff caused all the many disturbances. Usually there is a reason . . . they return for a good reason."

"Can anything be done?" Tim said.

"Jeff thinks that it is inevitable," the old lady said, after a time.

"Then what was the point of him coming back?" Kirsten said savagely; her face was white.

"He wanted to warn his father as well," the old lady said.

"About what?" I said.

Rachel Garret said, "He has a chance to live. No, Jeff says. His father will die soon after Kirsten. Both of you are going to perish. It won't be long. There is some uncertainty about the father but none about the woman. If I could give you more information, I would. Jeff is still with me but he doesn't know any more." She shut her eyes and sighed.

All the vitality, it seemed, had gone out of her as she sat in the old chair, her hands clasped together; then suddenly she leaned forward and picked up her teacup.

"Jeff was so anxious that you know," she said in a bright, chipper voice. "He feels so much better now." She smiled at us.

Still ashen, Kirsten murmured, "Is it all right if I smoke?"

"Oh, I'd prefer you didn't smoke," Dr. Garret said. "But if you feel you must —"

"Thank you." Her hand trembling, Kirsten lit her cigarette. She stared and stared at the old lady, with dislike and fury, or so it seemed to me. I thought: Kill the Spartan messengers, lady; hold them responsible.

"We want to thank you very much," Tim said to Dr. Garret in a level, controlled voice; he began, by degrees, to rouse himself, to take command of the situation. "So then Jeff is beyond any doubt whatsoever alive in the after-world? And it has been he who has come to us with what we call the 'phenomena'?"

"Oh, indeed," Dr. Garret said. "But Leonard told you that. Leonard Mason. You knew that already."

I said, "Could it have been an evil spirit posing as Jeff? And not actually Jeff?"

Her eyes bright, Dr. Garret nodded. "You are exceedingly alert, young lady. Yes, it certainly could have been. But it was not. One learns to tell the difference. I found no malice in him, only concern and love. Angel — your name is Angel, isn't it? — your husband apologizes to you for his feelings about Kirsten. He knows that it is unfair to you. But he thinks that you will understand."

I said nothing.

"Did I get your name right?" Rachel Garret asked me, in a timid and uncertain tone.

"Yes," I said. To Kirsten, I said, "Let me have a puff on your cigarette."

"Here." Kirsten passed it to me. "Keep it. I'm not supposed to smoke." To Tim she said, "Well? Shall we go? I don't see any reason for staying any longer." She reached for her purse and coat.

Tim paid Dr. Garret — I did not see how much, but it took the form of cash, not a check — and then phoned for a cab. Ten minutes later, the three of us rode back down the winding hillside roads to the house where we had accommodated ourselves.

Time passed and then, half to himself, Tim said, "That was the same eclogue of Virgil that I read to you. That day."

"I remember," I said.

"It seems a remarkable coincidence," Tim said. "There is no way she could have known it is a favorite of mine. Of course, it is the most famous of his eclogues . . . but that would scarcely account for it. I have never heard anyone else quote it but myself. It was as if I were hearing my own thoughts read back to me aloud, when Dr. Garret lapsed into Latin."

And I — I, too, had experienced that, I realized. Tim had expressed it perfectly. Perfectly and precisely.

"Tim," I said, "did you say anything to Dr. Mason about the Bad Luck Restaurant?"

Eying me, Tim said, "What is the 'Bad Luck Restaurant'?"

"Where we met," Kirsten said.

"No," Tim said. "I don't even remember the name of it. I remember what we had to eat . . . I had abalone."

"Did you ever tell anybody," I said to him, "anybody at all, at any time, anywhere, about Fred Hill?"

"I don't know anybody by that name," Tim said. "I'm sorry." He rubbed his eyes wearily.

"They read your mind," Kirsten said. "That's where they get it. She knew my health was bad. She knows I'm worried about the spot on my lung."

"What spot?" I said. This was the first I had heard about it. "Have you been in for more tests?"

When Kirsten did not answer, Tim said, "She showed a spot.

Several weeks ago. It was a routine X-ray. They don't think it means anything."

"It means I'm going to die," Kirsten said bitingly, with palpable venom. "You heard her, the old bitch."

"Kill the Spartan runners," I said.

Furiously, Kirsten lashed at me, "Is that one of your Berkeley educated remarks?"

"Please," Tim said in a faint voice.

I said, "It's not her fault."

"We pay a hundred dollars to be told we're both going to die," Kirsten said, "and then on top of that, according to you, we should be grateful?" She scrutinized me with what struck me as psychotic malice, exceeding anything I had ever seen in her or in anyone else. "You're okay; she didn't say anything was going to happen to you, you cunt. You little Berkeley cunt — you're doing fine. I'm going to die and you get to have Tim all to yourself, with Jeff dead and now me. I think you set it up; you're involved; goddamn you!" Reaching, she took a swing at me; there in the back of the Yellow Cab she tried to hit me. I drew back, horrified.

Grabbing her with both hands, Tim pinned her against the side of the cab, against the door. "If I ever hear you use that word again," he said, "you are out of my life forever."

"You prick," Kirsten said.

After that, we drove in silence. The only sound was the occasional racket of the cab company's dispatcher, from the driver's two-way radio.

"Let's stop somewhere for a drink," Kirsten said, as we approached the house. "I don't want to have to deal with those awful mousy people; I just can't. I want to shop." To Tim she said, "We'll let you off. Angel and I'll go shopping. I really can't take any more today."

I said, "I don't feel like shopping right now."

"Please," Kirsten said tightly.

Tim said to me in a gentle voice, "Do it as a favor to both of us." He opened the cab door.

"Okay," I said.

After giving Kirsten money — all the money he had with him, apparently — Tim got out of the cab; we shut the door after him, and, presently, arrived at the downtown shopping district of Santa Barbara, with all the many lovely little shops and their various handcrafted artifacts. Soon Kirsten and I sat together in a bar, a nice bar, subdued, with low music playing. Through the open doors we could see people strolling around in the bright midday sunlight.

"Shit," Kirsten said as she sipped her vodka collins. "What a thing to find out. That you're going to die."

"Dr. Garret worked backward from Jeff's return," I said.

"How do you mean?" She stirred her drink.

"Jeff had come back to you. That's the given. So Garret summoned up a reason to explain it, the most dramatic reason she could find. 'He returned for a reason. That's why they return.' It's a commonplace. It's like —" I gestured. "Like the ghost in *Hamlet*."

Gazing at me quizzically, Kirsten said, "In Berkeley there is an intellectual reason for everything."

"The ghost warns Hamlet that Claudius is a murderer, that he murdered him, Hamlet's father."

"What's Hamlet's father's name?"

"He's just called 'Hamlet's father, the late king.'"

Kirsten, an owlish expression on her face, said, "No, his father is named Hamlet, too."

"Ten bucks says otherwise."

She extended her hand; we shook. "The play," Kirsten said, "instead of being called *Hamlet* should properly be called *Hamlet, Junior*." We both laughed. "I mean," Kirsten said, "this is just sick. We're sick going to that medium. Coming all this way — of course, Tim is meeting with those double-domed eggheads from the think tank. You know where he really wants to work? Don't ever say this to anyone, but he'd *like* to work for the Center for the Study of Democratic Institutions. This whole business about Jeff coming back —" She sipped her drink. "It's cost Tim a lot."

"He doesn't have to bring out the book. He could drop the project."

As if thinking aloud, Kirsten said, "How do those mediums do it? It's ESP; they can pick up your anxieties. Somehow the old biddy knew I have medical problems. It goes back to that damn peritonitis . . . that's public knowledge that I had that. There's a central file they keep, mediums of the world. Media, I guess, is the plural. And my cancer. They know I'm plagued with a second-rate body, sort of a used car. A lemon. God sold me a lemon for a body."

"You should have told me about the spot."

"It's none of your business."

"I care about you."

"Dyke," Kirsten said. "Homo. That's why Jeff killed himself, because you and I are in love with each other." Both of us had begun laughing, now; we bumped heads, and I put my arm around her. "I have this joke for you. We're not supposed to call Mexicans 'greasers' any more; right?" She lowered her voice. "We're supposed to call them —"

"Lubricanos," I said.

She glanced at me. "Well, fuck you."

"Let's pick up somebody," I said.

"I want to shop. You pick up somebody." In a more somber tone she said, "This is a beautiful city. We may be living down here, you realize. Would you stay up in Berkeley if Tim and I moved down here?"

"I don't know," I said.

"You and your Berkeley friends. The Greater East Bay Co-Sexual Communal Free Love Exchange-Partners Enterprise, Unlimited. What is it about Berkeley, Angel? Why do you stay there?"

"The house," I said. And I thought: Memories of Jeff. In connection with the house. The Co-op on University Avenue where we used to shop. "I like the coffee houses on the Avenue," I said. "Especially Larry Blake's. One time, Larry Blake came over to Jeff and me; downstairs in the Ratskeller — he was so nice to us. And I like Tilden Park." And the campus, I said to myself. I can never free myself of that. The eucalyptus grove, down by Oxford. The library. "It's my home," I said.

"You'd get accustomed to Santa Barbara."

I said, "You shouldn't call me a cunt in front of Tim. He might get ideas."

"If I die," Kirsten said, "would you sleep with him? I mean, seriously?"

"You're not going to die."

"Dr. Spooky says I am."

"Dr. Spooky," I said, "is full of it."

"Do you think so? God, it was weird." Kirsten shivered. "I felt she could read my mind, that she was tapping it, like you tap a maple tree. Reading my own fears back to me. Would you sleep with Tim? Answer me seriously; I need to know."

"It would be incest."

"Why? Oh; okay. Well — it's already a sin, a sin for him; why not add incest? If Jeff is in heaven and they're preparing a place for me, apparently I'm going to go to heaven. That's a relief. I just don't know how seriously to take what Dr. Garret said."

"Take it with the entire output of salt from the Polish salt mines for one full calendar year."

"But," Kirsten said, "it is Jeff coming back to us. Now we have it confirmed. But if I'm going to believe that, don't I have to believe the other, the prophecy?"

As I listened to her, a line from *Dido and Aeneas* entered my head, both the music and the words:

> *"The Trojan Prince, you know, is bound*
> *By Fate to seek Italian ground;*
> *The Queen and he are now in chase."*

Why had that come to mind? The sorceress . . . Jeff had quoted her or I had; the music had been a part of our lives, and I was thinking about Jeff, now, and the things that had bound us together. Fate, I thought. Predestination; doctrine of the church, based on Augustine and Paul. Tim had once told me that Christianity as a Mystery Religion had come into existence as a means of abolishing the tyranny of fate, only to reintroduce it as predestination — in fact, double predestination: some predestined to hell, some to heaven. Calvin's doctrine.

"We don't have fate any more," I said. "That went out with astrology, with the ancient world. Tim explained it to me."

Kirsten said, "He explained it to me, too, but the dead have precognition; they're outside of time. That's why you raise the spirits of the dead, to get advice from them about the future: they know the future. To them, it's already happened. They're like God. They see everything. Necromancy; we're like Dr. Dee in Elizabethan England. We have access to this marvelous supernatural power — it's better than the Holy Spirit, who also grants the ability to foresee the future, to prophesy. Through that wizened old lady we get Jeff's absolute knowledge that I'm going to kick off in the near-future. How can you doubt it?"

"Readily," I said.

"But she knew about the Bad Luck Restaurant. You see, Angel, we either reject it all or accept it all; we don't get to pick and choose. And if we reject it then Jeff didn't come back to us, and we're nuts. And if we accept it he did come back to us, which is fine as far as that goes, but then we have to face the fact that I'm going to die."

I thought: And Tim, too. You've forgotten about that, in your concern for yourself. As is typical of you.

"What's the matter?" Kirsten said.

"Well, she said Tim would die, too."

"Tim has Christ on his side; he's immortal. Didn't you know that? Bishops live forever. The first bishop — Peter, I imagine — is still alive somewhere, drawing a salary. Bishops live eternally and they get paid a lot. I die and I get paid almost nothing."

"It beats working in a record store," I said.

"Not really. Everything about your life is out in the open, at least; you don't have to skulk around like a second-story-man. This book of Tim's — it's going to be clear as day to everyone who reads it that Tim and I are sleeping together. We were in England together; we witnessed the phenomena together. Perhaps this is God's revenge against us for our sins, this prophecy by that old lady. Sleep with a bishop and die; it's like 'See Rome and die.' Well, I can't say it's been worth it, I really can't. I'd rather be a record clerk in Berkeley like you . . . but then I'd have to be young like you, to get the full benefits."

I said, "My husband is dead. I don't have all the breaks."

"And you don't have the guilt."

"Balls," I said. "I have plenty of guilt."

"Why? Jeff — well, anyhow, it wasn't your fault."

"We share the guilt," I said. "All of us."

"For the death of someone who was programmed to die? You only kill yourself if the DNA death-strip tells you to; it's in the DNA . . . didn't you know that? Or it's what they call a 'script,' which is what Eric Berne taught. He's dead, you know; his death-script or -strip or whatever caught up with him, proving him right. His father died and he died, the exact same age.

It's like Chardin, who desired to die on Good Friday and got his wish."

"This is morbid," I said.

"Right." Kirsten nodded. "I just heard a while ago that I'm doomed to die; I feel very morbid, and so would you, except that you're exempt, for some reason. Maybe because you don't have a spot on your lung and you never had cancer. Why doesn't that old lady die? Why is it me and Tim? I think Jeff's malicious, saying that; it's one of those self-fulfilling prophecies you hear about. He tells Dr. Spooky I'm going to die and as a result I die, and Jeff enjoys it because he hated me for sleeping with his father. The hell with both of them. It goes along with the pins stuck under my fingernails; its hate, hate toward me. I can tell hate when I see it. I hope Tim points that out in his book — well, he will because I'm writing most of it; he doesn't have the time, and, if you want to know the truth, the talent either. All his sentences run together. He has logorrhea, if you want to know the blunt truth — from the speed he takes."

I said, "I don't want to know."

"Have you and Tim slept together?"

"No!" I said, amazed.

"Bull."

"Christ," I said, "you're crazy."

"Tell me it's due to the reds I take."

I stared at her; she stared back. Unwinkingly, her face taut.

"You're crazy," I said.

Kirsten said, "You have turned Tim against me."

"I *what?*"

"He thinks that Jeff would be alive if it hadn't been for me, but it was his idea for us to get sexually involved."

"You —" I could not think what to say. "Your mood-swings are getting greater," I said finally.

Kirsten said in a fierce, grating voice, "I see more and more clearly. Come on." She finished her drink and slid from her stool, tottered, grinned at me. "Let's go shop. Let's buy a whole lot of Indian silver jewelry imported from Mexico; they sell it here. You regard me as old and sick and a red freak, don't you? Tim and I have discussed it, your view of me. He considers it damaging to me and defamatory. He's going to talk to you about it sometime. Get prepared; he's going to quote canon law. It's against canon law to bear false witness. He doesn't consider you a very good Christian; in fact, not a Christian at all. He doesn't really like you. Did you know that?"

I said nothing.

"Christians are judgmental," Kirsten said, "and bishops even more so. I have to live with the fact that Tim confesses every week to the sin of sleeping with me; do you know how that feels? It is quite painful. And now he has me going; I take Communion and I confess. It's sick. Christianity is sick. I want him to step down as bishop; I want him to go into the private sector."

"Oh," I said. I understood, then. Tim could then come out in the open and proclaim her, his relationship with her. Strange, I thought, that it never entered my mind.

"When he is working for that think tank," Kirsten said, "the stigma and the hiding will be gone because they don't care. They're just secular people; they're not Christians—they don't condemn others. They're not saved. I'll tell you something, Angel. Because of me, Tim is cut off from God. This is terrible, for him and for me; he has to get up every Sunday and preach knowing that because of me he and God are severed, as in the original Fall. Because of me, Bishop Timothy Archer is recapitulating the primordial Fall in himself, and he fell voluntarily; he chose it. No one made him fall or told him to do it. It's my fault. I should have said 'no' to him when he first asked me to sleep with him. It would have been a lot better, but I didn't know a rat's ass about Christianity; I didn't comprehend what it signified for him and what, eventually, it would signify for me as the damn stuff oozed out all over me, that Pauline doctrine of sin, Original Sin. What a demented doctrine, that man is born evil; how cruel it is. It's not found in Judaism; Paul made it up to explain the Crucifixion. To make sense out of Christ's death, which in fact makes no sense. Death for nothing, unless you believe in Original Sin."

"Do you believe in it now?" I asked.

"I believe I've sinned; I don't know if I was born that way. But it's true now."

"You need therapy."

"The whole church needs therapy. Old Dr. Batshit could take one look at me and Tim and know we're sleeping together; the whole media-news network knows it, and when Tim's book comes out — he *has* to step down — it has nothing to do with his faith or lack of faith in Christ: it has to do with me. I'm forcing him out of his career, not his lack of faith; I'm doing it. That cracked old lady only read back to me what I already knew, that you can't do what we're doing; you can do it but you have to pay for it. I'd just as soon be dead, I really would. This is no life. Every time we go somewhere, fly somewhere, we have to get two hotel rooms, one for each of us, and then I slip up the hall into his room . . . Dr. Batshit didn't have to be a psychic to ferret it all out; it was written on our faces. Come on; let's shop."

I said, "You're going to have to lend me some money. I didn't bring enough along to shop."

"It's the Episcopal Church's money." She opened her purse. "Be my guest."

"You hate yourself," I said; I intended to add the word unfairly, but Kirsten interrupted me.

"I hate the position I'm in. I hate what Tim has done to me, made me ashamed of myself and my body and being a woman. Is this why we founded FEM? I never dreamed I'd ever be in this situation, like a forty-dollar whore. Sometime you and I should talk, the way we used to talk before I was busy all the time writing his speeches and making his appointments — the bishop's secretary who makes sure he doesn't reveal in public the fool that he is, the child that he is; I'm the one who has all the responsibility, and I'm treated like garbage."

She handed me some money from her purse, grabbed out at random; I accepted it, and felt vast guilt; but I took the money anyhow. As Kirsten said, it belonged to the Episcopal Church.

"One thing I have learned," she said as we left the bar and emerged into the daylight, "is to read the fine print."

"I'll say one thing for that old lady," I said. "She certainly loosened up your tongue."

"No — it's being out of San Francisco. You haven't seen me out of the Bay Area and Grace Cathedral before. I don't like you and I don't like being a cheap whore and I don't particularly like my life in general. I'm not sure I even like Tim. I'm not sure I want to continue with this, any of this. That apartment — I had a much better apartment before I met Tim, although I suppose that doesn't count; it's not supposed to, anyhow. But I had a very rewarding life. But I was programmed by my DNA to get mixed up with Tim and now some old skuzz-bag rails at me that I'm going to die. You know what my feeling is about that, my real feeling? It no longer matters to me. I knew it anyway. She just read my own thoughts back to me and you know it. That is the one thing that sticks in my mind from this séance or whatever we're supposed to call it: I heard someone express my realizations about myself and my life and what's become of me. It gives me courage to face what I have to face and do what I have to do."

"And what is that?"

"You'll see in due time. I've come to an important decision. This today helped clear my mind. I think I understand." She spoke no further. It was Kirsten's custom to cast a veil of mystery over her connivings; that way, she supposed, she added an element of glamour. But in fact she did not. She only murked up the situation, for herself most of all.

I let the subject drop. Together, then, we sauntered off, in search of ways to spend the church's wealth.

We returned to San Francisco at the end of the week, laden with purchases and feeling tired. The bishop had secured, covertly, not for publication, a post with the Santa Barbara think tank. It would be announced presently that he intended to resign from his post as Bishop of the Diocese of California; the announcement would be coming ineluctably, his decision having been made, his new job arranged for: nailed down. Meanwhile, Kirsten checked into Mount Zion Hospital for further tests.

Her apprehension had made her taciturn and morose; I visited her at the hospital but she had little to say. As I sat beside her bed, ill at ease and wishing I were elsewhere, Kirsten fussed with her hair and complained. I left dissatisfied, with myself, basically; I seemed to have lost my ability to communicate with her — my best friend, really — and our relationship was dwindling, along with her spirits.

At this time, the bishop had in his possession the galleys for his book dealing with Jeff's return from the next world; Tim had decided on the title *Here, Tyrant Death*, which I had suggested to him; it is from Handel's *Belshazzar*, and reads in full:

"Here, tyrant Death, thy terrors end."

He quoted it in context in the book itself.

Busy as always, over-extended and preoccupied with a hundred and one major matters, he elected to bring the galleys to Kirsten in the hospital; he left them with her to proofread and at once departed. I found her lying propped up, a cigarette in one hand, a pen in the other, the long galley-pages propped up on her knees. It was evident that she was furious.

"Can you believe this?" she said, by way of greeting.

"I can do them," I said, seating myself on the edge of the bed.

"Not if I throw up on them."

"After you're dead you'll work even harder."

Kirsten said, "No; I won't work at all. That's the point. As I read over this thing I keep asking myself, Who is going to believe this crap? I mean, it is crap. Let's face it. Look." She pointed to a section on the galley-page and I read it over. My reaction tallied with hers; the prose was turgid, vague and disastrously pompous. Obviously, Tim had dictated it at his rush-rush, speeded-up, let's-get-it-over-with velocity. Equally obviously, he had never once looked back. I thought to myself, The title should be *Look Backward, Idiot.*

"Start with the final page," I said, "and work forward. That way, you won't have to read it."

"I'm going to drop them. Oops." She simulated dropping the galleys onto the floor, catching them just in time. "Does the order matter on these? Let's shuffle them."

"Write in stuff," I said. "Write in, 'This really sucks.' Or, 'Your mother wears Army boots.'"

Kirsten, pretending to write, said, "'Jeff manifested himself to us naked with his pecker in his hand. He was singing "The Stars and Stripes Forever."'" Both of us were laughing, now; I collapsed against her and we embraced.

"I'll give you one hundred dollars if you write that in," I said, almost unable to talk.

"I'll just turn it over to the IRA."

"No," I said. "To the IRS."

Kirsten said, "I don't report my earnings. Hookers don't have to." Her mood changed, then; her spirit palpably ebbed away. Gently, she patted me on the arm and then she kissed me.

"What's that for?" I said, touched,

"They think the spot means I have a tumor."

"Oh, no," I said.

"Yep. Well, that's the long and the short of it." She pushed me away, then, with stifled — ill-stifled — anger.

"Can they do anything? I mean, they can —"

"They can operate; they can remove the lung."

"And you're still smoking."

"It's a little late to give up cigarettes. What the hell. This raises an interesting question . . . I'm not the first to ask it. When you're resurrected in the flesh, are you resurrected in a perfect form or do you have all the scars and injuries and defects you had while alive? Jesus showed Thomas his wounds; he had Thomas thrust his hand into his — Jesus' — side. Did you know that the church was born from that wound? That's what the Roman Catholics believe. Blood and water flowed from the wound, the spear wound, while he was on the cross. It's a vagina, Jesus' vagina." She did not seem to be joking; she seemed, now, solemn and pensive. "A mystical notion of a spiritual second birth. Christ gave birth to us all."

I seated myself on the chair beside the bed, saying nothing. The news — the medical report — stunned and terrified me; I could not respond. Kirsten, however, looked composed.

They have given her tranks, I realized. As they do when they deliver this sort of news.

"You consider yourself a Christian now?" I said finally, unable to think up anything else, anything more appropriate.

"The fox hole phenomenon," Kirsten said. "What do you think of the title? *Here, Tyrant Death.*"

"I picked it," I said.

She gazed at me, with intensity.

"Why are you looking at me like that?" I said.

"Tim said he picked it."

"Well, he did. I gave him the quotation. One among a group; I submitted several."

"When was this?"

"I don't know. Some time ago. I forget. Why?"

Kirsten said, "It's a terrible title. I abominated it when I first saw it. I didn't see it until he dumped these galleys in my lap, literally in my lap. He never asked —" She broke off, then stubbed her cigarette out. "It's like somebody's idea of what a book title ought to consist of. A parody of a book title. By someone who never titled a book before. I'm surprised his editor didn't object."

"Is all this directed at me?" I said.

"I don't know. You figure it out." She began, then, to scrutinize the galleys; she ignored me.

"Do you want me to go?" I said awkwardly, after a time.

Kirsten said, "I really don't care what you do." She continued with her work; presently, she halted a moment to light up another cigarette. I saw, then, that the ashtray by her bed overflowed with half-smoked, stubbed-out cigarettes.

# 11

I LEARNED OF HER suicide by hearing it from Tim on the phone. My little brother had come over to the house to visit me; it was on Sunday, so I didn't have to go to the Musik Shop that day. I had to stand there and listen to Tim telling me that Kirsten had "just slipped away"; I could see my little brother, who had really been fond of Kirsten; he was assembling a balsa-wood model of a Spad Thirteen — he knew the call was from Tim but, of course, he didn't know that now Kirsten, along with Jeff, was dead.

"You're a strong person," Tim's voice sounded in my ear. "I know you will be able to stand up to this."

"I saw it coming," I said.

"Yes," Tim said. He sounded matter-of-fact but I knew his heart was breaking.

"Barbiturates?" I said.

"She took — well, they're not sure. She took them and timed herself. She waited. Then she walked in and told me. And then she fell. I knew what it was." He added, "Tomorrow she was supposed to go back to Mount Zion."

"You called —"

"The paramedics came," Tim said, "and they took her right to the hospital. They tried everything. What she had done was build up the maximum amount in her system already, so that what she took as the overdose —"

"That's how it's done," I said. "That way pumping her stomach doesn't help; it's already in the system."

"Do you want to come over here?" Tim said. "To the City? I would really appreciate your being here."

"I have Harvey with me," I said.

My little brother glanced up.

To him I said, "Kirsten died."

"Oh." He nodded, and, after a moment, returned to his balsa-wood Spad. It's like *Wozzeck,* I thought. Exactly like the end of *Wozzeck*. There I go: Berkeley intellectual, viewing everything in terms of culture, of opera, of novel, oratorio and poem. Not to mention play.

> *"Du! Deine Mutter ist tot!"*

And Marien's child says:

> *"Hopp, hopp! Hopp, hopp! Hopp, hopp!"*

It will break you, I thought, if you keep this up. The little boy assembling a model airplane and not understanding: double horror, and both happening to me now.

"I'll come over there," I said to Tim. "As soon as I can find someone to take care of Harvey."

"You could bring him," Tim said.

"No." Reflexively, I shook my head.

I got a neighbor to take Harvey for the rest of the day, and, shortly, I was on my way to San Francisco, driving over the Bay Bridge in my Honda.

And still the words of Berg's opera percolated obsessively through my mind.

> *"The huntsman's life is gay and free,*
> *Shooting is free for all!*

*There would I huntsman be,*
*There would I be."*

I mean, I said to myself, George Büchner's words; he wrote the damn thing.

As I drove, I cried; tears ran down my face; I turned on the car radio and pressed button after button, station after station. On a rock station I picked up an old Santana track; I turned up the volume and, as the music rebounded throughout my little car, I screamed. And I heard:

*"You! Your mother is dead!"*

I narrowly missed rear-ending a huge American car; I had to swerve into the lane to my right. Slow down, I said to myself. Fuck this, I thought; two deaths are enough. You want to make it three? Then just keep driving the way you're driving: three plus the people in the other car. And then I remembered Bill. Dingaling Bill Lundborg, off in an asylum somewhere. Had Tim called him? I should tell him, I said to myself.

You poor miserable fucked-up son of a bitch, I said to myself, remembering Bill and his gentle, pudgy face. That air of sweetness, like new clover, about him, him and his dumb pants and dumb look, like a cow, a contented cow. The Post Office is in for another round of their windows smashed, I realized; he will walk down there and start hitting the great plate glass windows with his fists until blood runs down his arms. And then they'll lock him up again in one place or another; it doesn't matter which because he doesn't know the difference.

How could she do it to him? I asked myself. What malice. What abysmal cruelty, toward us all. She really hated us. This is our punishment. I'll always think I'm responsible; Tim will always think he's responsible; Bill likewise. And of course none of us is, and yet in a sense all of us are, but anyhow it is beside the point, after the fact, null and moot and void, totally void, as in "the infinite void," the sublime non-Being of God.

There is a line somewhere in *Wozzeck* that translates out to, roughly, "The world is awful." Yes, I said to myself as I shot across the Bay Bridge not giving a fuck how fast I drove, that sums it up. That is high art: "The world is awful." That says it all. This is what we pay composers and painters and the great writers to do: tell us this; from figuring this out, they earn a living. What masterful, incisive insight. What penetrating intelligence. A rat in a drain ditch could tell you the same thing, were it able to talk. If rats could talk, I'd do anything they said. Black girl I knew. Not rats with her; it's rats for me — for her, she said, it was spiders; *viz:* "If spiders could talk." That time she got the runs while we were up in Tilden Park and we had to drive her home. Neurotic lady. Married to a white guy . . . what was his name? Only in Berkeley.

*Viz,* a short form of Visigoths, the noble Goths. Visitation, as in, Visitation from the dead, from the next world. That old lady bears some real responsibility for this; if any one single person done did it she done did it. But that's killing the Spartan runners; now they have me doing it myself, after all the warnings. WARNING: THIS LADY IS NUTS. Get out of my way. May you all be fucked forever, all of you in your washed big cars.

I thought: *"Destructive War, thy limits know; here, tyrant Death, thy terrors end. To tyrants only I'm a foe, to virtue and her friends, a friend."* And then it says it again: *"Here, tyrant Death."* It's a great title; it's not a parody. That's what did it, Tim using my title and, of course — in his usual chickenshit fashion — not bothering or remembering to tell her. In fact, telling her that *he* thought of it. He probably thinks so. Every valuable idea in the history of the world was thought into being by Timothy Archer. He invented the heliocentric solar system model. We'd still have the geocentric one if it hadn't been for him. Where does

Bishop Archer end and God begin? Good point. Ask him; he'll tell you, quoting from books.

No single thing abides; and all things are fucked up, I thought. That's how it should have been worded. I'll suggest that to Tim for Kirsten's gravestone. Teaching school in Norway, the Swedish cretin. A million nasty things I said to her, in the guise of play. Her brain recorded them and played them back to her, late at night when she couldn't sleep, while Tim snoozed on; she couldn't sleep and took more and more downers, those barbiturates that killed her; we knew they would: the only issue was whether it would be an accident or a purposeful overdose, assuming there is a difference.

My instructions required me to meet with Tim at the Tenderloin apartment before going on with him, then, to Grace Cathedral. I had expected to find him red-eyed and distraught. However, to my surprise, Tim looked stronger, more powerfully put-together, even in a literal sense larger, than I had ever seen him before.

He said, as he put his arms around me and hugged me, "I have a terrible fight on my hands. From here on in."

"You mean the scandal?" I said. "It'll be in the papers and on the news, I guess."

"I destroyed part of her suicide note. The police are reading what's left. They've been here. Probably they'll be coming back. I do have influence but I can't keep the news quiet. All I can hope for is to keep it retained as speculation."

"What did the note say?"

"The part I destroyed? I don't remember. It's gone. It had to do with us, her feelings about me. I had no choice."

"Guess so," I said.

"As to it being suicide, there is no doubt. And the motive is, of course, her fear that she had cancer again. And they're aware that she was a barbiturate addict."

"Would you describe her that way?" I said. "An addict?"

"Certainly. That's not disputed."

"How long have you known?"

"Since I met her. Since I first saw her taking them. You knew."

"Yes," I said. "I knew."

"Sit down and have some coffee," Tim said. He left the living room for the kitchen; automatically, I seated myself on the familiar couch, wondering if any cigarettes could be found anywhere in the apartment.

"What do you take in your coffee?" Tim stood at the kitchen doorway.

"I forget," I said. "It doesn't matter."

"Would you rather have a drink?"

"No." I shook my head.

"Do you realize," Tim said, "that this proves Rachel Garret right."

"I know," I said.

"Jeff wanted to warn her. Warn Kirsten."

"So it would seem."

"And I'm going to die next."

I glanced up.

"That's what Jeff said," Tim said.

"Guess so," I said.

"It will be a terrible fight but I will win. I am not going to follow them, follow Jeff and Kirsten." His tone rang with harshness, with indignation. "This is what Christ came to the world to save man from, this sort of determinism, this rule. The future can be changed."

"I hope so," I said.

"My hope is in Jesus Christ," Tim said. "'While you still have the light, believe in the light and you will become sons of light.' John, twelve, thirty-six. 'Do not let your hearts be troubled. Trust in God still, and trust in me.' John, fourteen, one. 'Blessings on him who comes in the name of the Lord!' Matthew, twenty-three, thirty-nine." Breathing heavily, his great chest rising and falling, Tim, gazing at me, pointed at me saying, "I'm not going that way, Angel. Each of them did it intentionally, but I will never do it; I will never go like that, like a sheep to slaughter."

Thank God, I thought. You are going to fight.

"Prophecy or no prophecy," Tim said. "Even if Rachel were the sibyl herself — even then I wouldn't walk toward it willingly, like a dumb animal, to have my throat cut, to be offered up." His eyes blazed, hot with intensity and fire. I had seen him this way sometimes at Grace Cathedral when he preached; this Tim Archer spoke with the authority vested in him by the Apostle Peter himself: through the line of apostolic succession, unbroken in and for the Episcopal Church.

As we drove to Grace Cathedral in my Honda, Tim said to me, "I see myself falling into Wallenstein's fate. Catering to astrology. Casting horoscopes."

"You mean Dr. Garret," I said.

"Yes, I mean her and Dr. Mason; they're not doctors of any kind. That wasn't Jeff. He never came back from the next world. There is no truth in it. Stupidity, as that poor boy said; her son. Oh Lord; I haven't called her son."

I said, "I'll tell him."

"It will finish him off," Tim said. "No, maybe it won't. He may be stronger than we give him credit for. He could see through all that nonsense about Jeff coming back."

"You get to tell the truth," I said, "when you're schizophrenic."

"Then more people should be schizophrenic. What is this, a matter of the emperor's new clothes? You knew, too, but you didn't say."

I said, "It's not a matter of knowing. It has to do with evaluation."

"But you never believed it."

After a pause, I said, "I'm not sure."

"Kirsten is dead," Tim said, "because we believed in nonsense. Both of us. And we believed because we wanted to believe. I have not that motive now."

"Guess not."

"If we had ruthlessly faced the truth, Kirsten would be alive now. All I can hope is to put an end to it here and now . . . and accompany her at some later date. Garret and Mason could see that Kirsten was sick. They took advantage of a sick, disturbed woman and now she's dead. I hold them responsible." He paused and then said, "I had been attempting to get Kirsten to go into the hospital for drug detox. I have several friends who're in that field, here in San Francisco. I was well aware of her addiction and I knew that only professionals could help her. I had to go through this myself, as you know . . . with alcohol."

I said nothing; I merely drove.

"It's too late to stop the book," Tim said.

"Couldn't you phone your editor and —"

"The book is their property now."

I said, "They're a totally reputable publishing house. They would listen to you if you instructed them to withdraw the book."

"They've sent out promotional prepublication material. They've circulated bound galleys and Xerox copies of the manuscript. What I'll do —" Tim pondered. "I'll write another book. That tells about Kirsten's death and my reevaluation of the occult. That's the best avenue for me to pursue."

"I think you should withdraw *Here, Tyrant Death*."

His mind, however, had been made up; he shook his head vigorously. "No; it should be allowed to come out as planned. I've had years of experience with these matters; you should face up to your own folly — my own, I am referring to, of course — and then, after you've faced up to it, set about correcting it. My next book will be that correction."

"How much was the advance?"

Glancing swiftly at me, Tim said, "Not much, considering its sales potential. Ten thousand on my signing the contract; then another ten thousand when I delivered the completed manuscript to them. And there will be a final ten thousand when the book is released."

"Thirty thousand dollars is a lot of money."

Half to himself, reflecting, Tim said, "I think I'll add a dedication to it. A dedication to Kirsten. In memoriam. And say a few things about my feelings for her."

"You could dedicate it to both of them," I said. "Both Jeff and Kirsten. And say, 'But for the grace of God —'"

"Very appropriate," Tim said.

"Add me and Bill," I said. "While you're at it. We're part of this movie."

"'Movie'?"

"A Berkeley expression. Only it's not a movie; it's the opera *Wozzeck* by Alban Berg. They all die except the little boy riding his wooden horse."

"I'll have to phone in the dedication," Tim said. "The galleys are already back in New York, corrected."

"She finished, then? Her job?"

"Yes," he said, vaguely.

"Did she do it right? After all, she wasn't feeling too well."

"I assume she did it correctly; I didn't look them over."

"You're going to have a Mass said for her, aren't you?" I said. "At Grace?"

"Oh, yes. That's one of the reasons I'm —"

"I think you should get Kiss," I said. "It's a group, a very highly thought of rock group. After all, you had been planning a rock mass anyhow."

"Did she like Kiss?"

"Second only to Sha Na Na," I said.

"Then we should get Sha Na Na," Tim said.

We drove for a time in silence.

"The Patti Smith Group," I said suddenly.

"Let me ask you," Tim said, "about several things regarding Kirsten."

"I am here to answer any question," I said.

"At the service, I want to read poems that she loved. Can you give me the names of a few?" He got from his coat pocket a notebook and gold pen; holding them, he waited.

"There is a very beautiful poem about a snake," I said, "by D. H. Lawrence. She loved it. Don't ask me to quote it; I can't quote it just now. I'm sorry." I shut my eyes, trying not to cry.

# 12

AT THE SERVICE, Bishop Timothy Archer read the D. H. Lawrence poem about the snake; he read it wonderfully and I saw how moved the people were, although not many mourners had shown up. Not that many people knew Kirsten Lundborg. I kept seeking to locate her son Bill somewhere in the cathedral.

When I had phoned him to tell him the news, he had showed little response. I think he foresaw it. At this time, the hospital and the house of many slammers held no power over him; Bill had earned his freedom to walk around or to paint cars or whatever he did. However he currently amused himself in his earnest fashion.

The cobwebs departed Bishop Archer's mind when Kirsten killed herself, so, it would seem, her death had served a useful purpose, although a purpose unequal to our loss. It amazes me: the sobering power of human death. It outweighs all words, all arguments; it is the ultimate force. It coerces your attention and your time. And it leaves you changed.

How Tim could derive strength from death—the death of a person he loved—baffled me; I could not fathom it, but this was the sort of quality in him that made him good: good at his job, good as a human being. The worse things got, the stronger he became; he did not like death but he did not fear it. He comprehended it — once the cobwebs left. He had tried out the bullshit solution of séances and superstition and that hadn't worked; it simply brought on more death. So now he shifted gears and tried out being rational. He had a profound motive: his own life had been placed on the line, like bait. Bait to tempt what the ancients called "a sinister fate," meaning premature death, death before its time.

The thinkers of antiquity did not regard death per se as evil, because death comes to all; what they correctly perceived as evil was premature death, death coming before the person could complete his work. Lopped off, as it were, before ripe, a hard, green little apple that death took and then tossed away, as being of no interest — even to death.

Bishop Archer had by no means completed his work and by no means did he intend to be lopped off, severed from life. He now correctly perceived himself sliding by degrees into the fate that had overtaken Wallenstein: first the superstition and credulity, then run through with a halberd by an otherwise historically undistinguished English captain named Walter Devereux (Wallenstein had pleaded in vain for quarter; when the halberd is in the foe's hand, it is usually too late to plead for quarter). At that final instant Wallenstein, roused from sleep, had probably also been roused from his mental stupor; I would guess that the swift realization came to him as the enemy soldiers broke into his bedroom that all the astrological charts and all the horoscopes in the world had been of no use to him, for he had not foreseen this, and was caught. The difference between Wallenstein and Tim, however, was great and crucial. First, Tim had the advantage of Wallenstein's example; Tim got to see where folly led great men. Second, Tim was fundamentally a realist, for all his double-domed, educated flow of twaddle. Tim had entered the world with a wary eye, a keen sense of what benefited him and what worked to his disadvantage. At the moment of Kirsten's death he had cannily destroyed part of her suicide note; no fool he, and he had been able — amazingly — to conceal their relationship from the media and from the Episcopal Church itself (it all came out later, of course, but by then Tim was dead and probably did not care).

How an essentially pragmatic — even, it could be argued, opportunistic — man could involve himself in so much self-defeating nonsense is, of course, amazing, but even the nonsense had a sort of utility in the larger economy of Tim's life. Tim did not wish to be bound by the formal strictures of his role; he did not really define himself as a bishop any more than he had previously let himself be defined as an attorney. He was a man, and he thought of himself that way; not a "man" in the sense of "male person," but "man" in the sense of human being who lived in many areas and spread out into a variety of vectors. In his college days, he had learned much from his study of the Renaissance; once he had told me that in no way had the Renaissance overthrown or abolished the Medieval world: *the Renaissance had fulfilled it,* whatever T. S. Eliot might imagine to the contrary.

Take, for example, (Tim had said to me) Dante's *Commedia.* Clearly, in terms of brute date of composition, the *Commedia* emanated from the Middle Ages; it summed up the Medieval worldview absolutely: its greatest crown. And yet (although many critics will not agree) the *Commedia* has a vast span of vision that in no way can be bipolarized to, say, the view of Michelangelo, who, in fact, drew heavily on the *Commedia* for his Sistine Chapel ceiling. Tim saw Christianity reaching its climax in the Renaissance; he did not view that moment in history as the ancient world revived and overpowering the Middle Ages, the Christian Ages; the Renaissance was not the triumph of the old pagan world over faith but, rather, the final and fullest flowering of faith, specifically the Christian faith; therefore, Tim reasoned, the well-known Renaissance man (who knew something about everything, who was, to use the correct term, a polymath) was the ideal Christian, at home in this world and in the next: a perfect blend of matter and spirit, matter divinized, as it were. Matter transformed but still matter. The two realms, this and the next, brought back together, as they had been joined before the Fall.

This ideal Tim intended to capture for himself, to make it his own. The complete person, he reasoned, does not lock himself into his job, no matter how exalted that job. A cobbler who views himself only as one who repairs shoes is circumscribing himself viciously; a bishop, by the same reasoning, must therefore enter regions occupied by the whole man. One of these regions consisted of that of sexuality. Although the general opinion ran contrary to this, Tim did not care, nor did he yield. He knew what was apt for the Renaissance man and he knew that he himself constituted that man in all his authenticity.

That this trying out of every possible idea to see if it would fit finally destroyed Tim Archer can't be disputed. He tried out too many ideas, picked them up, examined them, used them for a while and then discarded them . . . some of the ideas, however, as if possessing a life of their own, came back around the far side of the barn and got him. That is history; this is an historical fact. Tim is dead. The ideas did not work. They got him off the ground and then betrayed him and attacked him; they dumped him, in a sense, before he could dump them. One thing, however, could not be obscured: Tim Archer could tell when he was locked in a life-and-death struggle and, upon perceiving this, he assumed the posture of grim defense. He did not — just as he had said to me the day Kirsten died — surrender. Fate, to get Tim Archer, would have to run him through: Tim would never run himself through. He would not collude with retributive fate, once he spotted it and what it was up to. He had done that, now: discerned retributive fate, seeking him. He neither fled nor cooperated. He stood and fought and, in that stance, died. But he died hard, which is to say, he died hitting back. Fate had to murder him.

And, while fate figured out how to accomplish this, Tim's quick brain was totally engaged in sidestepping through every mental gymnastic move possible that which perhaps held in it the force of the inevitable. This is probably what we mean by the term "fate"; were it not inevitable, we would not employ that term; we would, instead, speak of bad luck. We would talk about accidents. With fate there is no accident; there is intent. And there is relentless intent, closing in from all directions at once, as if the person's very universe is shrinking. Finally, it holds nothing but him and his sinister destiny. He is programmed against his will to succumb, and, in his efforts to thrash himself free, he succumbs even faster, from fatigue and despair. Fate wins, then, no matter what.

A lot of this Tim himself told me. He had studied up on the topic as part of his Christian education. The ancient world had seen the coming into existence of the Greco-Roman Mystery Religions, which were dedicated to overcoming fate by patching the worshipper into a god beyond the planetary spheres, a god capable of short-circuiting the "astral influences," as it had been called in those days. We ourselves, now, speak of the DNA death-strip and the psychological-script learned from, modeled on, other, previous people, friends and parents. It is the same thing; it is determinism killing you no matter what you do. Some power outside of you must enter and alter the situation; you cannot do it for yourself, for the programming causes you to perform the act that will destroy you; the act is performed with the idea that it will save you, whereas, in point of fact, it delivers you over to the very doom you wish to evade.

Tim knew all this. It didn't help him. But he did his best; he tried.

Practical men do not do what Jeff did and Kirsten did; practical men fight that drift because it is a romantic drift, a weakness. It is learned passivity; it is learned giving up. Tim could ignore his son's death as unique — reasoning that no contagion was involved — but when Kirsten went the same way, Tim had to change his mind, return to Jeff's death and reappraise it. He saw in it, now, the origins of later disaster, and he saw that disaster shaping up for himself. This caused him immediately to jettison all the claptrap notions that he had picked up beginning with Jeff's death, all the weird and shabby ideas associated with the occult, to borrow Menotti's apt phrase. Tim suddenly realized that he had seated himself at the table in Mme. Flora's parlor, for the purpose of contacting the spirits — for the purpose, really, of delivering himself over to folly. He now did what characterized him throughout his life: he abandoned that route and sought another; he dumped that malicious cargo and reached around for something more stable, more durable and sound, to replace it. If the ship is to be saved, cargo must sometimes be flung overboard; when something is jettisoned, it is dumped calculatedly — heaved away, to float off, leaving the ship intact. This moment only comes when the ship is in trouble, as Tim now was. Dr. Garret had pronounced doom on both himself and Kirsten, beginning with Kirsten. The first prophecy had come true. He could expect, then, to be next. These are emergency procedures. They are employed by the desperate and the smart. Tim was both. And out of necessity. Tim knew the difference between the ship (which was not expendable) and the cargo (which was). He viewed himself as the ship. He viewed his faith in spirits, in his son's return from the next world, as cargo. This clear distinction was his advantage, inasmuch as he could discern it. Throwing away his beliefs did not compromise him, nor did it vitiate him. And there existed a slight chance that it might save him.

I rejoiced in Tim's newfound lucidity. But I felt deeply pessimistic. I viewed his clearheadedness as a surfacing of his basic determination to survive. This is a good thing. You cannot fault the drive to endure. The only question that frightened me was: had it come soon enough? Time would tell.

When the ship is saved — if it is saved — necessary jettison gives the right of general salvage to the owner or owners of the goods. This is an international rule of the seas. This is an idea basic to human beings, of whatever place of origin. Tim consciously or unconsciously understood this. In doing what he was doing, he partook of something venerable and universally accepted. I understood him; I think anybody would. This was not the time to whine over lost battles involving the issue of whether or not his son had returned from the next world; this was the time for Tim to fight for his life. He did so, and he did the very best he could. I watched, and where possible I helped. It failed in the end, but not for want of effort, not for a failure of trying, a decline of nerve.

This is not expedience. This is rousing oneself to a final defense. To view Tim in his final days as a cheap man devoted to animal survival at all costs — abandoning all moral conviction — is to misunderstand totally; when your life is at stake, you act in certain ways if you are smart, and Tim acted in those ways: he dumped everything that could be dumped, should have been dumped — he bared his dog-tooth and offered to bite, and that is what a man does in the sense of man the creature who is determined to survive, and to hell with the cargo. Upon Kirsten's death, Tim stood in danger of imminent death himself and he understood it, and for you to understand him in that final period you must take his realization into consideration and you must also understand that his perception, his realization, was correct. He was, as the therapists put it, in touch with the reality situation (as if there is some kind of distinction between "situation" and "reality situation"). He desired to live. So do I. Presumably, so do you. Then you should be able to figure out what Bishop Archer had in mind during the period following Kirsten's death and preceding his own, the first a given, the second an ominous but dubitable possibility, not a reality, not then, at least, although from our standpoint now, as hindsight, we can comprehend it as inevitable. But this is the famous nature of hindsight: to it everything is inevitable, since everything has already happened.

Even if Tim regarded his own death as inevitable, willed by prophecy, willed by the sibyl — or by Apollo, speaking through the sibyl as a mouthpiece — he was determined to confront that fate and put up the best fight he could manage. I think that is quite remarkable and to be lauded. That he jettisoned a whole lot of claptrap that he once believed in and preached is of no importance; should he have hugged all that crap and died in a curled-up abreactive posture, his eyes shut, his dog-tooth not bared? I am of firm conviction in this; I saw it; I fathomed it. I saw the cargo go. I saw it heaved overboard the instant Dr. Garret's first prophecy came true. And I said, Thank God.

I think, though, he should have withdrawn that goddamn book from publication, that *Here, Tyrant Death,* as I had titled it. But he did have thirty thousand dollars riding on it, and perhaps this determination to let it get into print was simply further evidence of his practicality. I don't know. Some aspects of Tim Archer remain a mystery to me, even to this day.

It simply was not Tim's style to abort a mistake before it happened; he let it happen and then — as he put it — he filed a correction in the form of an amendment. Except insofar as his physical survival was involved; there he calculated activity in advance. There he looked ahead. The man who had run through his own life, outpacing himself, outdistancing himself as if urged on by the amphetamines he daily swallowed — that man now all at once ceased to run, turned instead, gazed at fate and said, as Luther is supposed to have said but did not, "Here I stand; I can do not otherwise *(Hier steh' Ich; Ich kann nicht anders)*." The German ontologist Martin Heidegger has a term for that: the transmutation of inauthentic Being to true Being or *Sein*. I studied that at Cal. I didn't think I would ever see it happen, but it did and I did. And I found it beautiful but very sad, because it failed.

Within my mind I conceived of the spirit of my dead husband penetrating my thoughts and being highly amused. Jeff would have pointed out to me that I viewed the bishop as a cargo ship, a freighter, baring its dog-tooth, a mixed metaphor which would have kept Jeff in a state of rapture for days; I would never have heard the end of it. My mind had begun to go, due to Kirsten's suicide; at work, comparing the content of shipments to the listings on the invoices, I barely noticed what I did. I had withdrawn. My fellow workers and my boss pointed this out to me. And I ate little; I spent my lunch hour reading Delmore Schwartz, who, I am told, died with his head in a sack of garbage that he had been carrying downstairs when he suffered his fatal heart attack. A great way for a poet to go!

The problem with introspection is that it has no end; like Bottom's dream in A *Midsummer Night's Dream*, it has no bottom. From my years at Cal in the English Department, I had learned to make up metaphors, play around with them, mix them, serve them up; I am a metaphor junkie, over-educated and smart. I think too much, read too much, worry about those I love too much. Those I loved had begun to die. Not many remained here; most had gone.

*"They are all gone into the world of light!*
*And I alone sit lingring here;*

> *Their very memory is far and bright,*
> *And my sad thoughts doth clear."*

As Henry Vaughan wrote in 1655. The poem ends:

> *"Either disperse these mists, which blot and fill*
> *My perspective (still) as they pass,*
> *Or else remove me hence unto that hill,*
> *Where I shall need no glass."*

By "glass" Vaughan means a telescope. I looked it up. The seventeenth century minor metaphysical poets constituted my specialty, during my school years. Now, after Kirsten's death, I turned back to them, because my thoughts had turned, like theirs, to the next world. My husband had gone there; my best friend had gone there; I expected Tim to go there, soon, and thus he did.

Unfortunately, I began now to see less of Tim. This for me acted as the worst strike of all. I really loved him but now the ties had been severed. They got severed from his end. He resigned as Bishop of the Diocese of California and moved down to Santa Barbara and the think tank there; his book, which in my eternal opinion should have been suppressed, had come out to indict him as a fool; this combined with the scandal about Kirsten: the media, despite Tim's tampering with evidence, had caught on to their secret relationship. Tim's career with the Episcopal Church ended suddenly; he packed up and left San Francisco, surfacing in (as he had put it) the private sector. There he could relax and be happy; there he could live his life without the repressive strictures of Christian canon law and morality.

I missed him.

A third element had blended in to terminate his relationship with the Episcopal Church, and that of course consisted of the goddamn Zadokite Documents, which Tim simply could not leave alone. No longer involved with Kirsten — she being dead — and no longer involved with the occult — since he recognized that for what it was — he now concentrated all his credulity on the writings of that ancient Hebrew sect, declaring as he did in speeches and in interviews and articles that here, indeed, lay the true origins of the teachings of Jesus. Tim could not leave trouble behind him. He and trouble were destined to join company.

I kept abreast of developments concerning Tim by reading magazines and newspapers; my contact came secondhand; I no longer had direct, personal knowledge of him. For me this constituted tragedy, more perhaps than losing Jeff and Kirsten, although I never told anyone that, even my therapists. I lost track, too, of Bill Lundborg; he drifted out of my life and into a mental hospital, and that was that. I tried to track him down but, failing, gave up. I was either batting zero or a thousand, whichever way you want to compute it.

Whichever way you want to compute it, the results came out to this: I had lost everyone I knew, so the time had arrived to make new friends. I decided that retail record selling was more than a job; for me it amounted to a vocation. Within a year, I had risen to the post of manager of the Musik Shop. I had unlimited powers to buy; the owners put no ceiling on me, none at all. My judgment alone determined what I ordered or did not order, and all the salesmen — the representatives of the various labels — knew it. That earned me a lot of free lunches and some interesting dates. I started coming out of my shell, seeing people more; I wound up with a boyfriend, if you can abide such an old-fashioned term (it would never be employed in Berkeley). "Lover" I guess is the word I want. I let Hampton move into my house with me, the house Jeff and I had bought, and began what I hoped was a fresh, new life, in terms of my involvements.

Tim's book, *Here, Tyrant Death,* did not sell as well as had been expected; I saw remaindered copies at the different book-stores near Sather Gate. It had cost too much and rambled on too long; he would have done better to shorten it, insofar as he had written it — most of it, when I finally got around to reading it, struck me as Kirsten's work; at least she had done the final draft, no doubt based on Tim's bang-bang dictation. That was what she had told me and probably it was the case. He never followed it up with an amending sequel, as he had promised me.

One Sunday morning, as I sat with Hampton in our living room, smoking a joint of the new seedless grass and watch-ing the kids' cartoons on TV, I got a phone call — unexpect-edly — from Tim.

"Hi, Angel," he said, in that hearty, warm voice of his. "I hope this isn't a bad time to call you."

"It's fine," I managed to say, wondering if I really heard Tim's voice or if, due to the grass, I was hallucinating it. "How are you? I've been —"

"The reason I'm calling," Tim interrupted, as if I had not been speaking, as if he did not hear me, "is that I'll be in Berke-ley next week — I'm attending a conference at the Claremont Hotel — and I'd like to get together with you."

"Great," I said, immensely pleased.

"Can we get together for dinner? You know the restaurants in Berkeley better than I do; I'll let you pick whichever one you like." He chuckled. "It'll be wonderful to see you again. Like old times."

I asked him, haltingly, how he had been.

"Everything down here is going fine," Tim said. "I'm ex-tremely busy. I'll be flying to Israel next month; I wanted to talk to you about that."

"Oh," I said. "That sounds like a lot of fun."

"I'm going to visit the *wadi*," Tim said. "Where the Zadokite Documents were found. They've all been translated now. Some of the final fragments proved extremely interesting. But I'll tell you about that when I see you."

"Yes," I said, warming to the topic; as always Tim's enthusiasm was contagious. "I read a long article in *Scientific American;* some of the last fragments —"

"I'll pick you up Wednesday night," Tim said. "At your house. Be formally dressed, if you would."

"You remember —"

"Oh, of course; I remember where your house is."

It seemed to me he was speaking ultra-rapidly. Or had the grass affected me? No, the grass would slow things down. I said, in panic, "I'm working at the store on Wednesday night."

As if he hadn't heard me, Tim said, "About eight o'clock; I'll see you then. Good-bye, dear." Click. He had rung off.

Shit, I said to myself. I'm working until nine Wednesday night. Well, I will just have to get one of the clerks to fill in for me. I am not going to miss having dinner with Tim before he leaves for Israel. I wondered, then, how long he would be over there. Probably for some time. He had gone once before, and planted a cedar tree; I remembered that: the news media had made quite a bit of it.

"Who was that?" Hampton said, seated in jeans and a T-shirt before the TV set, my tall, thin, acerbic boyfriend, with his black-wire hair and his glasses.

"My father-in-law," I said. "Former father-in-law."

"Jeff's father," Hampton said, nodding. A crooked grin appeared on his face. "I have an idea as to what to do with people who suicide. I think it should be a law that when they find someone who's suicided, they should dress him up in a clown suit. And photograph him that way. And print his picture in the newspaper like that, in the clown suit. Such as Sylvia Plath. Especially Sylvia Plath." Hampton went on, then, to recount how Plath and her girlfriends — according to Hampton's imagination—used to play games in which they'd see who could stick their head in the oven of the kitchen stove the longest, meanwhile all of them going "tee-hee," giggling and breaking up.

"You're not funny," I said, and walked from the room, into the kitchen.

Hampton called after me, "You're not sticking your head in the oven, are you?"

"Go fuck yourself," I said.

"—with a big red rubber bulb for a nose," Hampton was droning on, mostly to himself; his voice and the racket of the TV set, the kids' cartoons, assailed me; I put my hands over my ears to shut out the noise. "Head out of the oven!" Hampton yelled.

I walked back into the living room and shut off the TV set; turning to face Hampton I said, "Those two people were in a lot of pain. There's nothing funny about someone who's in that much pain."

Grinning, Hampton rocked back and forth, seated curled up on the floor. "And big floppy hands," he said. "Clown hands."

I opened the front door. "I'll see you. I'm going for a walk." I shut the door after me.

The front door swung open. Hampton came out on the porch, cupped his hands to his mouth and called, "Tee-hee; I'm going to stick my head in the oven. Let's see if the babysitter gets here in time. Do you think she'll get here in time? Anybody want to make a bet?"

I did not look back; I kept on going.

As I walked along, I thought about Tim and I thought about Israel and what it must be like there, the hot climate, the desert and the rock, the *kibbutzim*. Tilling the soil, the ancient soil that had been worked for thousands of years, farmed by Jews long before the time of Christ. Maybe they would direct Tim's attention to the ground, I thought. And away from the next world. Back to the real; back to where it belonged.

I doubted it, but perhaps I was wrong. I wished, then, that I could go with Tim — quit my job at the record store, just take off and go. Maybe never return. Stay in Israel forever. Become a citizen. Convert to Judaism. If they'd have me. Tim could probably swing it. Maybe in Israel I'd stop mixing metaphors and remembering poems. Maybe my mind would give up trying to solve problems in terms of recycled words. Used phrases, bits ripped from here and there: fragments from my days at Cal in which I had memorized but not understood, understood but not applied, applied but never successfully. A spectator to the destruction of my friends, I said to myself; one who records on a notepad the names of those who die, and did not manage to save any of them, not even one.

I will ask Tim if I can go with him, I decided. Tim will say no — he has to say no — but nonetheless, I will ask.

To root Tim in reality, I realized, they will first have to get his attention, and if he is still on the Dex it will not be possible for them to do that; his mind will be tripping and freewheeling and spinning forever out into the void, conceiving the great models of the heavens . . . they will try and, like me, they will fail. If I go with him, maybe I can help, I thought; the Israelis and I maybe could do what I never could do alone; I will direct their attention to him and they, in turn, will direct his attention to the soil under their feet. Christ, I thought; I have to go with him. It's essential. Because they will not have time to notice the problem. He will skim his way across their country, be first here, then there, never lighting, never coming to rest long enough, never letting them —

A car honked at me; I had wandered out onto the street, crossing unconsciously, without looking.

"Sorry," I said to the driver, who glared at me.

I am no better than Tim, I realized. I'd be no help in Israel. But even so, I thought, I wish I could go.

# 13

ON WEDNESDAY NIGHT, Tim picked me up in a rented Pontiac. I wore a black strapless gown and carried a little beaded purse; I wore a flower in my hair, and Tim, gazing at me as he held the car door open, remarked that I looked lovely.

"Thank you," I said, feeling shy.

We drove to the restaurant on University Avenue, just off Shattuck, a Chinese restaurant that had recently opened. I had never been there, but customers at the Musik Shop had told me it was the great new place to eat in town.

"Have you always worn your hair up like that?" Tim asked, as the hostess led us to our table.

"I got it done for tonight," I explained. I showed him my earrings. "Jeff got me these years ago. I usually don't wear them; I'm afraid I'll lose one."

"You've lost a little weight." He held my chair for me and I nervously seated myself.

"It's the work. Ordering far into the night."

"How is the law firm?"

I said, "I manage a record store."

"Yes," Tim said. "You got me that album of *Fidelio*. I haven't had much chance to play it . . . ." He opened his menu, then; absorbed, he turned his attention away from me. How easily that attention waned, I thought. Or, rather, alters its focal point. It isn't the attention that changes; it is the object of that attention. He must live in an endlessly shifting world. Heraclitus' flux world personified.

It pleased me to see that Tim still wore his clericals. Is that legal? I asked myself. Well, it's none of my business. I picked up my menu. This was Mandarin-style Chinese food, not Cantonese; it would be spiced and hot, not sweet, with lots of nuts. Ginger root, I said to myself; I felt hungry and happy, and very glad to be back with my friend again.

"Angel," Tim said, "come with me to Israel."

Staring at him, I said, "What?"

"As my secretary."

Still staring, I said, "Take Kirsten's place, you mean?" I began, then, to tremble. A waiter came over; I waved him away.

"Would either of you like a drink?" the waiter said, ignoring my gesture.

"Go away," I said to him, with menace in my voice. "The goddamn waiter," I said to Tim. "What are you talking about? I mean, what sort of —"

"Just as my secretary. I don't mean any personal involvement; nothing of that sort. Did you think I was asking you to become my mistress? I need someone to do the job Kirsten did; I find I can't manage without her."

"Christ," I said. "I thought you meant as your mistress."

"That's out of the question," Tim said, in the stern, firm tone that meant he was not joking. That, in fact, he disapproved. "I think of you still as my daughter-in-law."

"I run the record store," I said.

"My budget permits a fairly good outlay; I can probably pay you as well as your law office —" He corrected himself. "As the record store pays."

"Let me think about it." I beckoned to the waiter to come over. "A martini," I said to him. "Extra dry. Nothing for the bishop."

Tim smiled wryly. "I'm no longer a bishop."

"I can't," I said. "Come to Israel. I have too many ties here."

In a quiet voice, Tim said, "If you don't come with me, I will never —" He broke off. "I saw Dr. Garret again. Recently. Jeff came across from the next world. He says that unless I take you to Israel with me, I'll die there."

"That is pure nonsense," I said. "Pure, absolute bilge. I thought you gave all that up."

"There have been more phenomena." He did not elaborate; his face, I saw, looked strained and pale.

Reaching, I took Tim's hand. "Don't talk to Garret. Talk to me. I say, Go to Israel and the hell with that old lady. It isn't Jeff; it's her. You know that."

"The clocks," Tim said. "They've been stopped at the time Kirsten died."

"Even so —" I began.

"I think it may be both of them," Tim said.

"Go to Israel," I said. "Talk to the people there, to the people of Israel. If ever any people was embedded in reality —"

"I won't have much time. I've got to get right to the Dead Sea Desert and find the *wadi*. I have to be back in time to meet with Buckminster Fuller. I think it's Buckminster I'm supposed to meet with." He touched his coat. "It's written down." His voice trailed off.

"It was my impression that Buckminster Fuller is dead," I said.

"No, I'm sure you're wrong." He gazed at me; I gazed back, and then, by degrees, we both began to laugh.

"See?" I said, still holding the bishop's hand in mine. "I wouldn't be any help to you."

"They say you would," Tim said. "Jeff and Kirsten."

"Tim," I said, "think of Wallenstein."

"I have a choice," Tim said in a low but clear voice, a voice of brisk authority, "between believing the impossible and the stupid — on the one hand — and —" He ceased speaking.

"And not believing," I said.

"Wallenstein was murdered," Tim said.

"No one will murder you."

"I am afraid," Tim said.

"Tim," I said, "the worst thing is the occult crap. I know. Believe me. That's what killed Kirsten. You realized that when she died; remember? You can't go back to that stuff. You will lose all the ground —"

"'Better a live dog,'" Tim grated, "'than a dead lion.' By that I mean, Better to believe in nonsense than to be realistic and skeptical and scientific and rational and die in Israel."

"Then simply don't go."

"What I need to know is there at the *wadi*. What I need to find. The *anokhi*, Angel; the mushroom. It's there somewhere and that mushroom is Christ. The real Christ, whom Jesus spoke for. Jesus was the messenger of the *anokhi* which is the true holy power, the true source. I want to see it; I want to find it. It grows in the caves. I know it does."

I said, "It once did."

"It is there now. Christ is there now. Christ has the power to break the hold of fate. The only way I'm going to survive is if someone breaks the hold of fate and releases me; otherwise, I will follow Jeff and Kirsten. That's what Christ does; he unseats the ancient planetary powers. Paul mentions that in his *Captivity Letters* . . . Christ rises from sphere to sphere." Again his voice trailed off, bleakly.

"You're talking about magic."

"I'm talking about God!"

"God is everywhere."

"God is at the *wadi*. The Parousia, the Divine Presence. It was there for the Zadokites; it is there now. The power of fate is, in essence, the power of world, and only God, expressed as Christ, can burst the power of world. It's inscribed in the Book of the Spinners that I will die, except that Christ's blood and body save me." He explained, "The Zadokite Documents speak of a book in which the future of every human is written from before Creation. The Book of the Spinners; it's something like Torah. The Spinners are fate personified, like the Norns in Germanic mythology. They weave men's fortunes. Christ, alone, acting for God here on Earth, seizes the Book of the Spinners, reads it, carries the information to the person, informs him of his fate, and then, through his absolute wisdom, Christ instructs the person on the way his fate can be avoided. The road out." He was silent, then. "We'd better order. There are people waiting."

I said, "Prometheus stealing fire for man, the secret of fire; Christ seizing the Book of the Spinners, reading it and then carrying the information to man to save him."

"Yes." Tim nodded. "It's roughly the same myth. Except that this is no myth; Christ really exists. As a spirit, there at the *wadi*."

"I can't go with you," I said, "and I'm sorry. You'll have to go by yourself and then you'll see that Dr. Garret is pandering to your fears the way she pandered to—and viciously exploited—Kirsten's fears."

"You could drive me."

"There are drivers there in Israel who know the desert. I don't know anything about the Dead Sea Desert."

"You have an excellent sense of direction."

"I get lost. I am lost. I'm lost now. I wish I could go with you but I have my job and my life and my friends; I don't want to leave Berkeley—it's my home. I'm sorry but that's God's truth.

Berkeley is where I've always lived. I'm just not ready to leave it at this time. Maybe later." My martini came; I drank it down, all at once, in a spasmodic gulp that left me panting.

Tim said, "The *anokhi* is the pure consciousness of God. It is, therefore, Hagia Sophia, God's Wisdom. Only that wisdom, which is absolute, can read the Book of the Spinners. It can't change what is written, but it can discern a way to outwit the Book. The writing is fixed; it will never change." He seemed defeated, now; he had begun to give up. "I need that wisdom, Angel. Nothing less will do."

"You are like Satan," I said, and then realized that the gin had hit me in a rush; I had not meant to say that.

"No," Tim said, and then he nodded. "Yes, I am. You're right."

"I'm sorry I said that," I said.

"I don't want to be killed off like an animal. If the writing can be read, then an answer can be figured out; Christ has the power to figure it out, Hagia Sophia — Christ. They're homologized from the Old Testament hypostasis to the New." But, I could see, he had given up; he could not budge me and he knew it. "Why not, Angel?" he said. "Why won t you come?"

"Because," I said, "I don't want to die there in the Dead Sea Desert."

"All right. I'll go alone."

"Someone should survive all this," I said.

Tim nodded. "I would want you to survive, Angel. So stay here. I apologize for —"

"Just forgive me," I said.

He smiled wanly. "You could ride on a camel."

"They smell bad," I said. "Or so I've heard."

"If I find the *anokhi* I will have access to God's wisdom. After it has been absent from the world for over two thousand years. That is what the Zadokite Documents speak of, that wisdom that we once had open to us. Think what it would mean!"

The waiter approached our table and asked us if we were ready to order. I said I was; Tim glanced about him in confusion, as if just now aware of his surroundings. It made my heart ache to see his bewilderment. But I had made up my mind. My life, as it was constituted, meant too much for me; most of all, I feared involvement with this man: it had cost Kirsten her life, and, in a subtle way, my husband's. I wanted that all behind me; I had started over; I no longer looked back.

Wanly, without enthusiasm, Tim told the waiter what to bring him; he seemed oblivious of me, now, as if I had faded into the surroundings. I turned to my own menu, and saw there what I wanted. What I wanted was immediate, fixed, real, tangible: it lay in this world and it could be touched and grasped; it had to do with my house and my job, and it had to do with banishing ideas finally from my mind, ideas about other ideas, an infinite regress of them, spiraling off forever.

The food, when the waiter brought it, tasted wonderful. Both Tim and I ate with pleasure. My customers had been right.

"Mad at me?" I said, after we had finished.

"No. Happy because you will survive this. And you will stay as you are." He pointed at me, then, with a commanding expression on his face. "But if I find what I am after, *I will change.* I will not be as I am. I have read all the documents and the answer isn't in them; the documents point to the answer and they point to the location of the answer, but the answer is not in them. It is at the *wadi.* I am taking a risk but it's worth it. I am willing to take the risk because I may find the *anokhi* and just knowing that makes it worth it."

I said suddenly, with insight, "There haven't been any more phenomena."

"True."

"And you didn't go back to Dr. Garret."

"True." He did not seem contrite or embarrassed.

"That was to get me to come with you."

"I want you along. So you can drive me. Otherwise—I'm afraid I won't find what I'm looking for." He smiled.

"Shit," I said. "I believed you."

"I have had dreams," Tim said. "Disturbing dreams. But no pins under my fingernails. No singed hair. No stopped clocks."

I said, falteringly, "You wanted me to come with you that badly." For a moment I felt a surge in me, a need to go. "You think it would be good for me, too," I said, then.

"Yes. But you won't come. That's clear. Well—" He smiled his old familiar, wise smile. "I tried."

"Am I in a rut, then? Living in Berkeley?"

"Professional student," Tim said.

"I run a record store."

"Your customers are students and faculty. You're still tied to the university. You haven't broken the cord. Until you do, you will not fully be an adult."

"I was born the night I drank bourbon and read the *Commedia*. When I had that abscessed tooth."

"You *began* to be born. You knew about birth. But until you come to Israel—that is where you will be born, there in the Dead Sea Desert. That is where the spiritual life of man began, at Mt. Sinai, with Moses. *Ehyeh* speaking... the theophany. The greatest moment in the history of man."

"I would almost go," I said.

"Go, then." He reached out his hand.

I said, simply, "I'm afraid."

"That's the problem," Tim said. "That's the heritage of the past: Jeff's death and Kirsten's death. That's what it's done to you, done permanently. Left you afraid to live."

"'Better a live dog—'"

"But," Tim said, "you are not genuinely alive. You are still unborn. This is what Jesus meant by the Second Birth, the Birth in or from the Spirit; the Birth from Above. This is what lies in the desert. This is what I will find."

"Find it," I said, "but find it without me."

"'He who loses his life —'"

"Don't quote the Bible to me," I said. "I've heard enough quotations, my own and others'. Okay?"

Tim reached out and we solemnly, without speaking, shook hands. He smiled a little, then; after a bit he let my hand go and then examined his gold pocket-watch. "I'm going to have to get you home. I've still got one appointment left this evening. You understand; you know me."

"Yes," I said. "It's okay. Tim," I said, "you are a master strategist. I watched you when you met Kirsten. You brought it all to bear on me, here, tonight." And you almost persuaded me, I said to myself. In a few more minutes — I would have given in. If you had kept up just a little longer.

"I am in the business of saving souls," Tim said enigmatically. I could not tell if he spoke in irony or if he meant it; I simply could not tell. "Your soul is worth saving," he said, then, as he rose to his feet. "I'm sorry to rush you, but we do have to go."

You always were in a hurry, I said to myself as I also got up. "It was a wonderful dinner," I said.

"Was it? I didn't notice; I'm preoccupied, apparently. I have so many things to finish before I fly to Israel. Now that I don't have Kirsten to arrange everything for me . . . she did such a good job."

"You'll find someone," I said.

Tim said, "I thought I found you. The fisherman, tonight; I fished for you and didn't get you."

"Some other time, maybe."

"No," Tim said. "There will be no other time." He did not amplify. He did not have to; I knew that it was so, for one reason or another: I sensed it. Tim was right.

When Timothy Archer flew to Israel, the NBC network news mentioned it briefly, as they would mention a flight of birds, a migration too regular to be important and yet something the viewers should be told about, by way (it would seem) of a reminder that Episcopal Bishop Timothy Archer still existed and was still busy and active in the affairs of the world. And then we, the American public, heard nothing for a week or so.

I got a card from him, but the card arrived after the big news coverage, the late-breaking sensational story of Bishop Archer's abandoned Datsun found, its rear end up off the little rutted winding road, up on a jutting rock, the gas station map still on the right-hand front seat where he had left it.

The government of Israel did everything possible and did it swiftly; they had troops and — shit. They employed everything they had, but the news people knew that Tim Archer had died in the Dead Sea Desert because you cannot live out there, crawling up cliffs and down into ravines; you cannot survive, and they did eventually find his body and it looked as if, one of the reporters on the scene said, as if he knelt praying. But, in fact, Tim had fallen, a long way, down a cliff-side. And I drove, as usual, to the record store and opened it up for business and put money in the register and this time I did not cry.

Why hadn't he taken a professional driver? the news people asked. Why had he ventured out on the desert alone with a gas station map and two bottles of soda pop — I knew the answer. Because he was in a hurry. Undoubtedly getting hold of a professional driver took, in his view, too much time. He could not wait around. As with me in the Chinese restaurant that night, Tim had to get moving; he could not stay in one place; he was

a busy man, and he rushed on, he rushed out into the desert
in that little four-cylinder car that isn't even safe on California
freeways, as Bill Lundborg had pointed out; those subcompact
cars are dangerous.

I loved him the most of all of them. I knew it when I heard
the news, knew it in a different way than I had known it before;
before it had been a feeling, an emotion. But when I realized
he was dead, that knowledge made me into a sick person that
limped and cringed, but drove to work and filled the register
and answered the phone and asked customers if I could help
them; I wasn't sick as a human is sick or an animal is sick; I became ill like a machine. I still moved but my soul died, my soul
that, Tim had said, had never been fully born; that soul, not yet
born, but born a little and wishing to be born more, born fully,
that soul died and my body mechanically continued on.

The soul I lost during that week did not ever return; I am a
machine now, years later; a machine heard the news of John
Lennon's death and a machine grieved and pondered and drove
to Sausalito to sit in on Edgar Barefoot's seminar, because that
is what a machine does: that is a machine's way of greeting the
horrible. A machine doesn't know any better; it simply grinds
along, and maybe whirrs. That is all it can do. You cannot expect
more than that from a machine. That is all it has to offer. That is
why we speak of it as a machine; it understands, intellectually,
but there is no understanding in its heart because its heart is a
mechanical one, designed to act as a pump.

And so it pumps, and so the machine limps and coasts on,
and knows but does not know. And keeps up its routine. It lives
out what it supposes to be life: it maintains its schedule and
obeys the laws. It does not drive its car over the speed limit on
the Richardson Bridge and it says to itself: I never liked the Beatles: I found them insipid. Jeff brought home *Rubber Soul* and if
I hear . . . it repeats to itself what it has thought and heard, the

simulation of life. Life it once possessed and now has lost; a life now gone. It knows it knows not what, as the philosophy books say about a confused philosopher; I forget which one. Locke, maybe. "And Locke believes he knows not what." That impressed me, that turn of phrase. I look for that; I am attracted to clever phrases, which are to be regarded as good English prose style.

I am a professional student and will remain one; I will not change. My opportunity to change was offered to me and I turned it down; I am stuck, now, and, as I say, know but know not what.

# 14

FACING US, SMILING a moon-wide smile, Edgar Barefoot said, "What if a symphony orchestra was intent only on reaching the final coda? What would become of the music? One great crash of sound, over as soon as possible. The music is in the process, the unfolding; if you hasten it, you destroy it. Then the music is over. I want you to think about that."

Okay, I said to myself. I'll think about it. There is nothing on this particular day I'd prefer to think about. Something has happened, something important, but I do not wish to remember it. No one does. I can see it around me, this same reaction. My reaction in the others, here on this cushy houseboat at Gate Five. Where you pay a hundred dollars, the same sum, I believe, that Tim and Kirsten paid that crank, that quack psychic and medium, down in Santa Barbara, who wrecked us all.

One hundred dollars appears to be the magic sum; it opens the door to enlightenment. Which is why I am here. My life is devoted to seeking enlightenment, as are the other lives around me. This is the noise of the Bay Area, the racket and din of meaning; this is what we exist for: to learn.

Teach us, Barefoot, I said to myself. Tell me something I don't know. I, being deficient of comprehension, yearn to know.

You can begin with me; I am the most attentive of your pupils. I trust everything you utter. I am the perfect fool, come here to take. Give. Keep on with the sounds; it lulls me and I forget.

"Young lady," Barefoot said.

With a start, I realized he was speaking to me.

"Yes," I said, rousing myself.

"What's your name?" Barefoot asked.

"Angel Archer," I said.

"Why are you here?"

"To get away," I said.

"From what?"

"Everything," I said.

"Why?"

"It hurts," I said.

"John Lennon, you mean?"

"Yes," I said. "And more. Other things."

"I was noticing you," Barefoot said, "because you were asleep. You may not have realized it. Did you realize it?"

"I realized it," I said.

"Is that how you want me to perceive you? As asleep?"

"Let me alone," I said.

"Let you sleep, then."

"Yes," I said.

"'The sound of one hand clapping,'" Barefoot quoted.

I said nothing.

"Do you want me to hit you? Cuff you? To wake you up?"

"I don't care," I said. "It doesn't matter to me."

"What would it take to awaken you?" Barefoot said.

I did not answer.

"My job is to wake people."

"You are another fisherman."

"Yes; I fish for fish. Not for souls. I do not know of 'soul'; I only know of fish. A fisherman fishes for fish; if he thinks he fishes for anything else, he is a fool; he deludes himself and those he fishes for."

"Fish for me, then," I said.

"What do you want?"

"Not ever to wake up."

"Then come up here," Barefoot said. "Come up and stand beside me. I will teach you how to sleep. It is as hard to sleep as it is to wake up. You sleep poorly, without skill. I can teach you that as easily as I can teach you to wake up. Whatever you want you can have. Are you sure you know what you want? Maybe you secretly want to wake up. You may be wrong about yourself. Come on up here." He reached out his hand.

"Don't touch me," I said as I walked toward him. "I don't want to be touched."

"So you know that."

"I am sure of that," I said.

"Maybe what is wrong with you is that no one has ever touched you," Barefoot said.

"You tell me," I said. "I have nothing to say. Whatever I had to say—"

"You have never said anything," Barefoot said. "You have been silent all your life. Only your mouth has talked."

"If you say so."

"Tell me your name again."

"Angel Archer."

"Do you have a secret name? That no one knows?"

"I have no secret name," I said. And then I said, "I am traitor."

"Who did you betray?"

"Friends," I said.

"Well, Traitor," Barefoot said, "talk to me about your bringing your friends to ruin. How did you do it?"

"With words," I said. "Like now."

"You are good with words."

"Very good," I said. "I am a sickness, a word-sickness. I was taught it by professionals."

"I have no words," Barefoot said.

"Okay," I said. "Then I will listen."

"Now you begin to know."

I nodded.

"Do you have any pets at home?" Barefoot said. "Any dogs or cats? An animal?"

"Two cats," I said.

"Do you groom them and feed them and care for them? Are you responsible for them? Do you take them to the vet when they're ill?"

"Sure," I said.

"Who does all that for you?"

"For me?" I said. "No one."

"Can you do it for yourself?"

"Yes, I can," I said.

"Then, Angel Archer, you are alive."

"Not intentionally," I said.

"But you are. You don't think so but you are. Under the words, the disease of words, you are alive. I am trying to tell you this without using words but it is impossible. All we have is words. Sit down again and listen. Everything I say from now on, today, is directed at you; I am speaking to you but not with words. Does that make any sense to you?"

"No," I said.

"Then just sit down," Barefoot said.

I reseated myself.

"Angel Archer," Barefoot said, "You are wrong about yourself. You are not sick; *you are starved*. What is killing you is hunger. Words have nothing to do with it. You have been starved all your life. Spiritual things will not help. You don't need them.

There are too many spiritual things in the world, far too many. You are a fool, Angel Archer, but not a good kind of fool."

I said nothing.

"You need real meat," Barefoot said, "and real drink, not spiritual meat and drink. I offer you real food, for your body, so it will grow. You are a starving person who has come here to be fed, but without knowing it. You have no idea why you came here today. It is my job to tell you. When people come here to listen to me speak, I offer them a sandwich. The foolish ones listen to my words; the wise ones eat the sandwich. This is not an absurdity that I tell you; it is the truth. This is something none of you has imagined, but I give you real food and that food is a sandwich; the words, the talking, is only wind — is nothing. I charge you one hundred dollars but you learn something priceless. When your dog or cat is hungry, do you talk to him? No; you give him food, I give you food, but you do not know it. You have everything backward because the university has taught you that; it has taught you wrong. It has lied to you. And now you tell yourselves lies; you have learned how to do it and you do it very well. Take the sandwich and eat; forget about the words. The only purpose in the words was to lure you here."

Strange, I thought. He means it. Some of my unhappiness began, then, to ebb away. I felt a peacefulness come over me, a loss of suffering.

Someone from behind me leaned forward and touched me on the shoulder. "Hi, Angel."

I turned around to see who it was. A pudgy-faced youth, blond-haired, smiling at me, his eyes guileless. Bill Lundborg, wearing a turtleneck sweater and gray slacks and, I saw to my surprise, Hush Puppies.

"Remember me?" he said softly. "I'm sorry I didn't answer any of your letters. I've been wondering how you've been doing."

"Fine," I said. "Just fine."

"I guess we better be quiet." He leaned back and folded his arms, intent on what Edgar Barefoot was saying.

At the end of his lecture, Barefoot walked over to me; I still sat, unmoving. Bending, Barefoot said, "Are you related to Bishop Archer?"

"Yes," I said. "I was his daughter-in-law."

"We knew each other," Barefoot said. "Tim and I. For years. It was such a shock, his death. We used to discuss theology."

Coming up beside us, Bill Lundborg stood listening, saying nothing; he still smiled the same old smile I remembered,

"And then John Lennon's death today," Barefoot said. "I hope I didn't embarrass you, bringing you up front like that. But I could see something was wrong. You look better now."

I said, "I feel better."

"Do you want a sandwich?" Barefoot indicated the people gathered around the table at the rear of the room.

"No," I said.

Barefoot said, "Then you weren't listening. To what I told you. I wasn't joking. Angel, you can't live on words; words do not feed. Jesus said, 'Man does not live by bread alone'; I say, 'Man does not live by words at all.' Have a sandwich."

"Have something to eat, Angel," Bill Lundborg said.

"I don't feel like eating," I said. "I'm sorry." I thought, I'd rather be left alone.

Bending down, Bill said, "You look so thin."

"My work," I said remotely.

"Angel," Edgar Barefoot said, "this is Bill Lundborg."

"We know each other," Bill said. "We're old friends."

"Then you know," Barefoot said to me, "that Bill is a *bodhi-sattva*."

"I didn't know that," I said.

Barefoot said, "Do you know what a *bodhisattva* is, Angel?"

"It has something to do with the Buddha," I said.

"The *bodhisattva* is one who has turned down his chance to attain *Nirvana* in order to turn back to help others," Barefoot said. "For the *bodhisattva* compassion is as important a goal as wisdom. That is the essential realization of the *bodhisattva*."

"That's fine," I said.

"I get a lot out of what Edgar teaches," Bill said to me. "Come on." He took me by the hand. "I'm going to see that you eat something."

"Do you consider yourself a *bodhisattva?*" I said to him.

"No," Bill said.

"Sometimes the *bodhisattva* does not know," Barefoot said. "It is possible to be enlightened without knowing it. Also, it is possible to think you are enlightened and yet not be. The Buddha is called 'the Awakened One,' because 'awakened' means the same as 'enlightened.' We all sleep but do not know it. We live in a dream; we walk and move and have our lives in a dream; most of all we speak in a dream; our speech is the speech of dreamers, and unreal."

Like now, I thought. What I'm hearing.

Bill disappeared; I looked around for him.

"He's getting you something to eat," Barefoot said.

"This is all very strange," I said. "This whole day has been unreal. It is like a dream; you're right. They're playing all the old Beatles songs on every station."

"Let me tell you something that happened to me once," Barefoot said; he seated himself in the chair beside me, bent over, his hands clasped together. "I was very young, still in school. I attended classes at Stanford, but I did not graduate. I took a lot of philosophy classes."

"So did I," I said.

"One day I left my apartment to mail a letter. I had been working on a paper — not a paper to turn in but a paper of my own: profound philosophical ideas, ideas very important to me. There was one particular problem I couldn't figure out; it had to do with Kant and his ontological categories by which the human mind structures experience —"

"Time, space and causation," I said. "I know. I studied that."

"What I realized as I walked along," Barefoot said, "was that, in a very real sense, I myself create the world that I experience; I both make that world and perceive it. As I walked, the correct formulation of this came to me, suddenly, out of the blue. One minute I didn't have it; the next minute I did. It was a solution I'd been striving for over a period of years . . . I had read Hume, and then I had found the response to Hume's criticism of causation in Kant's writing — now, suddenly, I had a response, and a correctly worked-out response to Kant. I started hurrying."

Bill Lundborg reappeared; he held a sandwich and a cup of fruit punch of some sort; these he held out to me. I accepted them reflexively.

Continuing, Barefoot said, "I hurried back up the street toward my apartment as fast as I could go. I had to get the *satori* down on paper before I forgot it. What I had acquired, there on that walk, out of my apartment where I had no access to pen and paper, was a comprehension of a world conceptually arranged, a world not arranged in time and space and by causation, but a world as idea conceived in a great mind, the way our own minds store memories. I had caught a glimpse of world not as my own arrangement — by time, space and causation — but as it is in itself arranged; Kant's 'thing-in-itself.'"

"Which can't be known, Kant said," I said.

"Which normally can't be known," Barefoot said. "But I had somehow perceived it, like a great, reticulated, arborizing structure of interrelationships, everything organized according to meaning, with all new events entering as accretions; I had never before grasped the absolute nature of reality this way." He paused a moment.

"You got home and wrote it down," I said.

"No," Barefoot said. "I never wrote it down. As I hurried along, I saw two tiny children, one of them holding a baby-bottle. They were running back and forth across a street. A lot of cars came along very fast. I watched for a moment and then I went over to them. I saw no adult. I asked them to take me to their mother. They didn't speak English; it was a Spanish neighborhood, very poor . . . I didn't have any money in those days. I found their mother. She said, 'I don't speak English' and closed the door in my face. She was smiling. I remember that. Smiling at me beatifically. She thought I was a salesman. I wanted to tell her that her children would very soon be killed and she shut the door in my face, smiling angelically at me."

"So what did you do?" Bill said.

Barefoot said, "I sat down on the curb and watched the two children. For the rest of the afternoon. Until their father came home. He spoke a little English. I was able to get him to understand. He thanked me."

"You did the right thing," I said.

"So I never got my model of the universe down on paper," Barefoot said. "I just have a dim memory of it. Something like that fades. It was a once-in-a-lifetime *satori. Moksa,* it is called in India; a sudden flash of absolute comprehension, out of nowhere. What James Joyce means by 'epiphanies,' arising from the trivial or without cause at all, simply happening. Total insight into world." He was silent, then.

I said, "What I hear you saying is that the life of a Mexican child is —"

"Which way would you have taken?" Barefoot said to me. "Would you have gone home and written down your philosophical idea, your *moksa?* Or would you have stayed with the children?"

"I would have called the police," I said.

"To have done that," Barefoot said, "would have required you to go to a phone. To do that you would have had to leave the children."

"It's a nice story," I said. "But I knew someone else who told nice stories. He's dead."

"Maybe," Barefoot said, "he found what he went to Israel to find. Found it before he died."

"I very much doubt that," I said.

"I doubt it, too," Barefoot said. "On the other hand, maybe he found something better. Something he should have been looking for but wasn't. What I am trying to tell you is that all of us are unknowing *bodhisattvas,* unwilling, even; unintentional. It is something forced on us by chance circumstance. All I wanted to do that day was rush home and get my great insight down on paper before I forgot it. It really was a great insight; I have no doubt of that. I did not want to be a *bodhisattva.* I did not ask to be. I did not expect to be. In those days, I hadn't even heard the term. Anyone would have done what I did."

"Not anyone," I said. "Most people would have, I guess."

"What would you have done?" Barefoot said. "Given that choice."

I said, "I guess I would have done what you did and hoped I'd remember the insight."

"But I did not remember it," he said. "And that is the point."

Bill said to me, then, "Can I hitch a ride with you back to the East Bay? My car got towed off. It threw a rod and I —"

"Sure," I said; I stood up, stiffly; my bones ached. "Mr. Barefoot, I've listened to you on KPFA many times. At first, I thought you were stuffy but now I'm not so sure."

"Before you go," Barefoot said, "I want you to tell me how you betrayed your friends."

"She didn't," Bill said. "It's all in her mind."

Barefoot leaned toward me; he put his arm around me and drew me back to my chair, reseating me.

"Well," I said, "I let them die. Especially Tim."

"Tim could not have avoided death," Barefoot said. "He went to Israel in order to die. That's what he wanted. Death was what he was looking for. That's why I say, Maybe he found what he was looking for or even something better."

Shocked, I said, "Tim wasn't looking for death. Tim put up the bravest fight against fate I ever saw anybody put up."

"Death and fate are not the same," Barefoot said. "He died to avoid fate, because the fate he saw coming for him was worse than dying there on the Dead Sea Desert. That's why he sought it and that's what he found; but I think he found something better." To Bill he said, "What do you think, Bill?"

"I'd rather not say," Bill said.

"But you know," Barefoot said to him.

"What was the fate you're talking about?" I asked Barefoot.

Barefoot said, "The same as yours. The fate that has overtaken you. And that you're aware of."

"What is that?" I said.

"Lost in meaningless words," Barefoot said. "A merchant of words. With no contact to life. Tim had advanced far into that. I read *Here, Tyrant Death* several times. It said nothing, nothing at all. Just words. *Flatus vocis,* an empty noise."

After a moment I said, "You're right. I read it, too." How true it was, how terribly, sadly true.

"And Tim realized it," Barefoot said. "He told me. He came to me a few months before his trip to Israel and told me. He wanted me to teach him about the Sufis. He wanted to exchange meaning—all the meaning he'd piled up in his lifetime—for

something else. For beauty. He told me about an album of records that you sold him that he never got a chance to play.
Beethoven's *Fidelio*. He was always too busy."

"Then you knew who I was already," I said. "Before I told
you."

"That's why I asked you to come up front with me," Barefoot
said. "I recognized you. Tim had shown me a picture of you and
Jeff. At first, I wasn't sure. You're a lot thinner now."

"Well, I have a demanding job," I said.

Together, Bill Lundborg and I drove back across the Richardson
Bridge to the East Bay. We listened to the radio, to the endless
procession of Beatles songs.

"I knew you were trying to find me," Bill said, "but my life
wasn't going too well. I've finally been diagnosed as what they
call 'hebephrenic.'"

To change the subject I said, "I hope the music isn't depress-
ing you; I can turn it off."

"I like the Beatles," Bill said.

"Are you aware of John Lennon's death?"

"Sure," Bill said. "Everybody is. So you manage the Musik
Shop now."

"Yes, indeed," I said. "I have five clerks working under me
and unlimited buying power. I've got an offer from Capitol Records to go down to the L.A. area, to Burbank, I guess, and go to
work for them. I've reached the top in terms of the retail record
business; managing a store is as far as you can go. Except for
owning the store. And I don't have the money."

"Do you know what 'hebephrenic' means?"

"Yes," I said. I thought, I even know the origin of the word.
"Hebe was the Greek goddess of youth," I said.

"I never grew up," Bill said. "Hebephrenia is characterized
by silliness."

"Guess so," I said.

"When you're hebephrenic," Bill said, "things strike you as funny. Kirsten's death struck me as funny."

Then you are indeed hebephrenic, I said to myself as I drove. Because there was nothing funny about it. I said, "What about Tim's death?"

"Well, parts of it were funny. That little boxy car, that Datsun. And those two bottles of Coke. Tim probably had shoes on like I have on now." He lifted his foot to show me his Hush Puppies.

"At least," I said.

"But by and large," Bill said, "it was not funny. What Tim was looking for wasn't funny. Barefoot is wrong about what Tim was looking for; he wasn't looking for death."

"Not consciously," I said, "but maybe unconsciously he was."

"That's nonsense," Bill said. "All that about unconscious motivation. You can posit anything by reasoning that way. You can attribute any motivation you want, since there's no way it can be tested. Tim was looking for that mushroom. He sure picked a funny place to look for a mushroom: a desert. Mushrooms grow where it's moist and cool and shaded."

"In caves," I said. "There are caves there."

"Yes, well," Bill said, "it wasn't actually a mushroom anyhow. That, too, is a supposition. A gratuitous assumption. Tim stole that idea from a scholar named John Allegro. Tim's problem was that he didn't really think for himself; he picked up other people's ideas and believed they had come out of his own mind, whereas, in fact, he stole them."

"But the ideas had value," I said, "and Tim synthesized them. Tim brought various ideas together."

"But not very good ones."

Glancing at Bill, I said, "Who are you to judge?"

"I know you loved him," Bill said. "You don't have to defend him all the time. I'm not attacking him."

"It sure sounds like it."

"I loved him, too. A lot of people loved Bishop Archer. He was a great man, the greatest we'll ever know. But he was a foolish man and you know that."

I said nothing; I drove and I half-listened to the radio. They were now playing "Yesterday."

"Edgar was right about you, however," Bill said. "You should have dropped out of the university and not finished. You learned too much."

With bitterness I said, "'Learned too much.' Christ. The *vox populi*. Distrust of education. I get sick and tired of hearing that shit; I am glad of what I know."

"It's wrecked you," Bill said.

"You can just go take a flying fling," I said.

Bill said calmly, "You are very bitter and very unhappy. You are a good person who loved Kirsten and Tim and Jeff and you haven't gotten over what happened to them. And your education has not helped you cope with this."

"There is no coping with this!" I said, with fury. "They all were good people and they are all dead!"

"'Your fathers ate manna in the desert and they are all dead.'"

"What's that?"

"Jesus says that. I think it's said during Mass. I attended Mass a few times with Kirsten, at Grace Cathedral. One time, when Tim was passing the chalice around — Kirsten was kneeling at the rail — he secretly slipped a ring around her finger. No one saw but she told me. It was a symbolic wedding ring. Tim had on all his robes, then."

"Tell me about it," I said, bitterly.

"I am telling you about it. Did you know —"

"I knew about the ring," I said. "She told me. She showed it to me."

"They considered themselves spiritually married. Before and in the eyes of God. Although not according to civil law. 'Your fathers ate manna in the desert and they are all dead.' That refers to the Old Testament. Jesus brings —"

"Oh, my good God," I said, "I thought I'd heard the last of all this stuff. I don't want ever to hear any more. It didn't do any good then and it won't ever do any good. Barefoot talks about useless words — *those* are useless words. Why would Barefoot call you a *bodhisattva?* What is all this compassion and wisdom you have? You attained *Nirvana* and came back to help others, is that it?"

"I could have attained *Nirvana,*" Bill said. "But I turned it down. To return."

"Forgive me," I said, with weariness. "I don't understand what you're talking about. Okay?"

Bill said, "I came back to this world. From the next world. Out of compassion. That is what I learned out there in the desert, the Dead Sea Desert." His voice was calm; his face showed a deep calm. "That is what I found."

I stared at him.

"I am Tim Archer," Bill said. "I have come back from the other side. To those I love." He smiled a vast and secret smile.

# 15

AFTER A MOMENT of silence, I said, "Did you tell Edgar Barefoot?"

"Yes," Bill said.

"Who else?"

"Almost no one else."

I said, "When did this happen?" And then I said, "You fucking lunatic. It will never end; it goes on and it goes on. One by one, they go mad and die. All I want to do is run my record store and turn on and get laid now and then and read a few books. I never asked for this." My car's tires squealed as I swerved to pass a slow-moving vehicle. We had almost reached the Richmond end of the Richardson Bridge.

"Angel," Bill said. He put his hand on my shoulder, tenderly.

"Get your goddamn hand off of me," I said.

He withdrew his hand. "I have come back," he said.

"You have gone crazy again and belong back in the hospital, you hebephrenic nut. Can't you see what this is doing to me, to have to listen to more of this? You know what I thought about you? I thought: There, in a certain real sense, is the only sane one among us; he is labeled as a nut but he is sane. We are labeled as sane and we are nuts. And now you. You are the last one I would have expected this from, but I guess —" I broke off. "Shit," I said. "It's out of control, this madness process. I always said to myself: Bill Lundborg is in touch with the real; he thinks about cars. You could have explained to Tim why one does not drive out on the Dead Sea Desert in a Datsun with two bottles of Coke and a gas station map. And now you are as crazy as they were. More crazy." Reaching, I turned up the radio; the sound of the Beatles filled the car — Bill at once shut the radio off, entirely off.

"Please slow down," Bill said.

"Please," I said, "when we get to the toll gate, get out of the car and hitch a ride with somebody else. And you can tell Edgar Barefoot to go stick his —"

"Don't blame him," Bill said sharply. "I only told him; he didn't tell me. Slow down!" He reached for the ignition key.

"Okay," I said, putting my foot on the brake.

"You will roll this sardine can," Bill said, "and kill us both. And you don't even have your seat belt fastened."

"On this day of all days," I said. "The day they murder John Lennon. I have to hear this right now."

"I did not find the *anokhi* mushroom," Bill said.

I said nothing; I simply drove. As best I could.

"I fell," Bill said. "From a cliff."

"Yes," I said. "I read that, too, in the *Chronicle*. Did it hurt?"

"By that time, I had become unconscious from the sunlight and the heat."

"Well," I said, "apparently you are just not a very bright person, to go out there like that." And then, suddenly, I felt compassion; I felt shame, overwhelming shame at what I was doing to him. "Bill," I said, "forgive me."

"Sure," he said, simply.

I thought through my words and then I said, "When did —

what am I supposed to call you? Bill or Tim? Are you both, now?"

"I'm both. One personality has been formed out of the two. Either name will do. Probably you should call me Bill so that people won't know."

"Why don't you want them to know? I would think something as important and unique as this, as momentous as this, should be known."

Bill said, "They'll put me back in the hospital."

"Then," I said, "I will call you Bill."

"About a month after his death, Tim came back to me. I didn't understand what was happening; I couldn't figure it out. Lights and colors and then an alien presence in my mind. Another personality much smarter than me, thinking all sorts of things I never thought. And he knows Greek and Latin and Hebrew, and all about theology. He thought about you very clearly. He had wanted to take you with him to Israel."

At that, I glanced sharply at him and felt chilled.

"That night at the Chinese restaurant," Bill said, "he tried to talk you into it. But you said you had your life all planned out. You couldn't leave Berkeley."

Taking my foot from the gas pedal, I allowed the car to slow down; it moved more and more slowly until it came to a stop.

"It's illegal to stop on the bridge," Bill said. "Unless you're having motor trouble or run out of gas, something of that sort. Keep on driving."

Tim told him, I said to myself. Reflexively, I down-shifted, into low; I started the car up again.

"Tim had a crush on you," Bill said.

"So?" I said.

"That was one reason he wanted to take you to Israel with him."

I said, "You speak of Tim in the third person. So, in point of fact, you do not identify yourself with Tim or as Tim; you are Bill Lundborg talking about Tim."

"I am Bill Lundborg," he agreed. "But also I am Tim Archer."

"Tim wouldn't tell me that," I said, "about being sexually interested in me."

"I know," Bill said, "but I am telling you."

"What did we have for dinner that night at the Chinese restaurant?"

"I have no idea."

"Where was the restaurant?"

"In Berkeley."

"Where in Berkeley?"

"I don't remember."

I said, "Tell me what *hysteron proteron* means."

"How would I know that? That's Latin. Tim knows Latin; I don't."

"It's Greek."

"I don't know any Greek. I pick up Tim's thoughts and now and then he's thinking in Greek but I don't know what the Greek means."

"What if I believe you?" I said. "What then?"

"Then," Bill said, "you are happy because your old friend is not dead."

"And that's the point of this."

He nodded. "Yes."

"It would seem to me," I said carefully, "there would be a larger point involved. This would be a miracle of staggering importance, to the entire world. It is something that scientists should investigate. It proves there is eternal life, that a next world does exist — everything that Tim and Kirsten believed is, in fact, true. *Here, Tyrant Death* is true. Don't you agree?"

"Yes. I suppose so. That's what Tim is thinking; he thinks that a lot. He wants me to write a book, but I can't write a book; I don't have any writing talent."

"You can act as Tim's secretary. The way your mother did. Tim can dictate and you can write it all down."

"He rattles on and on a mile a minute. I've tried to write it down but — his thinking is fucked. If you'll pardon the expression. It's all disorganized; it goes everywhere and nowhere. And I don't know half the words. In fact, a lot of it isn't words at all, just impressions."

"Can you hear him now?"

"No. Not right now. It's usually when I'm alone and no one else is talking. Then I can sort of tune in on it."

"'*Hysteron proteron*,'" I murmured. "When the thing to be demonstrated is included in the premise. So it's all in vain, the reasoning. Bill," I said, "I've got to hand it to you; you have me tied up in a knot, you really have. Does Tim remember backing over the gas pump? Never mind; fuck the gas pump."

Bill said. "It's a presence of mind. See, Tim was in that area — the word 'presence' reminded me; he uses that word a lot. The Presence, as he calls it, was there in the desert."

"The Parousia," I said.

"Right." Bill emphatically nodded.

"That would be *anokhi*," I said.

"Would it? What he was looking for?"

"Apparently he found it," I said. "What did Barefoot say to all this?"

"That's when he told me — when he realized — I was a *bodhisattva*. I came back. Tim came back, I mean, out of compassion for others. For those he loves. Such as you."

"What is Barefoot going to do with this news?"

"Nothing."

"'Nothing,'" I echoed, nodding.

"There's no way I can prove it," Bill said. "To skeptical minds. Edgar pointed that out."

"Why can't you prove it? It should be easy to prove it. You have access to everything Tim knew; like you said — all the theology, details of his personal life. Facts. It should be the most simple matter on Earth to prove."

"Can I prove it to you?" Bill said. "I can't even prove it to you. It's like belief in God; you can know God, know he exists; you can experience him, and yet you can never prove to anyone else that you've experienced him."

"Do you believe in God now?" I said.

"Sure." He nodded.

"I guess you believe in a lot of things now," I said.

"Because of Tim in me, I know a lot of things; it isn't just belief. It's like —" He gestured earnestly. "Having swallowed a computer or the whole *Britannica,* a whole library. The facts, the ideas, come and go and just whizz around in my head; they go too fast — that's the problem. I don't understand them; I can't remember them; I can't write them down or explain them to other people. It's like having KPFA turned on inside your head twenty-four hours a day, without cease. In many respects, it's an affliction. But it's interesting."

Have fun with your thoughts, I said to myself. That is what Harry Stack Sullivan said schizophrenics do: they have endless fun with their thoughts, and forget the world.

There is not much you can say when someone unveils an account such as Bill Lundborg's — assuming that anyone ever unveiled such a narration before. It did, of course, resemble what Tim and Kirsten had revealed to me (that is the wrong word) when they returned from England, after Jeff's death. But that had been minor compared with this. This, I thought, consists of the ultimate escalation, the monument itself. The other narration was only the marker pointing to the monument.

Madness, like small fish, runs in hosts, in vast numbers of instances. It is not solitary. Madness does not remain content; it fans out across the landscape, or seascape, whichever.

Yes, I thought; it is like we are under water: not in a dream — as Barefoot says — but in a tank, and being observed, for our bizarre behavior and our more bizarre beliefs. I am a metaphor junkie; Bill Lundborg is a madness junkie, unable to get enough of it: he possesses a boundless appetite for it and will obtain it by whatever means possible. Just when it seemed, too, as if madness had passed out of the world. First John Lennon's death and now this; and, for me, on the same day.

I could not say, and yet he is so plausible. Because Bill was not plausible; it is not a plausible matter. Probably, even Edgar Barefoot recognized that — well, however a Sufi phrases such *moksa* to himself, that someone is sick and needs help, but is touchingly appealing, is guileless and not going to do any harm. This madness arose from pain, from the loss of a mother and what almost certainly amounted to a father in the true sense of the word. I felt it; I feel it; I always will feel it, as long as I live. But Bill's solution could not be mine.

Any more than mine — managing the record store — could be his. We each must find our own solution, and, in particular, we each must solve the sort of problem that death creates — creates for others; but not death only: madness also, madness leading to final death as its end-state, its logical goal.

When my original anger at Bill Lundborg's psychosis had subsided — it did subside — I began to view it as funny. The utility of Bill Lundborg, not just for himself but, as I viewed it, to all of us, consisted in his grounding in the concrete. This, precisely, he had lost. His showing up at Edgar Barefoot's seminar disclosed the change in Bill; the kid I had known, formerly known, would never have set foot in such surroundings. Bill had gone the way of the rest of us, not the way of all flesh but the way of our intellects: into nonsense and the foolish, there to languish without a trace of anything redemptive.

Except, of course, Bill could now emotionally deal with the assortment of deaths that had plagued us. Was my solution any better? I worked; I read; I listened to music — I bought music in the form of records; I lived a professional life and yearned to move into the A & R Division of Capitol Records down in Southern California. There my future lay, there were the tangible things that records had become for me, not something to enjoy but something to first buy and then sell.

That the bishop had returned from the next world and now inhabited Bill Lundborg's mind or brain — that couldn't be, for obvious reasons. One knows this instinctively; one does not debate this; one perceives this as absolute fact: it cannot happen. I could quiz Bill forever, trying to establish the presence in him of facts known only to me and to Tim, but this would lead nowhere. Like the dinner Tim and I had eaten at the Chinese restaurant on University Avenue in Berkeley, all data became suspect because there are multiple ways that data can arise within the human mind, ways more readily acceptable and explained than to assume that one man died in Israel and his psyche floated halfway across the world until it discriminated Bill Lundborg from all the other people in the United States and then dove into that person, into that waiting brain, and took up residence there, to sputter with ideas, thoughts and memories, half-baked notions; in other words, the bishop as we had known him, the bishop himself, like a sort of plasma. This does not lie within the domain of the real. It lies elsewhere; it is the invention of derangement, of a young man who grieved over the suicide of his mother and the sudden death of a father-figure, grieved and tried to understand, and one day into Bill's mind came — not Bishop Timothy Archer — but the *concept* of Timothy Archer, the notion that Timothy Archer was there, in him, spiritually, a ghost. There is a difference between the notion of something and that something itself.

Still, upon the lessening of my original anger, I felt sympathy toward Bill because I understood why he had gone this route; he had not willed it out of perversity: it did not consist of, so to speak, optional madness but, rather, madness compelled on him, thrust onto him forcibly, whether he liked it or not. It had simply happened.

Bill Lundborg, the first of us to be crazy, had become now the last of us to be crazy; the only genuine issue could best be phrased this way: could anything be done about it? Which raises a deeper question: *should* anything be done about it?

I pondered that during the next couple of weeks. Bill (he told me) had no major friends; he lived alone in a rented room in East Oakland, eating his meals at a Mexican café. Perhaps, I said to myself, I owe it to Jeff and Kirsten and Tim — to Tim, especially — to straighten Bill out. That way, there would be a survivor. That is, of course, in addition to myself.

Indubitably, I had survived. But survived, as I had for some time realized, as a machine; still, this is survival. At least my mind had not been invaded by alien intelligences who thought in Greek, Latin and Hebrew and used terms I could not comprehend. Anyhow, I liked Bill; it would not be a burden on me to see him again, to spend time with him. Together, Bill and I could summon back the people we had loved; these were the same people we had known, and our pooled memories would yield up a great crop of circumstantial details, the little bits that made of memory the semblance of the veridical . . . which is an ornate way of saying that my seeing Bill Lundborg would make it possible for me to experience Tim and Kirsten and Jeff again because Bill, like me, had once experienced them and would understand who I was talking about.

Anyhow, we both were attending Edgar Barefoot's seminar; Bill and I would run into each other there, for better or worse. My respect for Barefoot had climbed, due, of course, to the personal interest he had taken in me. I had warmed to that; I needed that. Barefoot had sensed it.

I interpreted Bill's statement that the bishop had been interested in me sexually as an oblique way of saying that he himself was interested in me sexually. I pondered that and came to the conclusion that Bill was too young for me. Anyhow, why get involved with someone classified as a hebephrenic schizophrenic? Hampton, who had had traces — rather more than traces — of paranoia and hypomania had been enough trouble, and it had been difficult to rid myself of him. In fact, it was not demonstrable that I had gotten rid of him; Hampton still phoned me, complaining aggressively that when I kicked him out of my house I had kept certain choice records, books and prints that, in truth, belonged to him.

What bothered me about my getting involved with Bill lay in my sense of the ferocity of madness. It can consume its owner, leave him, look around for more. If I was a rickety machine, I stood in danger of that madness, for I was not all that psychologically intact. Enough people had gone mad and died already; why add myself to the list?

And, perhaps worst of all, I discerned the kind of future that awaited Bill. He had no future. Someone with hebephrenia has dealt himself out of the game of process, growth and time; he simply recycles his own nutty thoughts forever, enjoying them even though, like transmitted information, they degenerate.

They become, finally, noise. And the signal that is intellect fades out. Bill would know this, having planned at one time to become a computer programmer; he would be familiar with Shannon's information theories. This is not the sort of thing you want to tie into.

Bringing my little brother Harvey along, I picked up Bill on my day off and drove up into Tilden Park, by Lake Anza and the clubhouse and barbecue stoves; there the three of us broiled hamburgers, and we tossed a Frisbie around and had a hell of a time. We had brought a Ghetto-blaster with us — one of those super sophisticated two-channel two-speaker combination radio and tape deck masterpieces that Japan turns out — and we listened to the rock group Queen and we drank beer, except for Harvey, and ran around and then, when it didn't seem anyone was watching or cared, Bill and I shared a joint. Harvey, while we did that, tried out all the heat-sensor controls of the Ghetto-blaster and then concentrated on picking up Radio Moscow on its shortwave.

"You can go to jail for that," Bill told him. "Listening to the enemy."

"Bull," Harvey said.

"I wonder what Tim and Kirsten would say," I said to Bill, "if they could see us now."

"I can tell you what Tim is saying," Bill said.

"What does he say?" I said, relaxed by the marijuana.

Bill said, "He says that — he's thinking that — it is peaceful here and he has finally found peace."

"Good," I said. "I could never get him to smoke grass."

"They smoked it," Bill said. "Him and Kirsten, when we weren't around. He didn't like it. But he likes it now."

"This is very good grass," I said. "They probably had local stuff. They wouldn't know the difference." I pondered over what Bill had said. "Did they really turn on? Is that true?"

"Yes," Bill said. "He's thinking about that now; he's remembering."

I regarded him. "In a way, you're lucky," I said. "To find your solution. I wouldn't mind having him in me. In my brain, I mean." I giggled; it was that kind of grass. "Then I wouldn't be so lonely." And then I said, "Why didn't he come back to me? Why to you? I knew him better."

After a moment of reflection, Bill said, "Because it would have wrecked you. See, I'm used to voices in my head and thoughts that aren't my own; I can accept it."

"It's Tim that's the *bodhisattva,* not you," I said. "It was Tim who came back, out of compassion." And then I thought with a start: My God; do I believe it, now? When you're high on good grass, you can believe anything, which is why it sells for as much as it does, now.

"That's right," Bill said. "I can feel his compassion. He sought wisdom, the Holy Wisdom of God, what Tim calls Hagia Sophia; he equates it with *anokhi,* God's pure consciousness. And then, when he got there and the Presence entered him, he realized that it was not wisdom that he wanted but compassion . . . he already had wisdom but it hadn't done him or anyone else any good."

"Yes," I said, "he mentioned Hagia Sophia to me."

"That's some of the Latin he thinks in."

"Greek."

"Whatever. Tim thought that with Christ's absolute wisdom he could read the Book of the Spinners and untangle the future for Tim, so Tim could figure out a way to evade his fate; that's why he went to Israel."

"I know," I said.

"Christ can read the Book of the Spinners," Bill said. "The

fate of every human is inscribed in it. No human being has ever read it."

"Where is this book?"

"All around us," Bill said, "I think, anyhow. Wait a sec; Tim is thinking something. Very clearly." He remained silent and withdrawn for a time. "Tim is thinking, 'The last canto. Canto Thirty-three of *Paradiso.*' *He's* thinking, '"God is the book of the universe"' and you read that; you read it the night you had the abscessed tooth. Is that right?" Bill asked me.

"That's right," I said. "It made a great impression on me, that whole last part of the *Commedia.*"

"Edgar says that the *Divine Comedy* is based on Sufi sources," Bill said.

"Maybe so," I said, wondering about what Bill had said, the statements about Dante's *Commedia.* "Strange," I said. "The things you remember and why you remember them. Because I had an abscessed tooth —"

"Tim says that Christ arranged that pain," Bill said, "so the final part of the *Divine Comedy* would impress itself on you in a way that would never wear off. 'One simple flame.' Oh, shit; he's thinking in a foreign language again."

"Say it out loud," I said, "as he thinks it."

Bill haltingly said:

> "'*Nel mezzo del cammin di nostra vita*
> *Mi ritrovai per una selva oscura,*
> *Che la diritta via era smarrita.*'"

I smiled. "That's how the *Commedia* begins."

"There's more," Bill said.

> "'. . . *Lasciate ogni speranza, voi ch' entrate!*'"

"'Abandon all hope, you who enter here,'" I said.

"He wants me to tell you one thing more," Bill said. "But I'm having trouble catching it. Oh; now I have it—he thought it again very clearly for me:

"*La sua volúntate e nostra pace . . .*"

"I don't recognize that," I said.

"Tim says it's the basic message of the *Divine Comedy*. It means, 'His will is our peace,' Meaning God, I guess."

"I guess so," I said.

"He must have learned that in the next world," Bill said. "He certainly didn't learn it here."

Approaching us, Harvey said, "I'm tired of the Queen tapes. What else did we bring?"

"Did you manage to pick up Radio Moscow?" I asked.

"Yeah, but the Voice jammed it. The Russians switched to another frequency—probably, the thirty-meter band—but I got tired of looking for it. The Voice always jams it."

"We'll be going home soon," I said, and passed the remains of the joint to Bill.

# 16

IT BECAME NECESSARY to rehospitalize Bill sooner than I had expected. He entered voluntarily, accepting this as a fact of life — a perpetual fact of his life, anyhow.

After they had signed Bill in, I met with his psychiatrist, a heavyset middle-aged man with a mustache and rimless glasses, a sort of portly but good-natured authority-figure who at once read me my mistakes, in order of descending importance.

"You shouldn't be encouraging him to use drugs," Dr. Greeby said, the file on Bill open before him across the surface of his desk.

"You call grass 'drugs'?" I said.

"For someone with Bill's precarious mental balance, any in-toxicant is dangerous, however mild. He goes into the trip but he never really comes out. We have him on Haldol now; he seems able to tolerate the side effects."

"Had I known the harm I was doing," I said, "I would have done otherwise."

He glanced at me.

"We learn by erring," I said.

"Miss Archer —"

"Mrs. Archer," I said.

"The prognosis on Bill is not good, Mrs. Archer. I think you should be aware of that, since you seem to be the one closest to him." Dr. Greeby frowned. "'Archer.' Are you related to the late Episcopal Bishop Timothy Archer?"

"My father-in-law," I said.

"That's who Bill thinks he is."

"Sufferin' succotash," I said.

"Bill has the delusion that he has become your late father-in-law due to a mystical experience. He does not merely see and hear Bishop Archer; he is Bishop Archer. Then Bill actually knew Bishop Archer, I take it."

"They rotated tires together," I said.

"You are a very smart-assed woman," Dr. Greeby said.

I said nothing to that.

"You have helped put Bill back in the hospital," the doctor said.

I said, "And we had a couple of good times together. We also had some very unhappy times together, having to do with the death of friends. I think those deaths contributed more to Bill's decline than did the smoking of grass in Tilden Park."

"Please don't see him any more," Dr. Greeby said.

"What?" I said, startled and dismayed; a rush of fear overcame me and I felt myself flush in pain. "Wait a minute," I said. "He's my friend."

"You have a generally supercilious attitude toward me and toward the world in all aspects. You obviously are a highly educated person, a product of the state university system; I'd guess that you graduated from U.C. Berkeley, probably in the English Department; you feel you know everything; you're doing great harm to Bill, who is not a worldly-wise, sophisticated person. You're also doing great harm to yourself, but that is not my concern. You are a brittle, harsh person, who —"

"But they were my friends," I said.

"Find somebody in the Berkeley community," the doctor

said. "And stay away from Bill. As Bishop Archer's daughter-in-law, you reinforce his delusion; in fact, his delusion is probably an introjection of you, a displaced sexual attachment acting outside his conscious control."

I said, "And you are full of recondite bullshit."

"I've seen dozens like you in my professional career," Dr. Greeby said. "You don't faze me and you don't interest me. Berkeley is full of women like you."

"I will change," I said, my heart full of panic.

"That I doubt," the doctor said, and closed up Bill's file.

After I left his office — ejected, virtually — I roamed about the hospital, at a loss, stunned and afraid and also angry — angry mostly at myself for lipping off. I had lipped off because I was nervous, but the harm was done. Shit, I said to myself. Now I've lost the last of them.

I go back now to the record store, I said to myself, and check the back orders to see what did and didn't arrive. There will be a dozen customers lined up at the register and the phones will be ringing. Fleetwood Mac albums will be selling; Helen Reddy albums will not be. Nothing will have changed.

I can change, I said to myself. Lard-butt is wrong; it isn't too late.

Tim, I thought; why didn't I go to Israel with you?

As I left the hospital building and walked toward the parking lot — I could see my little red Honda Civic from afar — I spotted a group of patients trailing along behind a psych tech; they had gotten off a yellow bus and were now returning to the hospital. Hands in the pockets of my coat, I walked toward them, wondering if Bill was among them.

I did not see Bill in the group, and I continued on, past some benches, past a fountain. A grove of cedar trees grew on the far side of the hospital, and several people sat here and there on the grass, undoubtedly patients, those with passes; those well enough to exist for a time outside of stern control.

Among them Bill Lundborg, wearing his usual ill-fitting pants and shirt, sat at the base of a tree, intent on something he held.

I approached him, slowly and quietly. He did not look up until I had almost reached him; suddenly, aware of me now, he raised his head.

"Hi, Bill," I said.

"Angel," Bill said, "look what I found."

I knelt down to see. He had found a stand of mushrooms growing at the base of the tree: white mushrooms with — I discovered when I broke one off — pink gills. Harmless; the pink gilled and brown-gilled mushrooms are, by and large, not toxic. It is the white-gilled mushrooms that you must avoid, for often they are the *amanitas,* such as the Destroying Angel.

"What have you got?" I said.

"It is growing here," Bill said, in wonder. "What I searched for in Israel. What I went so far to find. This is the *vita verna* mushroom that Pliny the Elder mentions in his *Historia Naturalis.* I forget which book." He chuckled in that familiar good-humored way that I knew so well. "Probably *Book Eight.* This exactly fits his description."

"To me," I said, "it looks like an ordinary edible mushroom that you see growing this time of year everywhere."

"This is the *anokhi,*" Bill said.

"Bill —" I began.

"Tim," he said, reflexively.

"Bill, I'm taking off. Dr. Greeby says I wrecked your mind. I'm sorry." I stood up.

"You never did that," Bill said. "But I wish you had come to Israel with me. You made a major mistake, Angel, and I did tell you that night at the Chinese restaurant. Now you're locked into your customary mind-set forever."

"And there's no way I can change?" I said.

Smiling up at me in his guileless way, Bill said, "I don't care. I have what I want; I have this." He carefully handed me the mushroom that he had picked, the ordinary harmless mushroom. "This is my body," he said, "and this is my blood. Eat, drink, and you will have eternal life."

I bent down and said, speaking with my lips close to his ear so that only he could hear me, "I am going to fight to make you okay again, Bill Lundborg. Repairing automobile bodies and spray-painting and other real things; I will see you as you were; I will not give up. You will remember the ground again. You hear me? You understand?"

Bill, not looking at me, murmured, "I am the true vine, and my Father is the vinedresser. Every branch in me that bears no fruit he cuts away, and every —"

"No," I said, "you're a man who spray-paints automobiles and fixes transmissions and I will cause you to remember. A time will come when you leave this hospital; I will wait for you, Bill Lundborg." I kissed him, then, on the temple; he reached to wipe it away, as a child wipes a kiss away, absently, without intent or comprehension.

"I am the Resurrection and the life," Bill said.

"I will see you again, Bill," I said, and walked away.

The next time I attended Edgar Barefoot's seminar, Barefoot noted Bill's absence and, after he had finished talking, he asked me about Bill.

"Back inside looking out," I said.

"Come with me." Barefoot led me from the lecture room to his living room; I had never seen it before and discovered with surprise that his tastes ran to distressed oak rather than to the Oriental. He put on a *koto* record which I recognized—that is my job—as a rare Kimio Eto pressing on World-Pacific. The record, made in the late Fifties, is worth something to collectors. Barefoot played *"Midori No Asa,"* which Eto wrote himself. It is quite beautiful but sounds not at all Japanese.

"I'll give you fifteen bucks for that record," I said.

Barefoot said, "I'll tape it for you."

"I want the record," I said. "The record itself. I get requests for it every now and then." I thought to myself: And don't tell me the beauty is in the music. The value to collectors lies in the record itself; this is not a matter that need be opened to debate. I know records: it is my business.

"Coffee?" Barefoot said.

I accepted a cup of coffee and together Barefoot and I listened to the greatest living *koto* player twang away.

"He's always going to be in and out of the hospital, you realize," I said, when Barefoot turned the record over.

"Is this something else you feel responsible for?"

"I've been told that I am," I said. "But I'm not."

"It's good that you realize that."

I said, "If somebody thinks Tim Archer came back to him, that somebody goes into the hospital."

"And gets Thorazine," Barefoot said.

"It's Haldol now," I said. "A refinement. The new anti-psychotic drugs are more precise."

Barefoot said, "One of the early church fathers believed in the Resurrection 'because it was impossible.' Not 'despite the fact that it was impossible' but 'because it was impossible.' Tertullian, I think it was. Tim talked to me about it one time."

"But how smart is that?" I said.

"Not very smart. I don't think Tertullian meant it to be."

"I can't see anybody going through life that way," I said. "To

me that epitomizes this whole stupid business: believing something because it's impossible. What I see is people becoming
mad and then dying; first the madness, then the death."

"So you see death for Bill," Barefoot said.

"No," I said, "because I am going to be waiting for him when
he gets out of the hospital. Instead of death, he is going to get
me. How does that strike you?"

"As much better than death," Barefoot said.

"Then you approve of me," I said. "Unlike Bill's doctor, who
thinks I helped put him in the hospital."

"Are you living with anyone right now?"

"As a matter of fact, I'm living alone," I said.

Barefoot said, "I'd like to see Bill move in with you when he
gets out of the hospital. I don't think he has ever lived with a
woman except with his mother, with Kirsten."

"I'd have to think a long time about that," I said.

"Why?"

"Because that's how I do things like that."

"I don't mean for his sake."

"What?" I said, taken by surprise.

"For your sake. That way, you would find out if it really is
Tim. Your question would be answered."

I said, "I have no question; I know."

"Take Bill in; let him live with you. Take care of him. And
maybe you'll find you're taking care of Tim, in a certain real
sense. Which — I think — you always did or anyhow wanted to
do. Or if you didn't, should have done. He is very helpless."

"Bill? Tim?"

"The man in the hospital. Who you care about. Your last tie
to other people."

"I have friends. I have my little brother. I have the people at
the store . . . and my customers."

"And you have me," Barefoot said.

After a pause, I said, "You, too; yes." I nodded.

"Suppose I said I think it may be Tim. Actually Tim come back."

"Well, then," I said, "I'd stop coming to your seminars."

He eyed me intently.

"I mean it," I said.

"You are not readily pushed around," Barefoot said.

"Not really," I said. "I've made certain serious mistakes; I stood there doing nothing when Kirsten and Tim told me that Jeff had returned — I did nothing and as a result they are now dead. I wouldn't make that mistake again."

"You genuinely foresee death for Bill, then."

"Yes," I said.

"Take him in," Barefoot said, "and I tell you what; I'll give you the Kimio Eto record we're listening to." He smiled. "'*Kibo No Hikari,*' this song is called. The Light of Hope.' I think it's appropriate."

"Did Tertullian actually say he believed in the Resurrection because it is impossible?" I said. "Then this stuff started a long time ago. It didn't begin with Kirsten and Tim."

Barefoot said, "You're going to have to stop coming to my seminars."

"You do think it's Tim?"

"Yes. Because Bill talks in languages he doesn't know. In the Italian of Dante, for instance. And in Latin and —"

"Xenoglossy," I said. The sign, I thought, of the presence of the Holy Spirit, as Tim pointed out that day we met at the Bad Luck Restaurant. The very thing Tim doubted existed any more; he doubted that it had ever existed, probably. According to what he, anyhow, could discern; to the best of his ability. And now we have it in Bill Lundborg claiming to be Tim.

"I'll take Bill in," Barefoot said. "He can live with me here on the houseboat."

"No," I said. "Not if you believe that stuff. I'll bring him to my house in Berkeley, rather than that." And then it came to me that I had been maneuvered and I gazed at Edgar Barefoot; he smiled and I thought: Just the way Tim could do it — control people. In a sense, Bishop Tim Archer is more alive in you than he is in Bill.

"Good," Barefoot said. He extended his hand. "Let's shake on it, to close the deal."

"Do I get the Kimio Eto record?" I asked.

"After I've taped it."

"But I do get the record itself."

"Yes," Barefoot said, still holding onto my hand. His grip was vigorous; that, too, reminded me of Tim. So maybe we do have Tim with us, I thought. One way or another. It depends on how you define "Tim Archer": the ability to quote in Latin and Greek and Medieval Italian, or the ability to save human lives. Either way, Tim seems to be still here. Or here again.

"I'll keep coming to your seminars," I said.

"Not for my sake."

"No; for my own."

Barefoot said, "Someday perhaps you'll come for the sand-wich. But I doubt that. I think you will always need the pretext of words."

Do not be that pessimistic, I said to myself; I might surprise you.

We listened to the end of the *koto* record. The last song on the second side is called *"Haru No Sugata,"* which means, "The Mood of Early Spring." We listened to that last and then Edgar Barefoot returned the record to its cover and handed it to me.

"Thank you," I said.

I finished my coffee and then left. The weather struck me as good. I felt a lot better. And I could probably get almost thirty dollars for the record. I had not seen a copy in years; it has long been out of print.

You must keep these things in mind when you operate a record store. And acquiring it that day amounted to a sort of prize: for doing what I intended to do anyhow. I had outsmarted Edgar Barefoot and I felt happy. Tim would have enjoyed it. Were he alive.

# BIBLIOGRAPHY

Aeschylus. *Agamemnon.* Quoted in *Bartlett's Familiar Quotations,* Fifteenth Edition. Boston: Little, Brown, 1980.

Aristophanes. *Lysistrata,* Jack Lindsay, trans. New York: Bantam, 1962.

Bible, the. *The Jerusalem Bible.* Garden City, New York: Doubleday & Co., 1966.

Büchner, Georg. *Wozzeck.* Alfred A. Kalmus, trans. by arrangement with Universal Edition of Eric Blackall and Vida Harford. 1836.

Cohen, Hermann. In *Contemporary Jewish Thought: A Reader.* Simon Noveck, ed. New York: B'nai B'rith Department of Adult Jewish Education, 1963.

Dante. *The Divine Comedy.* Laurence Binyon, trans., with notes by C. H. Grandgent. In *The Portable Dante.* New York: The Viking Press, 1947.

Donne, John. "Batter my Heart, three person'd God." Holy Sonnet XIV. In *The Complete Poetry and Selected Prose of John Donne.* New York: The Modern Library, 1952.

Geothe, Johann Wolfgang von. *Faust: Part Two.* Bayard Taylor, trans. Revised and edited by Stuart Atkins. New York: Collier Books, 1962.

Hertz, Dr. J. H. *The Pentateuch and Haftorahs.* London: Soncino Press, 5729[1967].

Huxley, Aldous. *Point Counter-Point*. New York: Harper & Row, 1965.

Jennens, Charles. *Belshazzar* [text of Handel oratorio]. 1744.

Kohler, Kaufmann. Quoted by Samuel M. Cohon in *Great Jewish Thinkers of the Twentieth Century*. Simon Noveck, ed. New York: B'nai B'rith Department of Adult Jewish Education, 1963.

Menotti, Gian Carlo. Liner notes to Columbia recording of Menotti's *The Medium*. Undated.

Plato. In *From Thaïes to Plato*. T. V. Smith, ed. Chicago: University of Chicago Press, 1934.

Prabhavananda, Swarni, and Isherwood, Christopher. *The Song of God: Bhagavad-Gita*. New York: NAL/Mentor, 1944.

Schiller, Friedrich. In *The New Encyclopedia Britannica*. Chicago: Encyclopedia Britannica, 1973.

Shakespeare. *Hamlet*. 1601.

Sonnleithner, Joseph, and Treitschke, Friedrich. *Fidelio* [text of Beethoven opera]. 1805.

Tate, Nahum. *Dido and Aeneas* [text of Purcell opera]. 1689.

Tertullian. Quoted in *Psychological Types, or The Psychology of Individuation* by C. G. Jung. London: Routledge & Kegan Paul, 1923.

Tillich, Paul. *A History of Christian Thought*. New York: Simon and Schuster, 1967.

Vaughan, Henry. "They are all gone into the world of light." 1655.

Virgil. Quoted in *Caesar and Christ* by Will Durant. New York: Simon and Schuster, 1944.

Yeats, W. B. "The Second Coming" and "The Song of the Happy Shepherd." *The Collected Poems of W. B. Yeats*. London: Macmillan, 1949.